JUST BY
LOOKING
AT HIM

Also by Ryan O'Connell

I'm Special

JUST BY
LOOKING
AT HIM

A Novel

RYAN O'CONNELL

ATRIA BOOKS

New York   London   Toronto   Sydney   New Delhi

ATRIA
BOOKS

An Imprint of Simon & Schuster, Inc.
1230 Avenue of the Americas
New York, NY 10020

First Atria Books hardcover edition June 2022

ATRIA BOOKS and colophon are trademarks of Simon & Schuster, Inc.

For information about special discounts for bulk purchases, please contact Simon & Schuster Special Sales at 1-866-506-1949 or business@simonandschuster.com.

The Simon & Schuster Speakers Bureau can bring authors to your live event. For more information or to book an event, contact the Simon & Schuster Speakers Bureau at 1-866-248-3049 or visit our website at www.simonspeakers.com.

Interior design by Yvonne Taylor

Manufactured in the United States of America

1 3 5 7 9 10 8 6 4 2

Library of Congress Cataloging-in-Publication Data
Names: O'Connell, Ryan, 1986¬ author.
Title: Just by looking at him : a novel / Ryan O'Connell.
Description: First Atria Books hardcover edition. | New York : Atria Books, 2022.
Identifiers: LCCN 2021062144 (print) | LCCN 2021062145 (ebook) |
ISBN 9781982178581 (hardcover) | ISBN 9781982178598 (paperback) |
ISBN 9781982178604 (ebook)
Subjects: LCGFT: Novels.
Classification: LCC PS3615.C5837 J87 2022 (print) |
LCC PS3615.C5837 (ebook) | DDC 813/.6--dc23
LC record available at https://lccn.loc.gov/2021062144
LC ebook record available at https://lccn.loc.gov/2021062145

ISBN 978-1-9821-7858-1
ISBN 978-1-9821-7860-4 (ebook)

For Jonathan

and for my father, who probably shouldn't read this

JUST BY
LOOKING
AT HIM

CHAPTER 1

My boyfriend Gus has a beautiful penis. It's big and thick without being *too* big or *too* thick. It has the right number of pulsating veins when hard (the correct number is two). It's not crooked or bent. It's not purple or pink. It's sun-dappled olive.

The rest of him is great too. High cheekbones, bee-stung lips, wavy brown hair, gentle eyes. Dressed neatly in cardigans and loafers like a true hot gay nerd. But if I'm being honest, his dick is the star. I loved it from the moment I saw it. Not like I was surprised. My best friend Augie dated Gus before me. "Elliott, if God is real, he's a fag," he told me. "A straight God would never make a penis this detailed and expressive. It's like the 'Beach House' episode of *Girls*. A work of art." I made a mental note. At the time I was dating someone else, someone whose penis I can no longer remember. His name was Hudson, which can you imagine? Yikes.

Anyway, we dated for three months and Augie dated Gus for four, which was generous of him really. He was doing the prep work, getting him ready for me. And when I broke up with Hudson, there

Gus was. My brain, which previously had been an unsafe neighbor-hood to walk around in at night, had carved out a nice space for him when I wasn't looking. It allowed me to have a nice patch of grass and sunshine, a Whole Foods even. And for five years, we were together, and everything was perfect. I don't even know how to write about this without slipping into platitudes, so I won't. I will say, however, that even with the best love, you could still wake up one day next to a beautiful man with a beautiful penis and be bored. You could start wishing for a smaller penis, an uglier one, with tons of veins and the color of sickness.

Everything gets boring after a while. The sun eventually goes down, the Whole Foods closes, and suddenly you're in a scary alleyway.

For the record: my penis is average.

CHAPTER 2

The walk to my office is fifteen minutes from the studio gate. An Uber drops me off, and I walk across the lot, usually accompanied by a mid-grade hangover, trying not to get run over by a trolley full of tourists getting fed such thrilling Hollywood tidbits as "This is where Hitchcock thought up new ways to torture Tippi Hedren." Then they all point to a sad, rundown office and everyone murmurs amongst themselves, impressed, and the trolley trudges on, as do I.

Someone invariably whizzes by me on a golf cart, stops, and reverses to ask, "Do you need a ride?"

"I'm fine," I say, drenched in sweat, looking like Reese Witherspoon in *Wild*.

They look me up and down. "Are you sure?"

I nod and keep walking. Having mild cerebral palsy and a limp means that strangers love to inquire about my well-being. But, like, I'm a gay man in his mid-thirties with an expensive haircut wearing A.P.C. jeans. I work very hard to appear palatable, easy to digest, the crostini of disability. Still, people see me and think I'm serving near-death realness.

As I approached my office that day, I thought about how nice it would be to turn back around, call an Uber, and crawl back into bed. I'm a writer for a television show called *Sammy Says*. It's about a woman named Sammy, who, it turns out, is a robot and, uh, hijinks ensue. Oh, and Sammy has kids. One who's a robot, one who's not. I don't even want to get into the weird sex that must have gone down for that to happen. Whatever. I make stupid amount of money.

Our offices take up an entire floor. On one side is the writers' room with all of the writers' offices. On the other is accounting and, well, me. I still have no idea why my office is so far away from the other writers, but being exiled really set the stage for the culture of the job. It's like I'm invisible and someone is dropping tiny turds on my heart all day long. The biggest turd-dropper is my boss, Ethan: a well-preserved gay man in his fifties who hates everyone almost as much as he hates himself.

Our relationship didn't start off so acrimonious. In the beginning, Ethan loved me. At my job interview in a Starbucks in Universal City ("This place is fucking disgusting, the studio made us meet here" was the first thing he said to me), I did my usual stand-up routine ("I grew up in Ventura. It's like Laguna Beach but with meth . . .") and Ethan said flatly, "You are so funny. . . ." Almost like it was a threat, but I took the compliment anyway. He then asked me why I walked like I'd just gotten railed by all the employees of a West Hollywood juice bar, and I was taken aback, of course, but I rolled with it, referring to my cerebral palsy as "cerebral lolzy." He thought that was *hilarious*. He loved all my slang! (Translation: He was seduced by how young I was and hoped that it would rub off on him.) Anyway, I landed the job and the first few months bordered on fun. People listened to my pitches and nodded approvingly. I got a fair amount of jokes in. And then, just like that, there was a shift. I'd seen Ethan turn on other writers arbitrarily out of boredom, but I thought I, the cerebral lolzy wunderkind, was safe.

I read somewhere that being neglected is, in some ways, worse than being abused. It was an odd, unfamiliar feeling because ever since I can remember, I have made a point to be the very best at my job. I was editor in chief of my high school newspaper, got all the coveted internships, always received straight As, except for math, but I'm convinced that's only because of the brain damage I incurred at birth. I've always been a type-A workhorse, eager to impress. When I first got staffed on a TV show at twenty-five, my mission was to get everyone absolutely OBSSESSED with me. "Who is this weird guy with a limp?" I'd imagine them saying as I accidentally drooled into my ramen at lunch. And I would respond with "Um, the funniest, most talented person you've ever met, babe!" Every day I tap-danced for people until I got blisters, and it worked. I developed a solid reputation in the industry and had been steadily employed for years, which is a rare feat for a television writer. But it seems at *Sammy Says*, my charms and talent had finally run out.

I entered the writers' room and took an empty seat next to Joan, my one and only ally. She used to be a doctor but then she wrote a spec script about a horse that solves murders and moved into TV. She's tiny and dry as a goddamn bone.

"I watched that doc about SeaWorld last night. *Blackfish*?" Joan said, yawning.

"Babe, um, update computer. That outrage is so 2013."

"I know," Joan said, leaning in and lowering her voice to a whisper. "But you know the trainers whose job it is to jack off the whales?"

I nodded.

"I feel like Ethan is Tilikum and we're all just the trainers jerking him off."

"True, but Ethan would be so offended that you compared him to a whale."

We chuckled. Our coworkers—Cindy, Amy, and Tom, aka Haunted Houses with Fillers, looked over and shot us death stares. Expressing joy was strictly forbidden here. Ethan then entered with his bite-sized dog, Monica (people who name their dogs regular people names will never not scare me), and took a seat at the head of the table.

"The network threw out the story about Sammy being unable to talk after her vocal chip goes missing."

"Why?" Cindy asked, leaning over to show her cleavage, despite Ethan's crystal queer homosexuality. "I thought they loved it in the run-through." Cindy was fifty-blank years old and dressed like a receptionist who had recently lost her moral center. On show nights, she wore six-inch heels and panty hose that looked like they were strangling her legs.

"Lisa didn't like that she wasn't going to have any lines for seven pages," Ethan said. Lisa is the lead of *Sammy Says* and a complete whacktress. She is prone to coming down with phantom illnesses. She once worried aloud that she might have gotten AIDS from touching a tiger on an African safari which, offensive, and, um, that's not how that works.

"Well, I suppose, maybe we could rework—" Amy stammered. Amy is six feet tall, from Scranton, Pennsylvania, and used to be a . . . zzzzzzzz, oh, gosh, sorry, my fingers fell asleep describing her because she is truly that unremarkable.

"We're done, Amy," Ethan yelled, causing Monica to jump in his lap. "Move on!"

"Totally hear you, Ethan," Tom said. "We can strategize a

plan B. Maybe do that story about Sammy going on a date with the dad from the trampoline park?"

Tom looks like he was picked out of an assembly line of television writers: white dude in a baseball cap who fails upward. He loves to tell stories about writing on the failed sitcom *Zoe, Duncan, Jack and Jane* at least once a day, and he's straight, but you wouldn't know it by how much he licks Ethan's ass. Also, I'm pretty sure Ethan wants to fuck Tom slash maybe already has.

"You." Ethan pointed at me. He only ever calls me "You," instead of my actual name, Elliott, these days. "What do you think?"

My soul left my body. Ethan hadn't asked me what I thought in months. The last time he spoke to me was when he forced me to try on his $75,000 watch, only to become enraged when he realized my wrists were thicker than his. Still, I took this as an opportunity to show him that I was worthy of being here and potentially get back in his good graces.

"Um," I cleared my throat. "Well, I think that—"

"GODDAMNIT, MONICA!" Ethan jumped up from his chair, revealing a piss stain in his lap. Everyone except for Joan and me leapt up in a show to help him.

Joan, side of mouth, said to me, "Feel that?"

"What?"

"Ethan's cum on our faces."

CHAPTER 3

That night, Gus and I ordered chopped salads from La Scala on Postmates, which cost, for reasons that remain unclear to me, $72.00. I am so bad with money. And not, like, in a cute "I'm too whimsical and wealthy to be bothered with budgets" kind of way. I grew up with a single dad (Mom left when I was young because she discovered that parenting a disabled child was taking time away from her real passion: emotionally terrorizing people on the East Coast). My father made a decent living as a social worker, enough to bring up one child in the sleepy Southern California beach town of Ventura, but I might as well have been one of the Boxcar Children. I could only order hamburgers, not cheeseburgers, at fast-food restaurants because my dad said he could grill the cheese himself at home. Lunch would often be served at Costco by eating free samples. My dad would travel five miles to save ten cents on a car wash, failing to understand that he'd be spending more on gas to get there. The second I started making my own money, I spent like crazy, partially to torture my father. After I wrapped my first TV job, I took my dad to Europe and put us up in five-star hotels. The entire time he looked like he was going to throw up. An expensive "fuck you" for sure but worth it.

"How was your day, Elly?" Gus asked, putting the dressing on my salad and shaking it up. Gus was, in a lot of ways, my caretaker. He prepared my meals for me, did the dishes, kept the household moving. At thirty-four, I did not know how to do a remarkable number of things (what is a duvet cover and why do I see it as a threat to my life?), and that's largely because I let Gus do everything. I feel guilty, almost like I am playing up my disability and asking to be infantilized, but Gus seems to genuinely enjoy it. Besides, they say in a relationship one is the garden and the other is the gardener and, well, gardening is a hard thing to do when you're disabled.

"Oh, my day was an absolute nightmare. But I added it up, and after taxes, I'm making over a thousand dollars a day. So, you know, I've suffered for far less."

"Yup. I'm doing it now." Gus took a swig of wine in a way that seemed unintentionally dramatic.

Gus was a story producer on *The Real Housewives: Orange County*, which meant he edited scenes of Republicans fighting at brunch and various costume parties. He hated the gig, obviously, but at thirty-five, he still didn't know what he wanted to do with his life, so he kept coming back season after season. I'm fascinated by people who haven't found their passion, especially the ones who appear fully developed and sure of themselves. Not to say that my passion is writing for *Sammy Says*, but being staffed on any television show is impressive. The number one dreaded question someone can ask a television writer in Los Angeles is "What are you working on?" If you say you're "developing a few things" that means you're unemployed, and you will be treated like a leper. I can say I'm a producer on *Sammy Says*—a network television show that gets millions of viewers each week (Yes, millions. It's depressing but America is profoundly dumb—the number one show on Netflix right now is about a sexy scary nanny who wants to steal a child's kidney because she lost her kidney in a fire as a teenager!), and people will know what that show is and, by extension, know that I matter, which gives me a greater quality of life in this nightmare city. And anyway, it's a stepping-stone to more creatively fulfilling writing jobs. Maybe one day I'll even create my own show.

"I'm sorry you had a bad day, honey."

"It's fine," he said, taking another swig of wine, less dramatic this time.

I squeezed his hand. "I *wuv* you," I said. A few years ago Gus and I developed the nasty habit of engaging in baby talk. It's like, you're with someone for so long, words become so dull that you decide to make them fun, but somehow you end up talking like you have brain damage, and any spark of desire you have for this person gets slowly snuffed out. Once I was fucking Gus's mouth, and I couldn't come, and he looked up at me, my uncooperative penis resting next to his cheek, and said in full-on baby voice, "It's okay, my *widdle dawin*."

Please, somebody help us. No one tells you that, in long-term relationships, you will never love someone more and want to fuck them less. It's like, what's designed to keep you in love and your heart full is also the thing that will keep your penis deflated.

Gus poured another glass of wine for me, and I absentmindedly picked at the price tag on the bottle, our second of the evening. Forty dollars.

After dinner, I always take a bath in our gorgeous clawfoot tub. I put on some music—Joni Mitchell, Karen Dalton, or something equally vintage and moody—and I use a bath bomb from Lush ($8) to make sitting in a body of water more interesting. Gus comes to visit with me. We don't really talk a whole lot during dinner. We're too busy stuffing our faces and guzzling wine, but now that our bellies are full and our brains are covered in the gauze known as alcohol, we can let our hair down and be relaxed. We talk about bigger things than How Was Your Day? We express anxieties and fears. Future plans. Past regrets. Whatever. There's something about being in a bath that is just, like, instant vulnerability. I blame the media.

Then, after about a half hour, Gus helps me out of the bath because I tried doing it once before on my own and fell, and it scared Gus more than it scared me—I'm used to falling—so he insisted on helping me every time after that. Or maybe I actually asked him to help me. In any case, I love and hate getting escorted out of the bath, because it makes me feel grand (like the Mariah Carey *Cribs* episode) and also kind of sad and pathetic (like the Mariah Carey *Cribs* episode). Gus then wraps a towel around me and dries me off because I never have enough patience to do it myself, and then I lie on the bed for ten minutes naked, smashing down on the soft parts of my body with my pruned hands, while Gus locks up the house and tidies up and takes all the decorative pillows off the bed. I'm telling you: the man loves to garden.

CHAPTER 4

This one time I had sex with a guy who wouldn't let me look at him, but I was young, and I didn't want to look at me either, and besides, it was kind of hot to be there on my stomach while this guy fucked me, because even when it hurt, the orgasm would still peek through, and after he finished inside me (no condom), he said I had "birthing hips" and laughed and fell asleep next to me but not before erecting this fort of pillows between us, and the next morning I woke up and he was gone. And I felt bad, mostly because I assumed that's how I was supposed to feel, that's what all the songs and TV shows and movies had taught me about degrading sexual experiences, and it wasn't until years later that I was able to admit that I liked the experience, I liked being told where to look or not to look, and sometimes when you have sex with someone and there's intense eye contact and he's gentle and you spoon before falling asleep, you can still feel like there's a fort of pillows between the two of you, and that makes you feel worse because at least the other kind of sex was honest: it knew what it was.

CHAPTER 5

The next day at work, we were discussing a male comedian who had been accused of sexual assault—the third one that week. This particular guy liked to masturbate into female colleague's desk drawers while they watched. I braced myself to weather Ethan's ice-cold take, which would be some variation of "We have gone too far, people!" and "It's just a drawer, Jesus, do we need consent from a fucking drawer?" #MeToo was a common point of conversation in the room because, well, all these years later, men still won't stop assaulting women in Hollywood. Ethan would cling to the same bad opinion, while Joan swallowed her rage, Cindy stared glassy-eyed at the wall, and Amy dreamed of Scranton. I knew Cindy, in particular, had been through some shit over the years (her first staff job was on a notoriously toxic eighties sitcom), but none of the men ever bothered to check in with her or ask any of the women how they felt about this long overdue reckoning. One time Tom said this was a moment for men to shut up and listen, to hear women's stories. Joan nodded and

started to open her mouth, and you know what Tom did? HE
CUT HER OFF.

I'd never been sexually harassed. In fact, I spent most of my
life feeling castrated from society because of my disability so, in
the very dark recesses of my brain, I almost felt a pang of envy for
people who had to swat away unwanted admirers. What did that
even feel like? I mean, I don't really wish to be sexually harassed.
It's just interesting how the absence of something can poison your
brain into desiring the excess.

"Anyway," Ethan said, after exhausting today's supply of out-
dated, misogynistic observations, "let's move on to one-hundred-
percent consensual sex. Me and Joe hired a hooker last night."

"Oh, um, cool," Tom stammered, clutching his heterosexuality
like a blanket on a snowstormy night. "Is this, like, a story idea for
Sammy?"

"What? No! We're doing a show about robots, not hookers. I
like your shirt, Tom," Ethan said, sizing him up.

"Really? I got it at Nordstrom's this weekend. Was kinda unsure
but ended up pulling the trigger."

"No, it's great. Fits you perfectly."

The audacity to act pervy to your employee right after a conversation about sexual harassment. Being rich is a helluva drug!

"The preferred term is sex worker, I think," Amy said, attempt-
ing to be more than a blank space.

"Oh, fuck off," Ethan said.

"Um, that's cool. My daughter's friend . . . well, I guess a friend of
a friend of hers does that," Cindy said. "Feels very new generation."

"What about you?" Ethan swirled his chair over to me. "Do you
and your boyfriend, Bobby, use them?" He unwrapped a piece of
gum and started angrily chewing, as if the gum owed him a script
or had told him he looked tired.

"Um, his name is Gus, and no," I said.

"He came to our house, but he brought his dog, which was weird, but okay, sure. And he was real fucking sexy, you know. I mean, of course he was. Well-defined arms, a nice big muscle ass. Anyway, we had a good time." Ethan paused for effect.

I imagined him topping the sex worker—there was no way Ethan has done enough therapy to be a bottom—on his luxe linen sheets while his husband—whom I'd met and who looks like a wax figure, and after a quick Google search, I discovered he once accidentally hit someone with their car and killed them à la Rebecca Gayheart/Brandy/Caitlyn Jenner—probably lay there telling Ethan what a big powerful dick he had. There's no way anyone in this scenario could have enjoyed themselves.

"What was his name?" I asked, surprising myself.

"Why?" Ethan asked, bemused.

"Oh. Um—" I honestly didn't know where my sudden interest had come from.

"Never mind. I don't want to know. His name was River. River Banks. Obviously not his real name. Anyway, in other news, I think my maid is stealing from me. Is that anything?"

CHAPTER **6**

After work, I went home and couldn't stop thinking about River Banks. I assumed sex workers were mostly used by straight married men or guys who were deemed too hideous by society to have sex for free. Having Ethan buy one like he was shopping at Saks seemed so empty and sinister. I bet he ordered River around. Told him where to sit. What to say. How to move his mouth. He was like Play-Doh for Ethan: a mound of flesh for him to touch and mold to his liking.

Out of curiosity, my dick opened my laptop, Googled "River Banks," and opened his rent boy profile. There he was—well-defined abs, thick legs, the big muscle ass Ethan had bragged about. My dick grew a little in my shorts. I imagined meeting River and telling him where to sit, how to move his mouth. Not in a cruel Ethan way. More like in a way that allowed me to feel safe and in control. Hiring a sex worker had never once occurred to me, but my wheels were starting to turn. You're essentially paying someone to not judge you and to have a safe space to explore your sexuality. There's no anxiety over whether or not you're doing it right. Like, who fucking cares if my legs can't go in a certain position? If River judged me, he'd be doing it silently, and besides, you can bet that he's seen it all, that any misstep I have, he's witnessed something way more egregious. How nice to not be the worst one for once.

I looked at a picture of River in a jockstrap. He was on a tractor for some reason, trying to approximate a farmer fantasy. It worked. I imagined wandering onto his farm, like Anne Heche stumbling upon that stranger's house in Indio allegedly on Ecstasy. I'm dehydrated and possibly have heatstroke. Suddenly, River appears. He's mowing something or doing whatever it is you do in a tractor, and he sees me and jumps off of it, all concerned. He's only in his jockstrap which is something he doesn't acknowledge so neither do I, and he takes me into his barn, where he has a makeshift bed made out of hay, and he brings me water and revives me back to health. "Thank you," I say to him. "You saved my life." River nods and then says gruffly, "Now as a thank-you, you work for me. Bring me hay for the horses." Stunned, I look around. There are literally no horses. But River's demeanor has shifted so profoundly it's unsettling and I know not to question it, so I bring some hay over and it's really heavy and I drop it a million times. "I can't do it," I whine. "I'm disabled!" And then River looks at me, mouth softening, and I expect him to help me—like Gus does, like strangers on the lot do—but instead he snarls at me, "I don't give a shit. Get to fucking work, you little disabled bitch." I'm shocked. What kind of a Neanderthal would not consider my cerebral palsy? But then, just as quickly, I become turned on. Here is someone treating me like a piece of shit, like he would anybody else. How novel. How hot. I spend a month at his farm doing manual labor (and also getting ripped—hey, I can get hot in the fantasy too . . .) and finally as a reward, River sits me down. At this point I'm exhausted and tan and—again, just to reiterate, really muscle-y—and he tells me thank you for the hard work. I say, "You're welcome. You pushed me to places I didn't know I was capable of. I'm proud of myself." And I'm being genuine. I mean, I somehow managed to put together a goddamn chicken coop while I was there. My self-esteem is flying high. River says he's proud of me too, and as a token of his appreciation, he takes off his jockstrap, revealing his gorgeous hard cock, and he asks me to kiss it. I do. Slowly. Hungrily. Then he lays me down on the hay and starts fucking me, until I have an orgasm so explosive that I end up screaming, and a horse finally comes rushing in—the first one I've seen the entire time I was there—and the horse says to me, "Thanks for the hay, bitch." And then, unfortunately, the horse speaking took me entirely out of the fantasy, and now I was back to reality in my apartment, and all I knew was that I suddenly wanted River so badly. I wanted to touch his perfect fucking body and get fucked by his perfect penis that paid for the rent on his apartment. In a horny daze, I picked up my phone and contemplated texting him. Then I looked at my spotless floors—wow, Gus must've cleaned after I left for work this morning—and was immediately reminded of my long-term romantic partner. Oh, wonderful, sweet Gus. We hadn't had any kind of "open relationship" discussion. We were strictly monogamous, so technically this would be against the rules. Maybe I should call Gus up and be like, "Hey babe, can I go get fucked by this hot sex worker? I'll be home before our rewatch of *Enlightened*!" But no, that would create a dialogue and become this big discussion about our relationship, and I don't think a sexual experience like this one even merits a deep dive. It isn't really cheating if you're paying for it. It's merely a transaction that has no potential to spill over into your normal life. It's an isolated incident, devoid of emotion. The definition of "just sex."

I looked at a picture of River's round, supple ass again. My dick grew larger in my shorts, eventually breaking through the fabric, grabbing my phone, and going rogue. My penis texted River: "Hi. Are you available today?"

Hmmm. That was a little too perfunctory and businesslike. I considered throwing in an emoji to convey that I was fun and normal. An eggplant? A peach? No. Too desperate. He'll get what I mean when I ask if he's available. A wink-y face? Ew. What am I, a creepy uncle that lets his hand linger too long on your lower back at Thanksgiving? I decided it was best to keep it simple. No emoji. Send.

My body filled with dread and joy. I couldn't believe I'd done that. What now? I looked at my outfit, which was expensive and well made, but plain and sexless. I changed into the kind of outfit one should wear if they were to hypothetically meet their first sex worker. Shorts with a five-inch inseam, because I thought my legs looked decent and I wanted him to see me as sexually viable, and a white Acne measure tee—the best white T-shirt to ever exist that retails for a hundred dollars and was discontinued but thankfully I bought it in bulk.

I stared at myself in the mirror: my average body made slightly better by well-tailored clothing, and I felt feelings that resembled satisfaction.

Then, *ping*. He texted me. "What do u Look like?"

What do I look like? If I were honest I would've said:

- Hair: Mousy brown with spots of dandruff from a psoriasis outbreak.

- Chest: Hairy with bits of acne sprinkled in to keep it intersectional. #HairyAcneChest #RepresentationMatters

- Arms: Tired of carrying everyone's expectations.

- Stomach: A wine cellar.

- Penis: Average. (I already told you, fuck!)

- Ass: Pretty good, actually.

Overall I think I look like the first draft of a cute person. My features all blend together with shades of potential. The ones that are pronounced stick out because of my scars or thick glasses. You know that 'NSYNC song "(God Must Have Spent) A Little More Time on You"? Well, God definitely got wasted and passed out while making me. Then he woke up, looked at the final product, shrugged, and said, "Meh. It'll do."

There's no way River would be attracted to me. I pictured him opening up his door and seeing my blah face and my wobbly CP knees and giving himself an internal pep talk that's like, "You can do this, River. This man will pay your utility bill for two months!" Or maybe he would actually be relieved. Because I was relatively young and, like I said, my ass is pretty good. I'm sure he gets a lot of older men with asses that are sagging no matter how many squats they do, so I might be like a paid vacation by comparison. Yes, let's go with that. With newfound optimism slash delusion, I got up the courage to write River a spare yet generous description—"young, lean cub"—and attached a recent selfie. He texted back his address. Okay. This was happening.

Would Gus fuck a sex worker behind my back? Absolutely not. The man is so sweet. I practically become diabetic when he talks. But Gus has had a lot more sex than me. He spent his twenties being a Hot Young Thing having numerous dalliances with men. I didn't. My sex was doled out sporadically and was punctuated by long stretches of celibacy. This is my way of making up for lost time in a considerate and contained way. It's mindful cheating. In TV-writer-speak, I was simply having my very own bottle episode.

I took a quick shower and attempted to clean my asshole in case a rimjob was in the cards. I love rimjobs—giving and receiving them—but I hadn't had one in years because Gus hates them. He says they're too dirty and he's afraid he'll lap up a speck of shit or something, but I'm like, yeah, hello: welcome to the world of assplay. Sometimes there's shit. Also, gay guys only have, like, three things to choose from on the sex menu. You can't afford to cross one off. After doing a deep clean, I removed my finger and sniffed it, satisfied.

I found River's Instagram (his handle: "ARiverRunsThruU") and did a deep dive in the Uber to his house. His content was pretty typical of an Instagay: workout videos, a photo in a Speedo with a long caption about his struggles with anxiety, at the dentist for teeth-whitening sponcon. (I clicked on the dentist, who was also hot and gay. It never ends.) Then I came across a photo of him with Zach on a sailboat. *The* sailboat. Of course, he's friends with Zach. Zach is a popular daddy influencer with no apparent job other than "Be extremely handsome and post photos to make other less handsome men feel bad about themselves." I think he occasionally builds furniture that he only sells to other dreamy gay men? Anyway, he and his gay posse all live in Santa Monica (the first sign of being unwell) and have this sailboat that they take out every Sunday and do poppers and get naked and, like, stare at the endless expanse of blue laid out before them and try to realize stuff. I want to fuck Zach very badly. It's in the top ten of things I hate about myself.

This one time at a party, he took my hand and, without a word, led me to his car (a Jeep—impractical, but okay, run me over with it). I was confused as to what his intentions were. Was he going to rob me? And if so, could we at least have sex first? But instead he played me this song by Tennis (an indie band that likes to ride around in a sailboat . . . all paths lead to sailboats) and sang all the lyrics to me. He grabbed my shirt the entire time, belting his fucking heart out. I may or may not have gotten middle-school hard. When the song ended, I was convinced we were going to make out, but he simply said, "Cool song, huh?'" and GOT OUT OF HIS STUPID, SEXY JEEP.

I sat alone in the car, my face all hot with humiliation, thinking, "I'll never get to step foot on that fucking sailboat." I'll never be invited because of my subpar bone structure and because I'm not disciplined enough to not eat pasta and my stomach is soft because I work out mostly for mental health reasons and don't hate myself enough to shrink my world in order to shrink my size, because I have a limp and scars and slightly yellow teeth that could never score teeth-whitening sponcon. Because they will talk about things I've never experienced, never had access to, and what would be the point? I have nothing to offer them besides a well-observed joke.

I would like for these Sailboat Gays to see me how I see them—as a *body*. If Zach saw me like that, he would've stayed in the car with me. He would've taken off my clothes, regarded me as a series of parts to use and enjoy. It would've meant so much to be seen for so little. And maybe that's why I looked up River that day. The potential to be seen as just a body. Gus can't see me like that. He's too close. He thinks my body is "crazy nice" and that I look like Clark Kent??? But he has long-term-relationship goggles on. He didn't even care when I gained ten pounds one winter, which I know I should've processed as *Wow, my man is so sweet . . . he loves me for me . . .* , but instead I thought, *Unconditional love? Disgusting. Your opinion is no longer reliable.* It's funny. All I ever dreamed of was finding a man who would love me for me—flaws, disability, and all. Now that I had it, I found it revolting. After all these years with Gus, I wanted an unbiased person to see my body, to take it in, to examine it, not knowing or caring what kind of brain it was attached to.

My Uber pulled up to River's apartment. The building was shitty-looking, definite *Vanderpump Rules* vibes before they all got rich and moved out of their soulless shoeboxes in West Hollywood for roomier soulless houses in the Valley.

I gave my driver five stars and texted River that I was outside. My phone pinged after a minute.

"Be right down 😊"

CHAPTER 7

Shortly after he texted, a dreamy boy walked out.

"Hi," I said, already vibrating and tingly. "Are you River?"

The guy grimaced like I had squeezed a lemon into his mouth. "Um, no."

I started to panic. Okay, that guy clearly knows River is a sex worker, I thought, and that I'm here to pay him money to fuck me, and oh my god, he probably thinks I'm a loser, and I should probably tell him that I have a cute boyfriend and have sex for free all the time. Well, maybe not all the time, but we've been together for a while, and things slow down, you end up having less sex, and anyway, the point is I am here to have a new experience because isn't that what life is all about and—

"Hey!"

I snapped out of my shame spiral to register what was in front of me. River. The real one. He was wearing basketball shorts (ironically?) and a plain white T-shirt that was suffocating his massive pecs. It wasn't as good quality as my beloved Acne, but his body filled it out better so, not like it's a competition, but he won.

"Come on up."

On the way in I was staring at his ass when River turned around, noticed my limp, and suggested that we could take the elevator if I wanted.

"Oh, I'm fine with stairs."

Cerebral palsy is my Regina George. The bitch can't let me have this one moment of bliss, an interrupted view of River's perfect butt. It has to send me crashing back down to earth, reminding me I'm someone who appears as if he's in constant need of help.

"Do you live nearby?" River asked. He sounded like he had a slight accent.

"Um, yeah. Kind of near Melrose and Fairfax."

"Cool."

"Yeah, it's a great neighborhood. Very central."

"Yup."

We then did the bravest thing two strangers can do, which is be silent until we walked into his apartment. His place smelled like air freshener: sickly sweet, chemical-y. Almost like cum, which is ironic considering that's probably what he was trying to cover up. There was a bookshelf with titles like *Gilead* by Marilynne Robinson, *Slow Days, Fast Company* by Eve Babitz, and *How Should a Person Be?* by Sheila Heti. River noticed me scanning the spines. "Those are my sister's. She's traveling for the next few months so I'm holding on to them for her," he said, almost sheepishly, before taking off his shirt.

"Oh," I said, slightly disappointed.

"I used to read a bunch, but I don't have time anymore between this and, y'know, other stuff." He shrugged, rubbing his stomach, absentmindedly. Then he took his basketball shorts off, revealing his penis. It wasn't erect, but I could see why he's able to make money with the thing. Gus's was prettier and more inviting, and like I said, you can't beat the correct number of veins—but this penis was new, and new trumps the most gorgeous dick.

How do you describe a perfect face and flawless body, the kind you masturbate to in porn and in fitness magazines? I mean, River was objectively handsome, like if James Franco fucked Dave Franco and gave birth to a less problematic Franco. And his body is familiar, in the way that the V starts on the sides of his lower abdomen to form a perfect on-ramp to his dick. We've all seen abs like his— six whole abs!—and countless broad hairless chests with jutting pecs. It's all very Abercrombie & Fitch Americana, no variation and almost fake-looking. There are no moles or dimples or an area that goes unexpectedly soft. Gus has two birthmarks on his back that look like little rashes, and he has the teensiest paunch. It's not hot, but it's also not *not* hot. His belly shows that he's chosen a life beyond his body, that he's decided to fill himself with other things, notably profiteroles. Still, you look at a body like River's, and you get hard because your dick is a basic bitch who wants to live in the new sleek house on the block with the floor-to-ceiling windows and central air, not the 1920s Spanish bungalow with character.

"Wow," River said. "You leak a lot of pre-cum."

"Huh?"

I looked down and saw wetness bleeding through my shorts.

"Oh, sorry."

"No need to apologize. It's the body doing what it wants."

I tried to take off my shoes, one hand on the bookshelf to steady myself, but I almost fell over.

"Sorry."

"Are you going to say sorry a lot? Is that, like, your thing?" River smiled and sat down on his couch.

I didn't answer and continued to stare.

"You can sit down if you want." River motioned to a metal chair in his little dining space. Everything looked like it was from IKEA, which made me feel sad and then classist for feeling sad. River stretched his arms and clasped his hands behind his head, his penis dangling lazily, like the thing was killing time before clocking into work, which, I guess, it technically was.

I sat down, took off my shoes, doing my best not to stare at him, as if this was a real date, and I didn't want him to know how much I wanted him. I took off my shorts, underwear, and shirt. The differences in our bodies was humbling, like a "before" and "after" in an infomercial. I stood there, naked, awaiting my instructions.

"Did you want to fuck on the dining room table?" River asked, misreading my apprehension but seemingly open to the idea.

"What? No. I was just . . . I can go wherever. I'm totally flexi." I flashed him a thumbs-up and immediately regretted it.

"Let's go to my bedroom." River got up from the couch, walked over, and took me by the hand.

"You have a nice ass," he practically whispered. "It's like two bubbles."

"Thank you, sir. I can't wait for you to, uh, pop it." SIR? POP MY BUBBLE? DEAR GOD, HOW AM I EVEN ALLOWED TO HAVE SEX WITH PEOPLE? HOW IS IT NOT ILLE-GAL? Oh yeah, in this case it *is* illegal.

We walked into his bedroom, which was carpeted. Carpet is like hardwood floor but with low self-esteem. Like it needs to get all pretty for you and feel good on your toes, but you're like, "Babe, you actually look way better when you're natural."

We sat on the bed. River asked what I was into.

"Um, well, I'm a writer and—"

"No, I mean, sex stuff."

"Oh! I'm sorry. Uh, that's a very good question. Hmmm . . ."

Suddenly, a dog's bark erupted from the closet. An adorable little cocker spaniel poked its head out.

"Honey! Quiet!" River yelled. Jesus, even his raised voice was kind of delicate and sensual. "Sorry. She likes to hang out in there sometimes. Is it okay if she stays? I can put her in the bathroom."

"No, no. That's fine." I put a hand on his arm, to reassure him slash establish physical contact. "Her name is Honey?"

"Uh-huh." River laughed. "I know it's weird, but I think people who name their dogs like regular people names are even weirder."

"Oh my god, same! I was just thinking that today."

"Yeah, I met this guy recently; his dog's name was Monica. Creepy, right?"

Ethan. Of course. Drag that corn husk of a human straight to hell.

"Anyway . . ." River put his hand on my chest, rubbing it a bit before drifting further down my stomach.

"Oh, right. Um, can you just fuck me? Like nothing crazy. Just regular?"

"Yes," River said. "One regular fucking coming right up."

CHAPTER 8

I tried to kiss him, but he politely dodged my lips and nibbled on my ear instead. Message received. Ear action is okay. Kissing on the mouth wasn't. I faced his closet door and could see Honey in the hamper, her nose peeking out occasionally from a mound of clothes. River put his mouth on my cock and gently bobbed his head up and down. Any longer, I might've come, so I asked him to stop, and he moved on to playing with my nipples, but when I didn't react, he graduated to fingering my asshole and loosening me up, but at a certain point I was so horny I told him to put it in, and he did, but he got some lube first—Astroglide, water-based, my preferred brand, I mean it's so much better than silicone, which just ruins my sheets—and he slapped it on his dick and painted the ring of my hole with it, and then he put a condom on, which always kills the mood but not more than when you realize you've fucked without one, and finally he gently inserted the head into my asshole, which sent an electric shock through my insides, and he whispered the filthiest, most mind-blowing shit into my ear, but I won't tell you what because it will just translate to cheesy, and then he pushed my head further into the pillows and everything went black, and it hurt but in a way that someone is clearly asking for, and he pulled my hair, and pushed my sweaty face back into the pillows as he came inside me, and then he flipped me over and jerked me off, but each time I was about to come he would stop for a few seconds and start up again, slowly, so fucking slowly. And at first I thought the whole thing was a mistake, a casualty of him not knowing the rhythm of my body, but he kept at it, which felt so good but also so fucking agonizing that I asked him what he was doing to me, and he laughed and was like, "You haven't edged before?" I said no and instead of explaining he continued to manipulate the ebb and flow of my pleasure, and at that moment I realized that River's voice was starting to sound normal, like he wasn't pretending to sound like a porn star from an unspecified Eastern European country, which turned me on even more, and when I came I made these noises that I didn't know were possible. I mean, even Honey started barking. River handed me a hand towel, satisfied with the work he had done.

"Oh," I said, looking behind me at the mess I made. "I'm so sor—"

"Nope. Don't say it."

"Um, how much?" I asked. I was putting on my shoes, all rushed, nervous we had gone over our allotted time.

"Four hundred," River said plainly, taking the sheets off his bed.

"Great," I said. I took out a wad of sweaty bills. I had $500 in cash and was paralyzed with how much to give for tip. I decided on a total of $480. After all, River really did a fantastic job and I also wanted him to like me.

"Do I just—um, I mean, where do I—" I said, waving the bills around.

"You can put it on the kitchen table," River said, starting a load of laundry.

I did as I was told and turned to wave. "Okay," I said. "Well, bye." River ran over to give me a hug. His body felt colder to me when there was a stack of my money nearby.

"Bye, babe," he said, rustling my hair, like you would to your kid brother. I turned to leave and River told me to hold on. My heart beat faster with anticipation. Maybe he was going to actually give me a kiss. I faced him. He was simply counting his money, making sure it was all there. When he finished, he gave a satisfied nod. "Thanks for the tip, cutie," he said.

CHAPTER 9

I walked home from River's, even though I was three miles from my apartment. All in all, I'd say my first paid sexual experience was a mixed bag, especially with that transactional ending. However, it did reignite this feeling I'd been trying to ignore, which is that I am a sexual person who wants to get fucked by a Port Authority's worth of people. How will that work within the confines of my relationship with Gus? TBD. In the meantime though, I gave myself permission to imagine a different kind of future for myself. I imagined Gus and I opening things up and me sharing nudes with a stranger on an app who will continue to message me dirty things after I've orgasmed, and I'll think, *HOW DARE YOU, YOU SEX-STARVED SICKO!!*—even though two minutes earlier I was straight up begging for a picture of his hole. I imagined a guy at my gym who I will let jerk me off in the steam room, even though I don't think he's that cute, and in exchange for a halfhearted hand-job I will have to see him multiple times a week and share a gross knowing smile forever. I imagined the guys I will take home from bars and have to avoid in the supermarket years later, and the places I will travel for dick ("Satan Monica at rush hour? C U soon!"), I imagined—god forbid—me and Gus breaking up and me behaving like a little slut to numb the pain and letting a stranger fuck me without a condom because let's burn it all down, honey. I imagined me FaceTiming a boy who lives in Chicago who liked my episode of *Sammy Says* and DMed me a picture of his dick, so here I am being polite and stroking my cock in return as he fingers his asshole on a broken futon, and I have to see the inside of his sad studio apartment and the fact that he . . . wait . . . is that a Joe Rogan poster on his wall? Jesus fucking Christ.

I imagined being single for years—the novelty of sluttiness having faded and been replaced with the low hum of loneliness—but then I have a hookup that leaves me feeling seen and satiated, maybe even happy, and then, of course I want more from this person, it's so rare to not want to leave, but then I realize he actually only sees me as another person he has to avoid at the supermarket. Try again.

I thought about River and how, in the grand scheme of things, it's really not that bad what we did, it was like sex therapy, and then I thought about it for a little bit longer, until I was back at my apartment, putting my key in the door, looking at my amazing boyfriend, whose eyes were glued to the television screen, having no clue that I just paid a man to fuck me while his dog watched from the hamper.

CHAPTER 10

Gus and I ordered Postmates again for dinner. We went for Chinese this time, thinking it would be cheaper, but the total ended up being $80. I played Chet Baker on our Alexa, which is probably recording our conversations and sending them to the government, and we talked about the one person in our friend group that everybody hated, Justin, who was going to Burning Man for the first time.

"People only go to festivals so they can identify as a person who goes to festivals," I said, as I gulped down hot-and-sour soup.

"Yeah, but that's Justin. He's sort of blank. He just adapts to whatever the setting is," Gus said, drinking his red wine, a gamay ($35). "I'm not sure there's any *there* there."

"Well, he's only going to Burning Man because Brian's going."

Brian was the twenty-six-year-old Justin was currently dating, who voted for Trump. Allegedly. No one has hard evidence, but he posts vaguely alt-right memes on Facebook and everyone is creeped out, but also grateful for any gossip to distract us from our own dark lives.

"Yeah, they need to break up. Did you hear about the fight he had over gun control with Charles at Akbar?"

"Uh-huh." Of course I'd heard. Gus and I discussed it last week with the rest of our friend group. I love all my friends. I've worked hard to bring together this tribe of like-minded gays, but the déjà vu of our conversations can be grating. We hit the familiar beats: work, *Drag Race*, a quick detour into politics, a big chunk dedicated to who's fucking whom (literally and figuratively), a bitch sesh about Justin, then back to work talk then back to goddamn Justin followed by some pop-star musings and, what do you know, we're all drunk, let's go home.

"Well, I just heard from Augie that after their fight, they all went into the bathroom and sucked each other off," Gus said, mildly horrified.

"Well, that's one way to end an argument," I said.

"Yeah, they're already open. Can you believe it? I don't think they even, like, had a moment where they were just sleeping with each other. It's like, uh, slow down."

A vision of River face-fucking me flashed in front of my eyes, and I nervously spilled some hot-and-sour soup on myself. Without missing a beat, Gus wiped it up with a napkin.

Gus and I were practically the lone holdouts on being open. After all these years, I didn't know why we hadn't taken the plunge. Lately I'd been feeling more and more that monogamy, like capitalism or keto, wasn't sustainable, but I couldn't be sure Gus was on the same page. Whenever Gus and I'd discuss our friends in open relationships, we would do it with a sort of judgmental eye-roll like, "Oh, those crazy kids! When will they get their shit together?" I think a part of us secretly prided ourselves on not being That Kind of Gay. We liked conforming to these heteronormative roles of Gus being more of the homemaker and me being the one who makes a lot of money and is career-driven, and yeah, we also don't fuck anyone else and we have vaguely unsatisfying sex, like all the straight couples that came (or, more importantly, didn't come) before us. I think Gus, in particular, likes to project this radicalized queer self but deep down likes the trappings of tradition, and he thinks I'm the same way, which brings him comfort. He's with someone who doesn't want to draw outside the lines and plans to eventually get married and adopt children. Maybe he's right. Maybe I do want those things. Or maybe I've only been okay with fucking one person because I didn't believe there'd be any other option for me. Either way, Gus acting vaguely bitchy about Justin and Brian hooking up with Charles reinforced my decision to not tell him about River. He's a Mister Rogers gay. He wouldn't understand.

"Well, good for Brian and Justin on their bathroom sex journey," I said, genuinely meaning it.

"Uh, yeah," Gus said, laughing. "Sure. Best of luck to them. Really sounds like it's going to end well."

When we finished dinner, I noticed we had only drunk three-quarters of a bottle of wine each. I felt proud of us for not finishing a whole bottle.

Gus and I have a fan in the bedroom. We call it Helga. I don't know why. In lieu of having kids or pets, we've decided to anthropomorphize a fan. It's so dumb, and I love it so much.

"Can you turn on Helga?" I asked Gus, tipsy in bed and Googling pictures of Parker Posey walking her dog Gracie (RIP) around New York.

"Yes, my widdle angel." Gus flipped Helga's switch.

"You always forget about her," I said. "She senses it, you know. She feels the distance from her father."

"WHAT? I CAN'T HEAR YOU!" Gus said.

Gus got naked and crawled into bed with me. I turned off the light and rolled onto my side. Gus sidled up behind me, rubbing his cock against my ass, which took me off-guard, considering that we usually had sex on Saturday mornings. Having come earlier with River, I was in no mood to fuck, but this was a big gesture for Gus—we never deviated from the schedule—and to reject him outright would be too devastating. So I went to work. I gave him a blowjob that was so dispassionate I would've fired me if I were Gus. But Gus, ever the giver, wanted to go down on me instead. In order to get hard, I consulted my emergency "I need to cum!!!!" file—scenarios that never failed to get me aroused, like getting fucked over a desk by my first boss, an aging narcissist with gorgeous hair and a lean, tight body, or hooking up with a maintenance worker named Saul from the first apartment I'd ever lived in who liked to take his shirt off and wasn't even that hot but gave off vibes that he could take care of me sexually, emotionally, and possibly even spiritually.

Neither of my fantasies was doing the trick. I could sense Gus growing concerned as he sucked my stage-one hard-on. He came up for air.

"You okay, my widdle angel?" he asked, out of breath.

More baby talk. A suicide note to accompany my already-dead erection.

"Yeah." I wiggled my body away. "I'm sorry. I just, I think my stomach is upset from the Chinese food earlier. I don't think we should order from there anymore. Too heavy."

Disappointment radiated from Gus's cock-hungry mouth. "Oh. Okay. No worries."

"But I can continue going down on you, if you want!" *Please don't take me up on that. That wasn't a real offer.*

"No, don't worry about it. I wuv you."

Relief.

"I wuv you too."

Gus rolled over and immediately fell asleep. If I had come when he blew me, I could've maybe confessed to him about River in that blissful shield of postcoital bliss because we would've felt stable, because I would've earned me getting railed by a stranger.

But I didn't come. I barely got hard as he talked to me in gibberish. You hear stories about couples losing their sexual spark, that you really have to Work At It, but I thought that mostly applied to repressed straight couples that consider a finger in the ass to be exotic.

One of the first things Gus and I did together as a couple was fly to San Francisco. No reason why. Just to celebrate being young and in love and all that. We spent the weekend in a sex cave, only leaving the hotel room once to drink strong, syrupy tiki drinks at the hotel bar. I got wasted and summoned the courage to tell him about my disability (my version of "meet the parents"), and Gus nodded and said the right comforting things, which then turned into us having Emotional Sex—the kind where you bare your soul and then have sex to reinforce that you just experienced an intimate thing together. We never really discussed my disability again— mostly because I think Gus sensed I didn't want to and he was right. Talking about it once and knowing he was okay with it was enough for me.

I'd brought three jockstraps, which were basically in tatters by the time our fuck festival had ended. The sex that weekend was funny, sexy, awkward, familiar, strange, and never boring. You think to yourself, as you're getting pummeled for the fourth time in twelve hours, I will never tire of this person being inside of me. We will be the exception.

I still think we can make our way back to the SF Fuck Festival or at least land somewhere close to it. The passion and the love are still there. But lying in bed with my limp dick and Gus snoring at a deafening volume, I knew that my experience with River wouldn't be enough. I needed to have my Cumspringa. I want to be with someone who, if I spilled hot-and-sour soup on myself, would tell me, "Clean it up yourself, you stupid widdle baby!!!" I want to be with someone who would tell me if I'm looking too thick in the midsection. I want to be with someone who could buy me an expensive dinner and then fuck me in his stunning palatial house while talking about his stock portfolio. Why not? Growing up gay and disabled, I was taught not to want much, to feel grateful for whatever came my way. A live-in boyfriend was above and beyond what I should've dared dream for myself. Meanwhile, all around me, straight white guys were taking giant chunks out of life and leaving no leftovers for the rest of us. They see what they want, they get it, they don't bother asking questions. I want that kind of confidence. I want to stop the everyday mental gymnastics of making everyone around me comfortable with my identity because I am Kerri Struggling.

It was time for me to become the boy with the most cake, I decided. It was time for me to get everything and anything I wanted.

Or not. I don't know. Cake has a lot of calories, and I have to get thin for my body-shaming fantasy/nightmare suitor.

CHAPTER 11

Some things to know about cerebral palsy: it's a group of neurological disorders that causes a loss of motor function and can manifest in a variety of ways like trouble walking, talking, and being accepted into our massive bitch of a society.

I didn't have a traumatic childhood. Well, besides my mom leaving. And my dad, while loving, was always kind of in his own world. But still, all things considered, it was pretty fucking solid. I remember getting teased only once for my disability in middle school, for drooling on Chelsea Comer during science class, but that was a fair criticism. Ultimately though, it didn't matter how idyllic my adolescence was, how supportive my friends were, how hard my dad tried to make me feel "normal." When I left my protective bubble, I had to deal with strangers walking up to me asking if I needed to go to a hospital, teachers assuming that I was mentally slow, bosses questioning if I could hack it. And forget about our sexuality, our desires. The only way someone with CP could get laid is if we paid for it. (Maybe that's why I never considered sex workers until recently. I didn't want to be a cliché.)

In high school, I came out of the closet to much fanfare and even scored a boyfriend. I mean, he was the only other out gay person in school so it wasn't the hugest achievement, but still I couldn't believe it. I had convinced myself that I was doomed liked the Elephant Man. (Sidebar: Have you seen the photos of Bradley Cooper playing the Elephant Man in a play but he didn't use any makeup, he just scrunched up his face? How unfortunate for everyone involved.) But Dylan came along and was so dreamy and nice (you have to be dreamy if you're named Dylan . . . it's the law), and we fucked like crazy, these two thirsty seventeen-year-olds lost in each other's bodies, with no idea that they were having terrible sex because in the beginning there's no such thing as good or bad sex, there's just sex or no sex, and, you know, we had fun, and did boneheaded things like say "I love you" after two weeks, even though I had quiet suspicions that he was slightly stupid and selfish—he always came first and didn't care if I finished, and one time he monologued to me about his "skin regime"—but again, I was just happy to be there, to be included. It was like I had been given temporary access to a world that was never meant for someone like me, and when I shared my fears with Dylan, revealed how insecure I was—are you sure you want to date me?—he would reassure me and we would start fucking and for two minutes (maybe five), I would feel deserving of my place with this possibly stupid definitely selfish hot person, until one day Dylan left me for a freshman who had decided to experiment with his sexuality after watching *Velvet Goldmine*, and any ounce of self-esteem I had managed to accrue was gone, just like that. What's worse, the biggest bitch in school, Kristy Sullivan, came up to me shortly after our breakup and hissed, "What did you expect, Elliott? You're, like, disabled."

Okay, wow. Was Kristy made in a lab by CW execs in search of the perfect teen villain? I wish I could have written off her comment and grieved my breakup like a "normal" gay teen in 2005 (read: go psycho for six months, make sad playlists, bleach my hair, stalk new guys on Myspace, get over it), but instead the experience instilled a permanent state of wanting inside of me.

I never doubted my career or being successful. I was driven, ambitious, did not fuck around, but it was more meaningful when a nobody from Delaware once commented "sit on my face" on my Instagram than when I got staffed on my first television show. How strange that we can saw off certain parts of ourselves, so we remain confident in one area, an area that is challenging for others, only to feel completely hopeless in another.

By the way, I recently looked up Dylan on Facebook. He's married to a woman who looks like she has a good skin regimen.

CHAPTER 12

Work was more unnerving than usual because whenever I looked at Ethan all I could think about was that we had both fucked River. When he was eating his sad lunch of low-fat cottage cheese and a bouillon cube, all I could picture was River's dick in his curd-filled mouth. When he complained that he was cold and demanded that Joan raise the thermostat, I wondered what the ideal temperature in his house was when his "brought to you by Barry's Bootcamp and, let's face it, possibly Sculptra" ass was naked with River.

I was relieved when we broke off to write individual scenes, because it meant I didn't have to dwell upon the dreaded Ethan (or Ethan with River, on River, in River) anymore.

"Come write with me," Joan said. "It's so wrong that your office is on the other side of the floor."

Joan and I sat crammed at her desk to work out scenes with Sammy and her crush, who—unbeknownst to Sammy—is a robot just like her. Fascinating.

"Joan, would you ever hire a sex worker? Like Ethan did?"

"It's different for women, I think. I need to know that the man I'm fucking wants me. Which is completely at odds with the fact that I've been with the same guy for the past twenty years, I admit."

"Well, what if he did want you?"

Joan is pretty. Like, objectively so. She's petite and has big boobs. Straight guys love that shit, right? But she's also in her late forties, living in Los Angeles, so there was that.

"Maybe back in my prime. But definitely not now. And anyway, I've never been that sexual of a person to begin with. I guess I prefer getting emotionally fucked by gay bosses over, you know, actual penetration. That's my kink."

"What's a good joke for when Sammy meets robot guy at the coffee shop?" I asked, realizing my scene was due in twenty minutes.

"Have you hired one?"

"Why?" I said, getting defensive. "Do I look like I need to?"

"I don't know. Is there a type?"

"Yeah, gross old men who have to pay for it. And people like Ethan who get off on the power dynamics."

Joan looked at me in all seriousness and said, "Girl, are you the coffee I ordered? Because you provide me with a brief window of optimism every day."

"Huh?"

"For your script. The coffee shop? I don't know. I'm not funny anymore, sorry."

The sunset was a stunning pink and juicy Starburst, so I didn't really mind the walk back to the gate, even though a tour bus did almost run me over while doling out Ray Romano trivia, and my hangover decided to show up like an inconsiderate yet not entirely unexpected houseguest.

Gus and I drink a full bottle of wine each every night, sometimes more on the weekends. It didn't used to be this way. We started off with the occasional visit to our local wine shop, which introduced us to all these insanely delicious natural wines. Have you heard of natural wines? It's wine with no added sulfites and no chemical intervention. This makes the wine taste of the earth and sometimes also literally smell like dirt. Anyway, we got obsessed and started stocking up at home, which we never really had. At best, we were social drinkers, but before we knew it there we were, getting cases of natural wine delivered, joining wine clubs. At first, we felt sinful for splitting a bottle of wine each night ("Is this a lot or is it just us being adults?"), and over time opening two bottles became the norm. For the last few years, I've basically had a constant hangover. Somehow it doesn't prevent me from going about my day, which I think is the scariest part. It's very doable. While I do genuinely love the taste of wine and talking about it and trying different varietals and vintages and fantasizing about visiting the Loire Valley, our hobby acts as a mask for what is most likely a real problem.

Drinking also fills the silence during those dinners when Gus and I don't have anything to say to each other—not because we're angry or upset but because there's only so much you can say to the person you've had dinner with almost every single night for the past five years. Wine helps erode the familiarity and boredom. It provides a sliver of promise even if it actually just gives each night a *Groundhog Day* quality. It didn't matter. Once you're drunk and realize nothing's different, you're too fucked up to care. I've suggested taking breaks from drinking to Gus. He says we don't need to, which, I mean, of course he does. Gus comes home every night wrapped in coils of anxiety and stress over his shitty job and goes straight to the bottle. I do too, but I'm a better drunk than Gus is. I just get mellow and giggly. Gus gets this dopey look in his eyes and starts slurring his words. He starts pawing at me and becomes affectionate to an obnoxious and unattractive degree. There's a bigger contrast between Sober Gus and Drunk Gus. Something larger is being released here. And, yes, a sick part of me enjoys that he's the messier one. It makes me feel like I have a better handle on things. At least I question our drinking. At least I'm trying to think critically about it.

I was fishing in my bag for Advil, knowing full well that I would be starting a new booze journey in a few hours, when I felt my phone buzz. I dug for it in my bag, as the pink streaks in the sky morphed into lavender, and when I found it, there was a one-word text from River.

"Hey."

The sudden urge to take a shit gripped me, when a woman whizzed up next to me in her golf cart, concern etched across her ruddy complexion.

"Are you okay? Do you need a ride somewhere, honey?"

At last. The condescension of strangers working in my favor.

Her name was Jen, and she was bringing Rachel Bilson her dinner (bone broth perched perilously on her lap), and she asked me if I had been hurt. I told her I had been, actually. Hurt by a society that didn't understand me or my body. She looked at me funny and laughed uncomfortably before saying, "The bathroom's in this building."

While shitting, I considered a response to River's text. What did he want? Could he have caught feelings for me during our session and be contacting me to have dinner or get a drink or maybe he wanted to fuck for free? (I realize I'm insane.) I wrote back: "Hey. How are ya?"

The text bubble popped up. This is it. It's happening.

"Think U left ur ID here?"

He texted a picture. Sure enough it was mine. Me at twenty-six, cross-eyed, head full of hair, pre-Propecia.

I wrote back: "Oh, god, thanks! I can pick it up now if you want."

Ping. "Got a client. 9:30?"

No. That was when Gus and I would be finishing dinner, pleasantly drunk, ready to watch some prestige television series that gets really good in season four. And, besides, what kind of excuse could I come up with to tell Gus? Catching drinks with someone this late on a work night would require an explanation.

I wrote back: "Sure. See you then."

CHAPTER 13

River's apartment looked better at night, like it had its makeup on. When he answered the door, he was wearing an Everlane tank top and gym shorts, and in the background I could hear his bathtub running. He acted surprised to see me there, even though he was the one who had buzzed me up, and went to retrieve my ID. When he came back, I took my ID, said thank you, and River suddenly looked like he was hiding something, and I said what's wrong, and he told me he was getting ready to give Honey a bath, but Honey freaks out, which usually makes it a two-person job, but the person who helped him was out of town, and he knew this was weird but could I maybe help him? I wouldn't have to do anything, just make sure Honey didn't hop out of the bathtub.

River was right. The second we brought Honey into the bathroom, she went ballistic and started whimpering, and I had to hold her still as River and I gently lowered her into the tub. River lathered her up as I kneeled on the bathroom floor, grasping her tight, trying to calm her down, getting my shirt wet. It was a profoundly uncomfortable position for my body to be in, but I didn't say anything. I wanted to appear to be the kind of limber person who could put his ankles behind his ears at a moment's notice.

"You have really bad vision," River said, briefly looking at me as he washed Honey's fur.

"How would you know?"

"I'm studying to be an optician. What are you, shortsighted, nearsighted?"

"Um, a little bit of both?"

"What's your prescription?" River squinted, as if in the middle of solving a math problem.

He guessed, rattling off a bunch of numbers, and I said I didn't know and laughed, but mostly I was annoyed because here was another person taking apart my body and examining its deficits, feeling a sense of ownership over me which I will never comprehend. Also, I was hunched over on my knees, swallowing the pain, thinking I was presenting as normal, and he was still able to find things that were wrong with me.

"Do people ask you about your prescription a lot?" River said, massaging Honey's ears. "You seem kinda miffed."

"I do?"

"Only a little."

"I'm sorry."

"What did I tell you about that word?"

Honey started barking.

"See?" He continued smiling. "Even Honey hates when you say it. Don't you, widdle girl?" River said, rubbing his nose against Honey's. River's baby talk reminded me of Gus, and for a second I remembered a life outside this bathroom, one that didn't involve giving my sex worker's dog a bath.

"Okay, fine." I took a deep, involuntary sigh. "I didn't mean to do that just now. It's like a tic," I said.

"K. I wouldn't care, either way." River started to rinse Honey.

"Actually, you know what? It did annoy me. I clearly do not have the greatest vision. My lenses are thick. So why even bring it up?"

"It's what I do for a living. Well, besides, you know, the other thing." He turned Honey's head. "Geez, she really hates this. Could you grab me a towel?"

"Sure." I got up from the floor and my knees immediately thanked me.

"They're in the hallway closet."

I got two towels, which, curiously, were stacked next to some lube and a butt plug. God, even his towel closet oozed sex. When I returned, River was draining the bathtub and complimenting Honey on a good job. I handed him one of the towels and we dried her off. I didn't want the night to end, even though I wasn't having any fun. When Honey was dry, River looked over and said thank you and then took my glasses from my face and cleaned them.

"I'm doing this just to annoy you," River said.

Before handing them back, he said, "You look really good without your glasses on." And I asked him what do I look like with my glasses on, and he said I also looked good, just a different kind of good, and then he chuckled and I smacked his arm playfully, which struck me as a boldly intimate move on my part, more intimate than someone fucking you, because there's no real goal other than bantering with a person, volleying and praying they'll serve back whatever you give them.

For a moment, our vibe seemed flirty, so I decided to go in for a kiss, even though I'd surmised from before that wasn't allowed. Sure enough, River stepped back, saying he didn't see clients after ten but we could schedule something for tomorrow.

I left River's apartment and decided to walk home. The whole way I couldn't stop feeling like I had just slimed myself, like a contestant on one of those Nickelodeon game shows you'd watch while home from school with a stomachache, and how much more desperate could I possibly be, not respecting River's boundaries by making a move on him as if this was normal and not an arrangement, and yeah, I made an appointment for the following night, but you know what? I'm not going to apologize for that.

CHAPTER 14

I had told Gus I was getting a drink with a recent college grad who was begging for advice on breaking into television writing. Needlessly complicated, but if I'd said I was off to see a mutual friend, the story could have been cross-referenced, and I couldn't afford the added risk. When I arrived home later that night, Gus was drunk and being overly affectionate, like a dog almost pissing himself in delight when his owner came home. I didn't need to ask what he had done all evening, because I knew he'd been lobotomizing himself in front of the television—scripted TV shows only, reality was too triggering for him to watch. He said it was like taking his work home with him. Gus asked me a million questions about the drinks, and I couldn't help but act inconvenienced, even though he was genuinely happy to see me, and I was just pissed because I had to lie yet again, which reminded me of what I'd done, what I'd been doing.

In bed, I answered emails and looked at my endless to-do list. Sometimes I long for that last gasp of quiet before your life starts.

You know, at twenty-two or twenty-three, when you graduate and, other than making rent, you have no real commitments or obligations. The days belong to you, only you. Not your boyfriend, not your boss, not your mortgage. (Just kidding, no one can afford a house.) I look around at everything I've built for myself, this for-the-most-part impressive life, and I feel proud. But there are times I would trade it in for another chance to sit on a friend's porch for five hours, drinking boxed wine and recapping last night's shenanigans—which is silly because you spent the whole evening together, and the only reason you did anything crazy was so you'd have something to talk about the next day, on the porch with the same people, before going out and doing it all over again. I guess I miss the inconsequential nothingness. The idea that you could take three months of your life and throw it in the trash because everything would pretty much end up the same either way. I miss being content with what was right in front of me. I miss being twenty-two and wearing a tank top and having muscles for no reason and still thinking I was a gargoyle. I miss having a choice and making the wrong one. I miss obsessing over boys whose names, in six months' time, would elude my grasp if I saw them in a bookstore. I miss assuming everything was meant for me: this T-shirt, this party, these streets, this weather, this song . . . they were all red carpets for my existence.

I did end up getting everything I wanted: a career, a boyfriend, Jonathan Adler pillows. Maybe if I hadn't, I wouldn't be romanticizing my early twenties. But existential crises like these make me think about Cookie Mueller, who was this cult actress in John Waters's early films, best friend to photographer Nan Goldin and 100 percent party girl, and I'm envious that she figured out how to sculpt an entire life out of her Nothing. She found a way to make her life belong to her and no one else.

She died at forty. AIDS complications. Because apparently, you can't charge experiences to the Life credit card forever. Eventually you pay or perish. I respect people who don't buy the insurance, who don't get the partner, the kids, the job, which to me are flimsy shields against the inevitability of death. It's to make sure when you're eighty and shitting your pants, someone will be there to change your adult diapers. They have no choice. You gave them life and in return they have to give you an easier death. I bought the insurance. I ordered the gay bougie package. Most of my furniture is from West Elm. Do you know how pitiful that is? It's a Nightmare on West Elm Street.

I've sat through so many pointless brunches with other upwardly mobile gays that our meals are basically a game of Mad Libs: *Insert adjective to describe your gay vacation here. Insert name of gay famous person whose house you recently went to for a dinner party.* (It's always Jesse Tyler Ferguson. WHY?) *Insert playful fight with your spouse designed to showcase that you two are REAL and FLAWED. Insert flirty comment to demonstrate that you haven't gone full snooze and are DTF outside the relationship.*

Make no mistake, I fought tooth and nail for this role. I auditioned for years for Rich Gay, eventually got it, and now I do shows daily, matinee and evening. Guess what? It's boring. Did a black trans woman really throw the first brick at Stonewall so cis white gays could eat $26 eggs Benedict as they unpacked the new Robyn album?

Gus likes it, though. I can tell. He loves playing the part. It goes back to him secretly being an assimilationist gay. He likes being "normal." He likes feeling secure. He likes talking to other gay men who have a big nice house in Los Feliz and are showing us pictures of their expensive wedding and, oh my god, kids? We're not sure. But probably! He gets access to this domesticated wealthy world through me, and he feels comfortable there—away from his lackluster job and his own confusion and lack of direction over his future. He can cosplay as an Affluent Gay whose biggest dilemma is Provincetown or Fire Island for the summer.

I don't know if I want the insurance anymore. And I certainly don't want to eat another brunch. Life is too short to spend a fortune on what is essentially eggs. It's just eggs.

CHAPTER 15

On my first date with Gus, I wore an expensive outfit that said, "I will be able to retire at sixty-five, so stick with me, baby!" Gus looked incredible too. His outfit was very "I'm the slutty camp counselor who gets killed first in the horror movie." He was thinner then. He didn't work out, but he had a youthful metabolism on his side and he was leading with his sexuality, and I responded to it because sexuality was what I didn't have and couldn't lead with. I really didn't want to fuck this up. Gus was a ticket to kindness and to love: a world my psychology had previously denied me access to. And if I could just keep my shit together, if I could ward off self-sabotage, I'd let myself be loved by this person and I'd be okay. I'd end up better than all the other sad gay disabled boys who'd come before me.

I'm realizing that so much of my existence was focused on outrunning what seemed to be a preordained fate of loneliness. Even on that first date with Gus, which ended up being genuinely amazing, I still couldn't fully relax. I was still running.

CHAPTER 16

When I showed up to River's, I sat down and took off my shoes almost immediately, and the first thing he said to me was "Your feet are filthy."

I looked at the bottoms of my feet and could not spot the lie. I'd walked there from my apartment (drinks with a friend, I told Gus, a woman he barely knew) and I didn't wear socks and it was summer, so yeah. Filthy.

"I won't apologize for that. I mean, of course I want to, but I can't. You won't let me, remember?"

"Very good," River said, taking off his crisp white Hanes V-neck, which showcased every muscle perfectly. "Now go rinse them off in the bathtub."

"Oh, really?" I said, smirking. "Is this some kind of sub/dom thing?"

"No. Your feet are black on the bottom and they smell. I don't want those things on my bed."

His comment is one that would've cut me deep, my insides spilling out onto his cracked linoleum floor, but his matter-of-fact delivery made getting mad difficult. Plus, it was sexy that he trusted me to do something, that he thought of me as capable. Gus would've licked the dirt off my feet himself.

I went into the bathroom and noticed River had terrible shampoo. Like, the kind you get at CVS that smells like melons and gives your hair an awful leather-y texture. It depressed me that he was still buying the cheap stuff. His hair was nice. It deserved better. I placed a foot under the running faucet and watched the dirt immediately wash off and circle the drain. River walked in, fully nude.

"How do we always end up in the bathtub doing nonsexual things?" I said, doing my best impression of someone who is casual and playful.

The setup did feel kind of erotic. I liked him wanting to make me better, wanting to make my feet smell nice, even though the request was more for his benefit than mine.

"Is this okay?" I said, trying to show him the bottoms of my feet, but I fell and came inches from hitting my head against the tub. River helped me up.

"Are you all right? Did you hurt yourself?" he asked, examining my face.

"No, I'm fine."

"You should wear socks," he said. "Why don't you?"

"I don't know."

I did, actually. I didn't wear socks because my CP made them hard to put on. CP: 1. Socks: 0.

"You ask a lot of questions," I said.

"Do you not want me to? This is your time."

"Oh, are we on the clock? Am I paying you to watch me wash my feet, because, um, that's not what I asked for." The second the words left my mouth, I regretted them. River got quiet and turned off the faucet.

"You're good to go."

"Thank you."

We stood next to each other for a moment. Me still in the bathtub, him outside of it.

"I don't mind when you ask me questions," I said. "In fact, I kind of like it."

"I have another one for you."

"All right."

"How would you like to get fucked tonight?" River grabbed my cock, which was just waking up from its slumber.

"I was actually thinking we could do some stuff with my feet," I said, teasing.

"Foot stuff is extra," River shot back.

"Okay, then, let's not reinvent the wheel." I grabbed River's dick. Two guys with clean feet just grabbing each other's dicks. Then we went to his bedroom. I asked River if I could give him a rimjob, and he said sure and got all on fours, sticking his butt out, and I approached it with trepidation because it was the first ass I'd eaten in years, and River sensed my nerves and turned to look back over his shoulder and say, "It's less about technique, okay? To give a good rimjob, all you need is a love of eating ass." I nodded and grabbed his cheeks for balance before diving into his waxed, hairless hole. I've talked about his ass before—it's fabulous, although up close I spotted one zit and felt relieved he was human—but if I had one complaint, it was almost too muscle-y. The ideal ass, in my opinion, has to have some jiggle and fat. You must have something to hold on to.

I gripped on as best as I could and went in with my tongue, circling River's hole, one, two, three times, before plunging in deeper. I was expecting a whiff of standard ass smells, but I got nothing. River's asshole tasted blank, scrubbed of any evidence of shit. It was remarkable. I couldn't believe it. I wanted to come up for air and ask River what his secret was. I spend like forty minutes cleaning my asshole, and here his was, smelling like a unisex perfume.

As I thrust my tongue, River began letting out these exaggerated loud moans, which motivated me to do a better job. He was going to give me real ones, dammit. I buried my face in even further, licking up every inch of his hole, spreading his cheeks and spitting into his ass before eating it like it was my last meal on execution day. I have a long, dexterous tongue, which helped, and it didn't take long before River's overblown moans of pleasure evolved into authentic ones. There was a hint of surprise in his voice; he hadn't expected to enjoy himself as much as he was. I was so fucking proud.

River offered to return the favor, but by that point I was itching to fuck. He slapped a condom on and I straddled his hips, slowly grinding my ass into his cock. My shorts were pulled down partway, leaving enough room for him to enter me. I wanted the opposite of our first time, for us to fuck face-to-face and for me to be the one in control, setting the pace, the depth, the rhythm. Cowgirl (Cowboy? Whatever. Gender is a construct.) is my favorite position, bottoming on top, even though my legs—tight from the cerebral palsy—start to ache after a while.

"Fuck my hole," I said.

"Oh, yeah, man. You are so fucking tight," River said, giving me BelAmi vibes.

I stopped riding him. "Use your regular voice," I said.

"Maybe I don't want to," he said. "Maybe I like talking like this."

I could feel Honey's eyes on me from her laundry pile in the closet.

"I don't care if you like it," I said, my voice unwavering. "Talk to me like you'd talk to your dry cleaner."

"Okay, fine," River said, an edge of nerves to his voice.

I resumed my ride.

"Does that feel good?" he said to me, softly, almost tenderly.

"Yeah."

"Kiss me on my mouth," River said.

Holy shit. I had been given permission to kiss. It felt very "And the Best Client of a Sex Worker award goes to . . ." I went in slowly, kissing the sides of his mouth until I'd teased him enough and went for his lips. I was expecting an aggressive tonguing experience, very alpha male, but instead he moved his in and out gently, gliding the tip of his tongue over mine, tracing the inside of my lips.

When he cupped my face with his hands, I sped up my rhythm. Eventually my thigh muscles began to burn, so I braced my hands on the mattress to outsource some support. All the while, River made the softest, sweetest noises. I was suddenly jealous of his dry cleaner. When his mouth contorted into those telltale "I'm going to come" shapes, I rode him for all I was worth. It energized me, being in charge of his pleasure. I could cut off his orgasm if I wanted to.

"Feel good?" I asked, between kisses.

River nodded, eyes closed, his face covered with sweat, both his and mine.

"You like this, don't you? With me?"

"I do," River said. "I like it."

He groaned as he came, bucking underneath me. His O-face was hideous, like he was reaching for an object on a high shelf that might not be there, but I was so grateful for it to not resemble the last shot of a porno. Once he emerged from his fugue state, he reached for my dick.

"No, no," I said, swatting his hand away. "I'm good."

River sighed, falling back into his pillow. Honey emerged from the closet and jumped on the bed. He pulled her close. I sat there, watching them cuddle in a world of their own, and knew that it was time to go home. I had someone to cuddle with too.

CHAPTER 17

At work, we were trying to break an impossible story about Sammy being bullied by a mom who was anti-robot (a half-baked metaphor for xenophobia), and I stayed silent most of the day, too nervous to engage and risk being under Ethan's scrutiny. I would think of a joke pitch, consider raising my hand to tell it, and then ultimately decide against it. Two minutes later Tom or Cindy would pitch the same exact joke or something similar and be met with praise. I'd kick myself, angry that Ethan was successfully whittling away my confidence, making me feel like I wasn't funny or smart enough to work on a show that had a 22% rating on Rotten Tomatoes. But it also wasn't surprising that Ethan was making me shut down and retreat inward. He was old school in that he thought cultivating a culture of fear would lead people to produce their best work. For some of the TV writers who'd, you know, written on *Car 54, Where Are You?* in 1962, this discomfort was familiar and actually didn't make their work suffer. But here I was, crazy for having not been brought up around a toxic envi-

ronment and instead metabolizing this for what it was—abuse—
rather than misguided motivation.

"Why don't Joan and Elliott tackle the episode?" Ethan said,
bemused. At least he finally said my name.

"Tackle what, Ethan?" Joan asked.

"If you guys can break this story on your own, I'll let you write it."

I was uneasy. I didn't want to write an episode. A month ago, I
would've. I would've leapt at the chance to prove Ethan wrong. But
I didn't have the fight in me anymore. The torture involved, Ethan's
criticism—none of it was worth the script fee, which, just so you
know, was $28,000.

"Oh, you mean you're going to let us do our jobs for once?"
Joan said, trolling. The air in the room went dead. Unlike me, Joan
didn't give two shits about Ethan and mouthed off to him whenever the mood struck. And I suspect a part of Ethan got off on
it. If you're that rich and successful, you're only surrounded by yes
people, which is good for your fragile ego but is also tedious as shit.
Ethan liked to spar, he needed it.

"Yes, Joan, exactly. I'd like the two of you to do the goddamn
job you're getting paid for. Now go break the episode and don't
come back until you're done."

"Yes, sir," Joan said, saluting him.

Joan and I broke the story in under two hours. I mean, this isn't
The Leftovers, honey. When we returned, no one bothered asking if
we had come up with anything.

That night Gus was out to dinner with friends and I sat at home
"accidentally" getting wasted while watching old episodes of *The
Real Housewives of Beverly Hills*. I wondered if someone like River
watched *The Real Housewives*, and if he did, would he have correct
opinions of the cast or would he break my heart and reveal himself
to be a Kyle Richards stan—a true mark of basicness? Was River

funny? Was he smart? You can tell a lot about a guy by the way he fucks you, but even that didn't give any clues because it was his job.

I finished *The Real Housewives* and took a fresh glass of wine to the bedroom to get drunker and listen to Mazzy Star. I opened the balcony doors that face our courtyard and took in all of our string lights twinkling and got emotional over nothing discernible, and then I started leaving comments on celebrities' Instagrams: "daddy" for Andy Cohen and "why aren't we friends IRL" for Andrew Rannells. I slid into the DMs of a hot bear Gus and I had met in passing in Provincetown. He sent me a picture of his hard dick poking out of his Levi's and I sent him an ass shot, almost falling off my bed in an attempt to capture the ideal angle for minimal back fat. The bear and I do this once every few months. It's our thing.

I imagine a lot of gay men have these types of interactions, little pockets of flirting with strangers and acquaintances. We just don't talk about it. Even with societal acceptance, gay men still indulge in secret behavior. You get drinks with them and eventually you'll hear one confess that he got fucked at a spa downtown, the one everyone gets fucked at. Or one'll recommend a massage place with twink therapists who jerk you off. Or you'll mention a guy, and your friend will be like, "Oh yeah, I went to an orgy at his house a few months ago. He has the nicest hardwood floors, oh my god, I still dream about them."

I love it. I love how gay men do sex. Before Gus and I got together, my dating history left a lot to be desired. There were no sex parties, there was no cruising a hunky guy on the street and going home with him. I once went two years without kissing. This was when I was living in New York, blogging for an unfortunate entertainment site, and I was truly the best I've ever looked. I look at photos from this era and I'm like, "How was I not walking around with a dick in my mouth 24/7?"

The only semi-slutty period I enjoyed was right before Gus and Hudson. I had just wrapped a TV writing job and lost thirty pounds. That was fairly easy to do, considering I'd never exercised before, so really, just moving my body six days a week at the gym and eating small portions made the pounds slip off. I was twenty-eight and skinny, and for the first time in my life I felt as powerful as someone with cerebral palsy could possibly feel. I bet I could've snagged an invite to hang with the sailboat gays in Santa Monica. Boys were paying attention to me in a way they never had. I went on three dates with Buck, a twenty-four-year-old personal assistant who outed himself as a Coldplay fan. And not just the first two albums. Their new stuff. I went out with a struggling thirty-something actor, Ned, and kissed him in the middle of the street and wished him luck on his Dove soap audition. Adam, a producer, I kissed at a restaurant over 3 p.m. margaritas. Craig, a trustafarian, I made out with in his Prius. People were asking me out, and I was saying yes and kissing them, and most of the time it felt like they were actually kissing me back, which was nice, even if I didn't really like them, because it cost me nothing and was proof I mattered that certain summer when my stomach was flat and I was hungry but feeling satiated off compliments and attention. I tried to savor the moment, to acknowledge how good I looked and felt, unlike in my early twenties. I took nudes, knowing that I'd contemplate them ten years later with a combination of pride and pain. Sometimes I think this was the happiest period of my life, but only when I'm drunk and don't know any better.

It all ended when I met Hudson followed by Gus and for a long time I didn't need to kiss Coldplay fans or actors who auditioned for soap commercials to feel okay about myself, but being with River, it was like I'd relapsed, and I wanted to experience him again and again and again. I wanted to experience everyone.

I fell asleep, a bottle and a half of wine deep, with my laptop open. Gus came home and saw what was undoubtedly a familiar scene (I always get the most fucked up when I'm home alone), and he probably laughed to himself, most likely also drunk from slurping down cocktails at dinner, and he took off my glasses and set down a glass of water for my morning hangover and tucked me in.

I used to be satisfied with this. I used to not need more than a boy who brings me water. I don't know if I should be mad at myself for suddenly wanting more or mad at myself for having been okay with less.

CHAPTER 18

I woke up to a headache that was rapidly finding its voice. I dressed gingerly, putting on workout clothes to run off the pain at the gym.

My gym is pretty bare-bones, but the minimalism is intentional. It doesn't have to show off with eucalyptus towels or, hell, even air-conditioning. The place is good enough as is. I've been working out there for six years, and at this point I'm pretty much a local celebrity. I'm the disabled boy who shows up five times a week, getting stronger and stronger, defying the odds!

I feel lucky to love exercise. Finally, an addiction that enhances my life. When I run, I stop returning my brain's texts and I feel fully present in my body: my beautiful, fucked-up, strong, gimp body. Each day some part of myself challenges me. My leg doesn't want to go this way. My arm won't extend fully. That's okay. Compensating is all about adaptation. I relax my mind by listening to podcasts, funny ones, nothing true crime or politics or the history of anything. I don't want to learn about the Ottoman Empire—stop, you can't make me. Sometimes I'll zone out to shoegaze: a genre featuring fuzzy guitars and layered vocals made famous by bands like Ride and My Bloody Valentine. I like to imagine that I'm high on painkillers—not hard to do since I spent a large chunk of my twenties on them—and I'll wait for my endorphins to wake up, nature's opioids, and conjure those old feelings. I don't get remotely close, but I feel pleasant. At some point, you have to make a choice to live inside your body. I spent so much time detached from and resentful of mine. I still am, to a certain extent, but when I started exercising and dropping the pounds, I could see for the first time what I was capable of. Today, exercise is my penance for my continued attempts to fuck with my body, for poisoning myself with a bottle of wine every night.

It's hard to tell if my relationship with substances has improved. Sometimes I worry that I merely swapped out one addiction for a more socially acceptable one. Having a pill problem is a logistical nightmare. They're impossible to get and prohibitively expensive and non–pill users are perpetually concerned about you, as they should be. Opiates are gnarly. You don't even have to be taking that many to experience withdrawals. Still, they are *the best*. They turn your world into a luscious down comforter. I got hooked when I was twenty, after I got my wisdom teeth out, and realized, oh! this was for sure the lens through which I wanted to see the world. At the beginning, getting prescriptions from doctors was easy. I mean, I have cerebral palsy. I should be in chronic pain, even though I'm not. The first few years are spectacular. High as fuck, suntanning in Central Park, then walking the eighty blocks downtown to your apartment, the sun on your skin like a thick coat of paint, feet covered in blisters that you can't feel. What heaven.

But the magic quickly becomes tragic. You begin taking them too often and your face tingles when you run out, so you find a drug dealer, any drug dealer, and you meet under bridges, in random apartments all over the city. Sometimes you don't link up because drug dealers are unreliable, so you get creative and text that girl Lindsay you aren't really close with but who you remembered had pills left over from oral surgery, and she didn't end up taking them because they made her nauseated, and bloop, here you are standing in Lindsay's apartment—Chelsea, doorman building, her parents are rich, everyone's parents are rich in New York—and she's handing them over, but you can tell she's uncomfortable, and you've done your best job acting casual, but desperation is peeking through, and she can see how badly you want it, and you're embarrassed, but that doesn't stop you from taking the pills and hanging out with Lindsay for at least half an hour, that way you can justify why you're here, because Lindsay's a good friend, you're here to chill, the pills are a surprise bonus. Eventually you end up isolating and making promises you know you won't keep and throwing up and nodding off at lunches with friends who don't do drugs and have boyfriends and do fucking yoga and have no idea this has become your entire life.

Until it isn't. I moved to Los Angeles, got a job, and lost all my drug contacts. I get my hands on them occasionally, but the experience is different, and I've already built a bigger life for myself in LA than I ever had in New York and I don't want to lose it. Enough was enough. Simple as that.

Or was it? I used to be so proud of myself for kicking painkillers, especially without rehab or getting truly sober, but alcohol has replaced the pills, let's be honest, which means I've spent over a decade addicted to *something*. And now it looks like I've acquired a third addiction: River. How I'm queasy or need to take a shit before we meet up, that's what would happen when I'd score. The drug may have changed, but everything else is familiar. *You've been here before. When are you going to go somewhere else?*

When I got off the elliptical, my hangover seemed to have grown in size, and my sweat smelled like wine that had fucked a barnyard.

Post-workout, my limbs were shredded and I collapsed on the bed.

"What are you doing?" Gus said, scooting away from me. He was watching *The Sopranos* under the covers.

"I just ran six miles," I said. "I need a second to lie down."

"But you're making the bed all sweaty," Gus said, a tinge of whiny baby in his voice. "Get up please?"

Gus doesn't work out. At all. His idea of exercise is carrying home two bottles of wine from the grocery store, and I can't help myself, it makes me fucking livid. Here he is with a perfect body, all his parts working together as they should, and he doesn't even work out. He lets his muscles atrophy. It's like squandering a beautiful gift. I mean, the things I would do if I were able-bodied, holy shit. I would sit Indian-style, 24/7. I would do advanced yoga. I would buy a mountain bike and ride, baby, ride. I'd go rock climbing for, like, fun. I work so hard every day to achieve the bare minimum. My body is an ever-evolving bag of tricks I have to figure out, and here he is with a body that's the definition of no assembly required, and he's happy to let the whole thing waste away in bed while watching Edie Falco gun for an Emmy nomination.

Unlike me, Gus doesn't have to think about his body. He doesn't have to think about his muscles tightening. He doesn't have to think about stretching. Why would he? His body has never caused him any trouble. It has always been an all-access pass. He doesn't know what it's like to not be able to cook a nice dinner for your boyfriend because your subpar hand-eye coordination means you really shouldn't be wielding a knife. He doesn't know what it's like to be at an unfair disadvantage in bed, to constantly wonder if you're able to provide good sex to your partner. He doesn't know what it's like to feel constant guilt over the things you're unable to do, even though it's not your fault. It's the culture's for making the world with zero consideration of bodies like mine.

Sometimes with Gus, when he cleans up my messes, does all the chores, helps me out of the bath, it feels like my disability is this unbearable presence in our relationship. And then, in frustrating moments like these, it feels like my disability doesn't exist at all.

I lurched off our bed, calves stiff, and limped my way to the bathroom to shower. I looked back at Gus, lying in bed, and watched him discover the tiniest crumb of breakfast toast buried in his chest hair and eat it off his unmoving, able body.

CHAPTER 19

"Fuck that little gay bitch," Joan said, storming into my office.

"You can call me by my name, Joan," I said. "I'm right here."

"No. Ethan," Joan said, plopping down on the side of my desk. "Yesterday was such bullshit. He finally sends us off to break a story. We do it. And we do a damn good job, I must say. . . ."

"No, I know. I'm obsessed with our story. You think she's being bullied for being a robot, but it turns out *she's* the bully and making the mom's life hell."

"Which is real! When you're marginalized, the abuse you endure can turn you into the mean girl."

"Classic defense mechanism. Send us off to script, honey."

"But then, of course, he never even asks about it! He's fucking with us! He never intended to hear us out. We went on a fool's errand."

"I love the word 'fool.'"

"I know," Joan said, eating a fistful of gummy worms. "As a burn, it's so underutilized."

"Well, let's go in there and give him our story. He'll hate it, I'm sure, but fuck him. Also, could you stop eating my candy?"

"Sorry," Joan said, putting the mashed gummies back in their bowl. "I'm in a rage daze."

"Let's do it, Joan. I'm serious!" I then chuckled, surprised by my resolve. "Wow. Look at me, trying to care about my job again. Golly, I still have a flicker of life in me!"

"You know, I should've taken that job on *Grey's Anatomy*. I'm a doctor for fuck's sake. It would've been so much easier than this shit."

"Is that show still on?"

"I think so?" Joan looked at me, like really looked at me for the first time in our conversation, and said, "Are you hungover?"

"A little. . . ," I said, panicked that my high-functioning alcoholism was on display.

"Jesus. What'd you do last night?"

"A friend's birthday party at Pump," I lied.

"Do you and your friends ever go to places not ironically?" Joan asked before adding, "Never mind. Let's go do the pitch. Just don't vomit on anyone, okay?"

By the time we walked into the writers' room, work had already started and no one had bothered to tell us.

"Hi, all, sorry to interrupt, but Ethan, remember when you told us to go break that story yesterday?" Joan said, trying her best to not bubble over with righteous fury.

"Huh?" Ethan cocked his head, petting a stoned-looking Monica in his lap.

"Ethan, honey, baby, you remember," Joan said.

"Oh, right." Ethan smiled. "The bullying thing. Yeah, okay, I assumed you guys didn't do it."

Ethan laughed. Then Cindy laughed. Then Tom, that *Zoe, Duncan, Jack and Jane* motherfucker, laughed. A chorus of laughter like we were in a high school cafeteria, but instead these punks were in their mid-fifties and owned multimillion-dollar properties. My blood boiled.

"Why wouldn't we do it?" I snapped, fed up with all the emotional bottoming I'd been doing. "It's our job. You gave us an assignment. You're our boss, you asked, we did it."

Ethan's eyes lit up in delight, but for the sake of reinforcing the power dynamic, he feigned anger.

"Don't fucking do that," he said. "You don't want to be doing that with me."

Joan pivoted. "Okay, so do you wanna hear our story or not?"

Ethan maintained a pregnant pause like we were about to be voted off a reality show, then said sure, why not. We told him our story. We performed the whole thing, actually, and we did a damn good job, and after practically finishing with fireworks and jazz hands, you know what he said?

"Hey, did you ever end up reaching out to my call boy?"

"What?" I said, the adrenaline draining from my body.

"You asked me for his full name. What was it again? River something?"

"River Banks," Tom said. Leave it to Tom to have an encyclopedic knowledge of everyone Ethan has ever slept with.

"Bingo," Ethan said. "River Banks. Well, did you find him?"

"Ummm, no."

"Shame. He's a good time."

I wanted to punch him. Ethan plowed forward, saying, "All right, your story doesn't work but you get points for trying. Let's move on. Should I buy a house in Vermont? People say it'll be great when the rest of the world is ravaged by climate change."

Joan and I retreated to our seats, resenting the fucks we still had to give.

CHAPTER 20

"I think we should go somewhere," I said to River. We were lounging in bed, postcoital.

"Where? Like, the kitchen?"

"No," I laughed. "Like to a museum or something."

"Okay. A museum. Sure. I can do overnights, you know."

"Well, I don't need an overnight. I mean, more like an afternoon."

"Oh, cool. Well, that will be hourly then."

"Okay."

River squeezed me tighter. "Do you have a boyfriend?"

"Huh?"

"A lot of my regulars have boyfriends. I was just curious."

"Well, I don't," I said, not exactly sure why I was lying. "What about you?"

"Same. I mean, between optometry school and this, I'm pretty busy."

You know how sometimes you wake up in the middle of the

night and forget where you are and for a second you freak out? That's kind of how I felt in bed with River. There I was, in an apartment with someone I didn't really know, and no one besides River knew I was there. Nothing about this resembled my life up to this point, and the setting made me vulnerable, like I could get lost forever and never find my way back home.

"So," River said, kissing me. "Which museum is your favorite?"

The way payment usually works is this. I enter River's apartment and place the money on the dining table without making a big deal of it. Our first time, when I paid after sex, it was an unwelcome reminder of the reality of our arrangement, and I decided I didn't want to feel that way again.

When I went to meet River at LACMA, it was one of those gorgeous days that turns you into mush, making you want to scream "I LUV LA!!!!" out of the sunroof of a convertible cruising down the PCH. My heart swelled three sizes that day when I saw River leaning against a wall ("Don't you love how he leans?"—Rickie Vasquez, 1994). River could do a TED Talk on how to look sexy propped against various support structures. I basically galloped up to him, feeling less cute in a bright Dries shirt and short-shorts from Bonobos (#sponsored, no, but really, they're the only shorts that can tackle my giant ass), and River squinted and smiled, and I smiled too, before realizing my mistake.

"Oh, shit," I said.

"What?"

"I forgot . . . I forgot the money."

"Oh."

"Do you take Venmo?"

"Uh, no." He hated this conversation. I did too.

"Okay. Well, what about PayPal?"

"Yup!" River lit up. "I fuck with PayPal."

"I actually don't have an account," I said, filling with dread. "I could sign up . . ."

"It's cool," River said. "Let's just go inside." He grabbed my hand and we made our way to the entrance. My heart fluttered at the thought of him waiving his fee for me. Me! This was disability rights.

As we went inside, I was reminded that museums, second only to bookstores, are the horniest places on Earth. I mean, they're filled with a bunch of beautiful people looking at erotic things. Everything painted in The Olden Days is sexual. Like, even if it's just a painting of a goat, the artist gave the goat a giant cock and boobs for some reason, and you're like, "Okay?" So you're leisurely walking from expensive room to expensive room, looking at hot goats that just ooze sexuality, all the while stealing glances at other beautiful people looking at all the other beautiful things. Plus, it's a natural litmus test. Everyone here is naturally smart and interesting because, duh, we're in a museum. I basically walk around with the beginnings of a boner the entire time.

I was checking out a painting that was nothing but a white dot on a black canvas (cum splatter or am I projecting?) when River came up behind me and whispered in my ear, "Whoa, this one is really moving, don't you think?"

I nodded politely, even though I considered the piece to be pretentious trash, and then River burst out laughing. "I was only kidding," he said, speaking loudly in his non-museum voice. "It's a white fucking dot. Are you kidding me? Dude, it's so dumb."

People looked over and rolled their eyes. Some laughed. I laughed too.

"I was nervous for a second there," I said, turning and putting my arm around River's waist. River didn't recoil. Instead, he leaned into me.

"Awww." River nuzzled my ear with his nose. "I'm not stupid, baby. Come on."

We moved from room to room, ending up in the Robert Mapplethorpe exhibit. We stopped at a portrait. Mapplethorpe's naked in the bathtub looking up at the camera. His hair curly, his eyes menacing, his torso lean, and then the jackpot, his stunning penis surrounded by a serious full bush. Flaccid yet powerful. Defiant, I say! Like, the thing could be four inches fully erect, but it wouldn't matter because it's still going to be the biggest small penis you've ever seen, you know?

"Did you read *Just Kids*?" I asked.

"No," River said, transferring his attention to an S&M photo. "What is that?"

"Patti Smith's memoir. She writes all about being a starving artist in the seventies, and a lot of the book covers her friendship with Robert."

"That's this guy?" River asked, pointing to the cock photo.

"Yeah. You've never heard of these people?"

"Nope."

For a second, I enjoyed feeling superior to River. He may have a better body and dick than me, but I knew things he didn't. Important things. Then, as if reading my mind, River said, "Oh, God. Are you judging me right now because I didn't know who Patti Smith is?"

"No, of course not!"

"Yes, you are," River said, giving me a quick kiss. "You little bitch."

"All right," I said. "Maybe a little. Although I don't know why because I seriously hated her book. It was so overwrought and self-serious."

"I'm recording you," River said. "You're gonna get yourself canceled."

"Shut up!"

"It's over for you, buddy. Fuck, how sad. *Just Canceled.*"

"C'mere, you little jerk." I brought River in for a long kiss. We broke apart, and he admitted that the pictures were turning him on, and did I want to fuck in the bathroom? He didn't ask quietly. I tried to shush him, but I liked everyone knowing we were going to go have crazy museum sex. River doubled down, explaining that you can't showcase dicks and full-on seventies bush and not expect people to fuck afterward, Robert Maple Syrup would be proud. Robert Mapplethorpe, I corrected, and he said stop talking and led me into a bathroom and told me to blow him and who am I to refuse—his dick was the best piece of art I'd seen all day—and then he turned me around and fucked me using spit which hurt like hell and the stall smelled liked dried piss and shit. It was one of the best sexual experiences of my life.

When we left, I asked River if he wanted to grab a drink.

"I'm sober," he said.

"Oh," I said, trying not to sound so surprised and disappointed. "That's amazing, good for you."

"Thanks," he said, plainly. "But I can just, like, get a seltzer or something."

I said no, that's okay, and we were quiet for a moment, and I wasn't sure if there was enough left to keep the day going, given that we'd already had sex, and in the end I decided there wasn't, so I thanked him for a great day, and River said he had a lot of fun, and I believed him because he seemed like a person who wasn't wired to lie, and he offered me a ride home, and I got into his sensible

Nissan Versa, and the interior smelled like greasy fast food, which surprised me—I was expecting piles of empty protein shake cups—and we listened to "When the Sun Don't Shine" by Best Coast and held hands over the center console, and the moment was so normal, very "two people on a date on a gorgeous LA afternoon." Eventually River asked if I "do Bank of America," and I said yes, confused, and he said great, and before I knew it we were pulling into the parking lot of my bank so I could pay River, which I did, and when I gave River his money and said goodbye, I vowed to never see him again.

CHAPTER 21

"Dad, I cheated on Gus," I said while we were in line at Sweetgreen.

"What?" he said, noticeably irritated.

"I know, it's totally fucked up, but I put an end to it and—"

"No, I can't hear you. The music in here is loud for a fucking salad bar place."

"Dad, we're not at a salad bar. This is Sweetgreen. There's a big difference; show some respect. Besides, it's nobody's fault you're half-deaf."

"Excuse me," he said, his irritation building. "I am not half-dead."

"No, that's not . . ." I calculated the emotional energy it would cost in clarifying and decided to move on. "I CHEATED ON GUS." Suddenly it seemed like everyone in Sweetgreen had now turned to stare at me.

"Wow, that's messed up. Why'd you do that, ya idiot?"

Before I could answer, our salad artist asked for our order. Dad pointed to a salad on the menu but proceeded to make substitutions for every ingredient.

"Dad," I said, my own frustration mounting. "You know you can just build your own, right?"

"Shush, son."

Dad asked for roasted chicken. I begged him at least to try the blackened chicken, despite his bizarre prejudice against dark meat. He acquiesced and tried a sample. I could tell by the brief look on his face that he liked it, but he doubled down on the roast chicken breast.

We got our salads (his $11, mine $17) and sat down.

"You shouldn't cheat," Dad said, sampling the five different sides of dressing he somehow snagged for free. "Is that, like, big in your community or something?"

"My community?!?" I stabbed a plastic fork into my salad.

"Oh, you know what I mean. Don't be so sensitive."

"It's not a 'gay' thing, Dad. In fact, most people are in open relationships these days instead of cheating behind each other's backs."

"Well, why can't you be in that?" Dad said, having tried all the sauces by this point without a bite of salad. He then took a can of Coke out from his coat jacket and opened it.

"Dad!" I exclaimed, shrinking in my seat. "Did you smuggle that in here?"

"I called in advance. Said they don't sell Coke. Can you believe it? What idiots," Dad said, taking a giant swig.

"Uh, anyway, what if Gus says no to being open? I don't think I believe in monogamy—"

"Clearly."

"Rude." I took a bite and didn't wait to chew before continuing. "And I think he actually does. He's secretly a little retro. And if he said he wanted to keep things closed, that would probably be, like, the end for us."

"So your plan then is to just keep on cheating? Elly, you might want to cover up. Your brain damage is showing."

"Ew, shut up. I stopped."

"Who was it?"

"A sex worker. Since I paid for everything, maybe it doesn't count?"

"Dear God." Dad sighed then took his first bite of salad. "Why do you tell me these things? Don't you have friends?"

"Yes, but you're not involved. It's safer to tell you."

"Gee, thanks, how flattering. Look, you have to tell him. There's no other way. Either he's on the same page or he's not."

"Do you like your eleven-dollar salad?" I asked, in a desperate attempt to change the subject.

"It's okay. I could've made this at home, ya know."

"God, you're impossible."

"And you're a cheater. There, we're even." Dad laughed. The man is endlessly amused with himself.

When I was dating Dylan in high school, I asked Dad if we should wear condoms even if we were both virgins. He said no, but that we should try to establish safe practices for the future. Four years earlier, when my mom left us and my dad went on his dating rampage, he came down with herpes and genital warts in the span of six months. The man knew what he was talking about. Dylan and I never used condoms, but I appreciated having a father I could talk candidly to about sex, especially gay sex, without him acting all skittish.

"Okay," I said. "I'm not going to tell him, but I have stopped seeing River."

"His name is River?"

"Not his real name, obviously. Most sex workers have aliases."

"What's his real name?" Dad said, putting down his fork.

"I have no idea."

"Delightful. You're risking your relationship for a guy whose name you don't even know." He picked up one of his salad dressings and began to drink it.

"Are you going to eat any of your salad?"

"I don't think so. The chicken's too dry," he said.

Dad drove me home, blasting his favorite song, Alanis Morissette's "Thank U." When he pulled up to the house, he said that he was too tired to make the drive to Ventura and asked or rather announced that he was going to take a nap in my bed. I loved it when my dad napped in my apartment. It made the place cozier. Gus didn't understand it at all—his family isn't very warm because they're religious and repressed, which also means they have boundaries for days—but he also gets that everyone has their own definition of normal, so he doesn't make a fuss.

Gus read in the living room while Dad slept and I lay next to him working on my laptop. I inspected his face, which, at sixty-five, looked like a crumpled-up sheet of paper, and his big belly peeked out of the bottom of his Kirkland polo shirt, which now sported a kaleidoscope of stains from assorted salad dressings. My dad was never that attractive to begin with. I remember, during his single days, how he temporarily eschewed his cheapness for a fancy gym and hundred-dollar haircuts. He liked to explain that dating is all a numbers game and because he identified as average-looking, he would have to work that much harder to attract women. He had a point. How else to explain all the asymmetrical gays who can get away with buzzing and/or bleaching their hair thanks to the support of amazing facial structure. Meanwhile, I'm here spending a fortune on clothes to showcase my body in the most flattering way possible, while getting my own pricey haircuts because a bad one will take me from a 7 to a 5 in seconds. That kind of upkeep is exhausting.

Dad never did find someone. Eventually the dates petered out and he settled into being somebody who was okay with being alone. I couldn't tell if that was because he's still not over Mom leaving us or if he's a genuine weirdo who can't connect with 99.9 percent of society. A few years back he got prostate cancer and now his dick doesn't even work anymore. (He told me this while we were both standing at urinals.) I imagine that's why he gave up. Once your dick leaves the party, what's the point? At a certain age, more things get taken away from you than are given. They don't ask for permission. Sometimes it happens slowly, sometimes all at once.

He doesn't need to worry, though. I'll be his life insurance.

CHAPTER **22**

I was on day five of not seeing River and my body was still going through withdrawals, so I tried to distract myself by going on open houses with Gus. We can't afford to buy because we spend approximately $40,000 a day on wine, Uber, and Postmates, but looking and pretending we're very rich garbage homosexuals rather than comfortable garbage homosexuals is a fun way to howl against the void.

"What's your name?" I whispered to Gus as we entered a seven-hundred-square-foot shithole in the hills of Silver Lake with a price tag of $999,000. It would likely go for $1.2 million.

"My name is Blaine," Gus said. "I'm in PR. I publicly do relations."

"Oooh, nice. My name is Brian Michael. Not Brian. Not Michael. Brian Michael."

"Look at you, two names! What do you do?"

"Stocks. Bonds. Derivatives. Oh, and imports-slash-exports!"

"Sounds bone-chilling."

The house was very "hipster coffin," and we could tell the owner was trying to flip the place with minimal effort. The master bedroom barely fit a full-sized bed.

"Brian Michael, are you feeling this backsplash?" Gus asked, dragging one finger across the kitchen counter.

"I don't know, Blaine," I said, sighing a big beautiful gay bitch sigh. "I imagine we'd have to reno everything."

"Reno?" Gus gasped.

"Honey? Total reno."

"Babe? I hear you on the reno. I suppose we could make do with the Malibu house for a few months."

"I prefer Sunset Tower. You know how I hate being so far away from town."

Nikki, the Realtor, with a fire engine–red dye job (to signify that she's fun), interrupted with "You gentlemen in the market for a second home?"

Gus and I nodded in tandem. "We've been out in Malibu for a few years now," I said, solemnly.

"We're just too isolated out there, you know?" Gus said, lazily scratching the back of his head.

"Well, I can assure you, buying in Silver Lake is a great investment!" Nikki said, her eyes like slot machines.

"Yes, all our friends seem to be moving here for some reason. Honestly, we don't really get it—"

"But, like, at the end of the day, we don't need to, you know?" I said.

Nikki nodded, clearly confused but determined to make a commission. She had us sign the guest book and handed us her card in case we wanted to make an offer. Gus and I practically skipped out of the open house, holding hands, delighted that after all these years, we could still have such ridiculous fun together. We were in the hills of Silver Lake and had an afternoon to kill. Neither of us drives—me, cerebral palsy; Gus, who knows? It's annoying. If I could drive, I would literally train to be a NASCAR driver, but whenever I gently suggest Gus get a driver's license he gets defensive and says he's too scared, that it feels like playing a real-life video game where one false move could literally be the end of your life. I can't argue with that, but it still pisses me off and serves as an example of him not taking advantage of his able-bodied privilege.

We started walking. We walked for an hour, checking out all the gorgeous mid-century homes and, if we were lucky, the people who lived there, people who have artisanal chocolate lines and actors who star in *CSI*-like shows that run for a million seasons and earn them a boatload of cash, even though no one knows who they are besides your aunt Betty, and maybe publicists do live here with their stockbroker husbands. We made our way down to Silver Lake Boulevard and had some nibbles and enjoyed the view upstairs at L & E Oyster Bar, then ventured to Salazar in Frogtown and met up with our friends Harry and Augie and ate nachos and didn't even drink! There seemed to be this unspoken agreement between us that this day was special and we did not need to numb ourselves with alcohol. The sunset acted like a little show-off with blasts of cotton candy and orange sherbet, and by the time we called an Uber we were tired but we were happy. It felt like Gus and I were able to see each other clearly again and rise above the mundanity of our usual routine. In fact, the whole evening I didn't think of River at all, and I felt kind of bad that for the last few weeks I'd neglected my life with Gus to hang in someone's boxlike apartment while getting penetrated. Gus was real. River was not. He was an obsession, I told myself. A compulsion. Like playing a game repeatedly, trying your best to win, the prize being the true affection I already got for free from Gus.

The second Gus and I walked through our front door, we tore

off each other's clothes. I face-dived into Gus's cock, giving him an enthusiastic blowjob, but I remembered how amazing I felt when River edged me, so I jerked off Gus, slowly, and at first he was thrown by the pacing as I saw his pleasure build and build before I cut it off and started stroking again and cutting it off and starting the game again. Gus stopped me, wild-eyed with desire, and asked me where I had learned to edge and I shrugged and told him Xtube.

Emboldened by my sudden sexual adventurousness, Gus asked, "Hey, do you think you would be into topping me tonight?"

I'm very bad at topping. It acts as a sort of blacklight for my disability. The first time I did it, we attempted every position, but my dick would not make friends with Gus's hole. Finally, we landed on one position that I could do adequately, which is Gus on top of me and me just lying there thrusting and grunting like a fish gasping for air. When we finished, we both pretended that the sex was mind-blowing. ("HOLY SHIT. THAT WAS AWESOME. I DIDN'T KNOW YOU HAD THAT IN YOU!" Gus said, with the acting range of Melissa Joan Hart.) In reality, we both knew that this was Very Bad Sex and that topping required too much Cirque du Soleil movement for my gimpy body.

Still, on the rare occasion Gus asked to revisit it, I had to comply, so I said yes and Gus took my cock and rammed it into his asshole (I don't have the dexterity to direct it myself). He bounced up and down on it with oversized enthusiasm while I looked at the ceiling and made the appropriate noises of so-called pleasure. It was awful. I knew I couldn't fuck Gus the way he wanted to be fucked. He knew it too, but occasionally he would do these check-ins to see if anything had magically changed. I felt so bad about the terrible job I was doing that I suggested a consolation prize: he could fuck me standing up. It was one of Gus's favorite positions but, unbeknownst to him, absolute hell for my body. We got up from the bed and Gus inserted his cock. The position was manageable at first—for a second I even wondered, *Did my legs get stronger? Those lunges are paying off!*—but after a few minutes, the familiar burn returned and my legs began to tremble. Wanting to be done, I told Gus the words that would guarantee he came quickly (you don't want to know), but for some godforsaken reason it didn't work, so I stood there, biting down on my lip, my hands balled into fists, my body submerged in pain. Why didn't Gus notice? Why, after five years, could he not know when I hurt? In the beginning of a relationship, it seems like all you do is look. You want to know this person, figure them out so you can carve out the perfect-sized space for them to fit into your life. This involves paying attention, making notes, asking questions. Then, after a certain point, when you've created the space and they fit, you get complacent. You become convinced this person has shown you everything you need to know. You neglect to realize that everything takes maintenance. Nothing runs completely on its own.

Just when I thought Gus and I were seeing each other clearly again, I realized, with my legs about to buckle underneath me and my back seizing in pain right in front of him, that the parts of me that mattered were invisible.

Eventually, Gus came. Out of habit, I almost left money on the table.

"Where are you going?" Gus asked me as I walked naked toward the kitchen.

"Getting some wine," I said, with a hint of defeat. "Want some?"

There was a pause before Gus responded with a mumble, "Yeah."

CHAPTER **23**

River-free days turned into River-free weeks. Going cold turkey didn't stop me from indulging in my other habits: getting drunk and checking out rent-boy websites. I was perusing the wares but never buying the merchandise. Until one afternoon when Ethan eviscerated me for talking over him (I hadn't spoken a single word in over three hours) and I found myself texting Dave, a fifty-something former porn star living in Van Nuys whose ad I'd been returning to a few times a day. I took an Uber after work to his house. The place was shabby, with popcorn ceilings, but still, you know, a house. He was aggressive from the beginning, which usually I like but today I was feeling sensitive. Dave ordered me down onto his bed and then shoved his cock in my mouth, pushing my head off the mattress and fucking my throat. When he presented his ass to my face expectantly, I gave him a courtesy rim, but his hole wasn't anything like River's and my heart wasn't in it. When he asked if I wanted him to fuck me, I declined and said goodbye, and when I got home I took a scalding hot shower, and Gus and I drank a skin-contact white ($48) and watched the episode of *Sex and the City* where Steve's mom eats pizza out of the garbage and turns to Miranda and says, "This pizza tastes like garbage."

CHAPTER 24

Spas are hard to navigate when you have a disability. First, you must undress and change into a robe, which, lol, good luck with my projects. Thanks to piss-poor hand-eye coordination, I can't tie one correctly and inevitably I flash my penis to unsuspecting bystanders. And then there's the unfortunate issue of flip-flops. My left foot goes in no problem, but my right turns out at an angle and doesn't fully slip in, so I stumble over and over before finally taking them off in frustration and risking a nasty bout of athlete's foot. Then, of course, we have the biggest obstacle: the steam rooms. The second I enter, my glasses fog up, but if I take them off, I'm even more blind.

None of these roadblocks, however, could impede me from trying out the gay spa where all our friends have gotten off. I called in sick in the middle of the week, when the spa wouldn't be so crowded with picky muscle gays, but I might've been too cautious, because when I showed up at 3:30 p.m. on a Tuesday, there was only a smattering of naked old men milling about. I made the rounds, a towel around my waist, feeling a few sets of eyes on me. It felt good to be leered at for once, to be reduced to just dick and ass. I hopped in the Jacuzzi across from a portly man who told me he owned a car dealership in Camarillo with his husband. Pleasantries went from zero to sixty when he started pulling on his cock. There was no logical bridge from "We sell Toyotas mostly. . . ." to "You like my dick, boy?" Out of politeness, I let him masturbate for a minute, but when he made a grab for my dick, I wished him a nice afternoon and went on my way.

Everywhere I turned, there were men staring and circling. Overwhelmed, I hightailed it to the steam room, where, like clockwork, my glasses fogged up and, predictably, I slipped and ate absolute shit.

"Are you okay?" a voice called out from the steam.

I looked around, squinting, trying to make out a face.

"I'm fine! Thanks!" I was actually in a comical amount of pain. I scrambled, trying to get back on my feet. My knees were throbbing. Suddenly, a hand touched mine, gently, sweetly.

"Here," the voice said. "Sit down."

"Thank you," I said. "Wow, it's so slippery in here and—"

"You can't see a damn thing. I know. I wear glasses too."

I felt immediate comfort, secure in the knowledge that I was in the holy presence of a fellow gay nerd.

"I would take a look at your knee," the voice said, "but I can't see it."

"That's okay," I said. "I'm sure I'm fine."

"Cool."

A few seconds passed and a hand landed on my thigh, inching toward my penis. Part of me was flattered that I could fall on my ass in a steam room and still be desirable.

I reached for his cock. It was average, like mine. I tried going down on him, but the steam made me cough, so we jerked each other off, our backs against the wall, our eyes (presumably) glazed over. The whole experience was so lifeless, it was the sexual equivalent of a shrug emoji. Men have probably been giving each other unsatisfying handjobs since the dawn of time. It's almost moving, in a way, how we can help each other out this way without passing judgment. I decided to dedicate this mediocre sexual act to all the gay men who came (pun always intended) before me.

After we both finished, the voice said, "Don't forget to put some Neosporin on that," and left. I never saw what he looked like, which probably was for the best.

I walked home from the spa, feeling energized rather than guilty. Sleeping with sex workers, anonymous steam-room sexcapades— look at me participating in queer culture!

This feeling of discovery got me thinking of all the things that were formative to my gay development. Danny from *The Real World: New Orleans*'s gray turtleneck, paparazzi nudes of a sunbathing Brad Pitt, the movie *White Squall*, Matt Dillon's short-shorts in *Wild Things*, Kevin Bacon's fresh-from-the-shower dick in *Wild Things*, okay every scene in *Wild Things*, Ryan Phillippe's ice cream–scooped ass in *Cruel Intentions* and *54*, and his lesser-known-but-equally-brilliant ass work in the movie *Little Boy Blue*, my friendship with my fifth-grade teacher, the AIDS episode of *90210* with Rosie O'Donnell, knowing not to trust Ellen without fully understanding why, Fruit Gushers snacks (you bite into one and sticky liquid explodes in your mouth—foreshadowing much?), wearing a T-shirt on my head to mimic long hair, getting picked last for any sport, intense passion for decorating binders, deleting my search history on the family desktop, sensing that any foreign film equaled gay on some level, my ideal female being Parker Posey, a friend's mom loving me.

Three blocks from our apartment, I ran into Gus carrying a bag full of wine from the grocery store. I actually saw him before he saw me. He had a spring in his step, knowing that the permanent anxiety he felt would soon be deferred to the next morning. I watched him for a few more moments, smiling at his classically handsome face and his expressive eyes while also feeling a sprinkle of pity for him. For both of us. Finally, Gus's vision narrowed and he saw me. He asked where I was coming from, and I said I went for a walk, and he believed me because why wouldn't he, but I couldn't fight the urge to guilt-splain, so I said that I'd had a hard day at work and needed to clear my head. I put on a mini performance of feeling distressed, and Gus said, "Come here, my widdle angel . . . ," and brought me into his arms but not before saying, "Careful . . . don't hit the wine."

Gus and I wound up getting pretty blotto that night. Gus became his usual slurry stupid self and started talking about how much he hated his job and how he wanted to take painting classes. I was ashamed that my gut reaction was: *Be better. You're too old not to know what you want to do in life.*

As we got ready for bed, he inquired about my scratched knees.

"I went to the spa. The gay one," I said. All that wine had empowered me, bypassed my filter. No more Brita brain. I was serving straight-up tap.

"Whatever, so I went to Blick's and bought all these colored pencils and some fancy paper. Look!" Gus took some art supplies out of his backpack and arranged them on the bed.

"Hellooooo, did my *widdle baby* hear me?" I said, slapping his hand.

"What?" Gus was busy sketching on the bed.

"I said I scraped up my knees at the *gay spa*," I said. "GAY. SPA. KNEES."

"You're speaking gibberish. This is you right now." Gus displayed his sketch. It was me with scabbed-up knees, holding a comically large glass of wine. It looked like a five-year-old drew it.

"That's not good," I said. "I can say with complete objectivity that it is not a good drawing."

I had intended it as teasing, but his wounded face said otherwise. I flashed back to a memory from a few years ago when Gus and I were on a hike with friends in Provincetown and I was feeling a lot of anxiety about being able to keep up—hiking might seem like no big deal to most people, but I was making myself hugely vulnerable by putting my body's limitations on display like that—and Gus stayed glued to my side, and every time I fell down, he picked me up and told me I was okay. It was one of those rare moments when the help didn't feel like a condescending crutch. Rather, it was a person showing up for someone. And now here Gus was, putting himself out there, showing vulnerability, and not only was I not showing up for him, I was the asshole pushing him down into the dirt.

"I was just . . . I'm sketching, okay? It's not meant to be in a fucking museum. Jesus." Gus crumpled up the picture and tossed it off the bed. He rarely got mad like this.

"I'm sorry," I said. "I love it. I was kidding. You believe me, right? Honey, I will support you in whatever you want to do." I buried my head in Gus's chest.

"Did you really go to a gay spa? The one Augie goes to?" The way Gus asked—tentatively, softly—told me how I needed to answer him, but I couldn't bring myself to lie. I'd given him a sliver of honesty after weeks of lies, and I couldn't take it away. I was scared to look him in the eyes, so I picked up a colored pencil and started to draw.

"Yeah, I did. Is that okay?" I asked.

"I guess so." Gus was lost in thought for a moment. "You didn't, like, fuck anyone, did you?"

"Like anal?" I asked, horrified, as if I wasn't capable of such a vile act. "No! God, no. This guy and I . . . well, it's kind of funny."

"Good," Gus said, dripping with sarcasm. "I mean, because if you did, I mean if you wanted to . . ."

Gus grabbed the bottle of wine by the bed and reached for my glass.

"I'm okay," I said.

"No, you're not," Gus quipped, pouring wine into my glass and handing it to me. "So," he sighed. "What happened?"

"Well, I walked into the steam room and couldn't see anything, so of course I fell, but then this guy, I don't even know what he looked like, but he helped me up and then he promptly jerked me off. I think it was his way of being a Good Samaritan. Isn't that sweet?"

"Was he at least cute?"

"I couldn't see his face because of the steam," I said, drawing a mess on the page.

"Oh, yeah, you mentioned that. Well, okay. I mean, you've never done something like this before, right?"

"No," I lied. "Of course not. But this is normal, Gus. This is, like, the plus side of being gay. That we can do little things like this without it becoming a big deal."

Gus didn't say anything.

"Are you mad at me?" I asked.

"No. No, no. I mean, someone jerked you off. You're right. It's whatever. It's fine."

"That's kind of how I felt?"

"But let's not make, like, a habit out of it? Getting handjobs in steam rooms across greater Los Angeles. Having it become one giant gay slut free-for-all."

Gus's response confirmed what I'd always felt. In relationships, he is more *Leave It to Beaver* than *Caligula*. Still, I'm glad we talked about it. Made me feel 2 percent less like a liar.

"It won't become like that. And you can get jerked off too."

"Maybe. I don't know. I don't really need to."

"Well, it's not really about needing to. It's about wanting to."

Gus looked away from me and to my paper. "What are you drawing?"

I held up a sketch.

"Who is that?"

"You. Are you really that drunk?"

"That doesn't look like me at all," Gus said. "It's objectively not a good drawing."

"Okay, I deserved that one." I studied my picture. Gus was right. I hadn't drawn him. I'd drawn River.

CHAPTER 25

"We're going on a work retreat," Ethan announced, as he waltzed into the writers' room cradling Monica, who was wearing a onesie that read "MY OWNER IS THE REAL BITCH."

Everyone looked uncomfortable. The thought of having to spend time with one another off-the-clock was profoundly bleak. This we could all agree on.

Cindy tittered nervously and sipped at her third iced latte of the day. (She has four total instead of lunch. Ethan likes to call her lattes "doody water" because once the ice melts, they look like liquid shit.) "Ethan, a work retreat? Where?"

"Ojai Valley Inn," he said. "At brunch this weekend I was talking with David Geffen about how the chemistry in the room feels off. . . ."

Because you're emotionally abusive.

"And Geffen swears that work retreats help bond people together or whatever. Plus, the network agreed to pay and I really wanna go to Ojai."

"Wow, I love Ojai too," Tom said. "But these work retreats can be kind of hit-or-miss. We went on one during midseason hiatus for *Zoe, Duncan, Jack and Jane,* and—"

"Tom, for fuck's sake stop talking about that fucking show!" Ethan barked. "No one gives a shit. It makes me sad how often you bring up a show that was canceled after one season. Move on."

Ethan had never snapped at Tom like that. The guy looked like he was fighting tears, but he couldn't resist digging a deeper hole. "Well, the show did go off the air briefly, but it relaunched as *Zoe*—"

"Tom, stop," Ethan said, putting up his hand. "I love you, but you're embarrassing yourself."

"Right. Sorry," Tom said, his voice quavering. "Sure. Let's go to Ojai. I bet it'll be dope."

Ethan turned to me and Joan, who was playing Candy Crush on her iPhone.

"You two aren't required to go," Ethan said, focusing his attention on Monica. "Did you hear that, Monica? They don't have to go. No, they don't." He scratched under her chin.

"I'm in," I said, surprising myself.

Look, my personal life was a loaded mess—that was fine, I was used to it—but work was always the one place that made sense, and I refused to continue letting Ethan take that away from me. He needed to finally acknowledge my basic humanity and accept that I was a valued writer on this "too horrible to even be rebooted in ten years" show. What better place to do that than some forced quality time in Ojai.

"Seriously? You want to go?" Joan said, looking up from her phone.

"Yeah," I said, through gritted teeth. "Tom's right. I bet it'll be dope."

Joan sighed. "Fine, I'll go."

"Listen, I know we all hate hanging out, but if we spend most of the time getting massages instead of doing trust falls, we should come out of this weekend alive," Ethan said.

Ladies and gentlemen: I present to you our inspiring leader.

CHAPTER 26

Ethan arranged for *individual limos* to drive us to Ojai. Glass houses and all, I know, but I find the way Ethan spends money to be so 1980s-level gross. Like a Bret Easton Ellis novel. All cocaine on mirrored coffee tables and sushi platters on naked women. I mean, the man literally lives in Beverly Hills. Who would do that? Beverly Hills is best experienced as a thought or an idea. Maybe you go there for a salad or a dermatologist appointment, but it's not meant to be the headquarters for your life.

The drive up to Ojai was breathtaking. I listened to Snail Mail as I looked out the window and felt myself growing vaguely depressed for no reason, which was actually nice because I've always wanted to feel emotionally intense in the back of a limo. Ojai is ten minutes away from my hometown of Ventura, and it has more tarot readers than restaurants. More swimming holes than swimming pools. No one has a real job and they all dress like they wash dishes in a river. Ojai is sun-kissed and tranquil with a splash of psycho.

I'd never been to Ojai Valley Inn, but Oprah fucks with it so I figured it must be divine. When we pulled up, my immediate thought was "Wow. Nancy Meyers got drunk on some buttery Chard and went full ham at Costco." It was beautiful. Spanish-style tiles, acres and acres of green. But the furniture was mostly overstuffed wicker and the art was uninspired. I don't know why it continues to stun me when rich people can't get their shit together to display a modicum of taste.

My room was handicapped-accessible, meaning there was a huge shower with a railing, a high-as-fuck toilet, and no bath-tub. My reservation may have been a secret troll from Ethan, but I decided to be grateful and let it go. Earlier that morning Ethan had texted us all, saying "Arriving at noon. Eating food I'll regret and at spa till six. Don't bother me. C u 4 dinner at 7. Plz forward 2 Joan, as I don't believe she's on thread." Joan responded within seconds. "Despite your best efforts, I remain on the thread. Can't wAiT fOR a FuN WeEkend!!!" In a show of camaraderie, I texted that famous meme of Homer Simpson walking backward and disappearing into the bushes. No one responded. Forty minutes later, Cindy asked if she should bring her bathing suit. I wondered if she'd be out of the knee brace she got from her injury while running her daily 5K on the beach in Malibu. Tom texted back, "Maybe but I feel fat rn." Cindy texted: "rn?" Tom texted: "Right now." And then Amy—I hope you remember her because I try not to—texted, "Ugh, I'm dreading the whole thing but maybe we can meet up in Calabasas after?" She responded a second later with "oh sorry that was for my friend LOL. C u all soon, can't wait!" With that, our text exchange ended and I could sense the collective relief in the air to be free of this cursed thread. The one and only time I ever texted Ethan directly was when *Sammy Says* was nominated for a People's Choice Award and I needed a suit for the ceremony. I texted Ethan a photo of a Tommy Bahama's window display and wrote, "Think they'll have good suits here?" A JOKE, CLEARLY, but two days passed before Ethan responded. "On slopes in Aspen. Can't c pic thru goggles. Probs fine."

I whiled away the afternoon in my room by Googling things like "What happened to Claire Forlani?" After solving that mystery (she's working—in things you'll never see), I Googled Kirsten Dunst and Jake Gyllenhaal from the two years they dated. She gives off such miserable vibes in practically every photo, the most iconic of which is the shot where she's angrily chomping on salad. Kirsten met Jake when she turned twenty, and for the first few months how #blessed she must have felt to be with a fellow movie star of her stature, but then the blinders fell off and Jake turned out to be just another idiot who liked women to watch him do things. And that's what Kirsten did. She watched him emote in invite-only acting classes, play poker with the boys. She even cheered watching Jake conquer his gym's climbing wall! How proud she must have been until, eventually, she was like, "Wait, I'm a working A-list actress. Why am I losing my shit when Jake climbs four fake rocks? "

I made a mental note to check out how Cindy would eat her salad at dinner, if she chomped in spite like Kirsten had, but there was a high probability she wouldn't be eating anything at all.

"Watch your step. I hear you're one clumsy girl," Ethan said, extending a hand as we walked down a flight of stairs to dinner. I reluctantly took his over-moisturized hand.

Ojai apparently has the best sunsets—"the pink moment" it's called—and when Ethan, Joan, Tom, Cindy, Amy, and I sat down for dinner, Ojai did not disappoint. Despite the Zen-like setting, I couldn't seem to relax in front of my coworkers and focus on getting chummy with Ethan. I suspected that he was silently grading us, and any misstep would be weaponized later. I coped by ordering a cocktail. A gin martini. A spicy margarita. A healthy pour of Cab. (No natural wine in Ojai? "Wow, Bethenny. Wow."—Ramona Singer, *Real Housewives of New York*) Eventually, I was drunk enough to feel steady or, better yet, feel nothing at all.

"My family, we call ourselves the House of Bits," Cindy said, laughing to herself. "Did I tell you about the time a Nielsen guy came to our house and wanted to install a ratings tracker? My husband said yes while the kids and I ran around hiding our Emmys. They eventually found out we worked in television, and oh my God, it was like something out of a sitcom!" She shook her head.

I looked up from my drink and saw a famous man who'd been accused of sexual assault being seated at a table across from us.

"Ew," I said. "Look who the fuck is here."

All heads turned, taking him in.

"Amazing. I love that everyone made a huge deal of his career being over and it's like, 'Boo-hoo, I'm exiled at some five-star resort,'" Joan said.

"Who gives a shit?" Ethan grunted. "Let the man eat his chicken paillard in peace."

Suddenly it felt like we were back in the writers' room and all the men were reacting as they did when diving into #MeToo territory: by getting defensive, but also, um, totally listening to women, and by looking at both sides of the story, but also, sure, believing victims, totally! It was exhausting to watch. I imagine at night they flip through their mental "Past Aggressions" files, wondering if talking about a star's breasts for an hour in the room made the women writers uncomfortable or if rubbing the back of their female coworker on show night was out of line. But instead of admitting any kind of culpability, they double down in anger and blame cancel culture.

It was disheartening to see Ethan, a gay man, co-opt the straight bro's position, but it speaks to our generational divide. The more time I spend with Ethan, the more I think he believes, underneath his Gucci cardigan and layers of queer bitchiness, that being gay is actually shameful. The way he gravitates toward Tom, it goes beyond finding him attractive. It's wanting approval from The Boys Club. I don't say this in an accusatory way. I can't imagine what it was like for Ethan to come up in the nineties with a bunch of straight men, having to learn to assimilate into their world and use his sexuality mostly as a punchline to make everyone else around him feel comfortable. Actually, I sort of can because I do it today with my cerebral palsy.

Cindy, who, only seconds ago, was so upbeat, regaling us with her (admittedly boring) stories now sat in silence, her mouth a tight line, like she had in the past, and I regretted ever judging her appearance, or judging her at all. I took in her big platinum hair and skintight outfits and the plastic surgery that hadn't yet settled and maybe never would and her Great Lake's worth of doody water, and thought, *Why the fuck does she do that to herself?* To do a different version of what Ethan does by satisfying the patriarchy, if you wanna be all liberal arts about it, sure, but does any of the torture or discipline bring her actual joy, separate from the thrill of male validation?

I'm critical of Cindy and Ethan because I see the parts of myself in them that I'm trying to extract and destroy, the parts that are trying to please a world that will never love me back. In an ideal world, we would be allies, not enemies, but our world isn't ideal. It's a cishet hellscape and us minorities are all competing against each other, vying for that one seat at the table.

"Can we talk about something else?" Cindy said through a pinched smile, after Tom started a sentence with "If I can be devil's advocate here . . ."

I'd never seen Cindy assert herself like this—nobody had—so Ethan took her request seriously by moving to a more inclusive topic of discussion: Who was the biggest asshole in Hollywood? Ironic, I know, considering the prime candidates around the table. Here is a group of people who've been working for decades in a fickle, demanding business that has little by little chipped away at their self-worth. God knows how many skeevy scenarios Cindy has found herself in as the only woman in a writers' room. Even Tom and Ethan both had bosses that at one time or another made them feel worthless. But guess what? If you spend half of your professional life being treated like shit and the other half treating others like shit you become the representation of power that kept you down. And then nothing gets better. Nothing changes.

Dinner slogged on with gossip, subtle putdowns, followed by more gossip. By the time our entrées were served, Tom had begun to look fuckable, which meant that I was officially wasted. Ethan, who'd been keeping one cocked eyebrow on me all evening, asked if I was okay, which prompted the rest to turn and look at me, trying out their best "concerned" faces.

"Yeah, honey. " Joan said, rubbing my hand under the table. "Do you want me to take you back to your room?"

"I'm fine," I said, now too scared to stand up.

"No, you look really out of it. I'm worried," Amy said, turning to mouth something to Cindy.

"Oh, shut up, Amy," Joan hissed. "Keep pretending to eat your fish."

"Wow," Cindy said, clutching her chest in a gesture that was more performative than sincere. "Amy was just making an observation, Joan. This is a time to bond, not divide. Right, Ethan?"

Ethan was too busy checking out the waiter's ass to respond.

"And besides," Amy added, "I ordered the chicken."

The room began to spin, faster and faster. I couldn't focus my eyes.

"Shut up," Ethan said, ping-ponging back and forth from the waiter's ass to the dinner table. "All of you. I'll take him back. Panna cotta is for dessert, which couldn't be more of a letdown."

Before I could protest, Ethan was grabbing my upper arm and lifting me out of the chair. His frame was sturdier than I'd expected, and I thought, *It should be illegal for people who are two decades older than you to have better bodies.*

We moseyed on through the resort to my room, Ethan dragging me along like a rag doll.

"I can walk by myself," I said, pouting.

"That is an incorrect assessment of your capabilities at this given moment," Ethan said.

Feeling mischievous, I broke free from Ethan's grip and started running through the resort. Clusters of rich people dodged me as I ran toward them. I heard Ethan yell something about how he ran after Sarah Paulson once at the Independent Spirit Awards and vowed to never do it again. I laughed. It felt good to be sticking it to Ethan. To be drunk and free, soaking in the balmy rarefied air of the Ojai Valley Inn. But then I heard something go "pop" in my body, and pain filled my leg, pain I knew would be much worse if I wasn't pumped full of the anesthesia known as alcohol.

Ethan caught up to me and said, "Hey dum-dum, you almost ran over Elon Musk and a woman who looked like a very expensive alien."

"Good," I said, wincing and out of breath.

Ethan registered something was wrong and asked if I was okay. I wasn't. But I'd rather be in excruciating amounts of pain than confirm Ethan's perception of me that I was clumsy and needed help. I took a deep breath and said I was fine. I must've just pulled something. NBD. Ethan, out of either perceptiveness or boredom, dropped it, and we continued on.

Ethan pulled my key card from my right front pocket as the pain continued to sear through my leg. When we got inside my room, he ordered me to sit down on the bed. Even through my drunkenness, obeying Ethan was like muscle memory. He brought me a glass of water from the bathroom.

"Drink," Ethan said. "All of it. Now."

I sipped and grimaced. "Ew," I slurred. "Is this regular water?"

"What's regular water?" Ethan asked.

"Tap."

Ethan sighed and said, "You have a drinking problem, you know that?"

I continued sipping my regular water.

"Look," Ethan said, fluffing my pillows, "I'm not going to fire you. Most of the idiots on staff are functioning addicts. It is what it is. Lie down."

I bent over to fumble with my shoes. Impatient, Ethan huffed, pulling them off for me. "Jesus," he said. "Why do you have Velcro? Are you a sixth grader from 1983?"

"I can't tie my shoes, you fucker!" I said, falling backward on the bed.

"Don't worry. I'm not taking off your pants," Ethan said. "Not in this climate. Go to sleep."

My body was somehow too heavy to move. Ethan helped me onto my back.

"Look, get help or don't. I don't care. Just know that I see you."

"No, you don't," I said, drooling. "You don't have a clue who I am."

"Okay, cue the theatrics," Ethan said, grabbing my legs and plopping them on the bed.

"Ow," I yelped. Ethan had touched my hamstring, which I now realized was the source of my discomfort.

"Don't be such a baby," Ethan said, continuing to situate my legs. They felt more like oars than appendages. "I'm not your fucking daddy, okay? I don't do heart-to-hearts with my staff. I'm just saying, you know, you strike me as someone who is miserable. That's all."

"Maybe you're the reason why I'm so sad, huh? You ever think of that, Bucko?"

"You called me Bucko. Now that's a fireable offense." Ethan began fussing with my tangled sheets. "Jesus Christ, is this a drunk thing or a disability thing? Would you please get under the covers?"

I fumbled for either five seconds or five hours, but I did it. Ethan tucked me in.

"Does your boyfriend do this for you? I bet he does," Ethan said, taking off my glasses and placing them on the bedside table.

"Sometimes," I said. "He also takes off my shoes sometimes if I'm wearing, like, boots. And he does the dishes and laundry and then he folds the laundry and he hangs up my clothes for me and if I have salad he always shakes it up for me so the dressing can be distributed proportionately."

"Sounds hot," Ethan said, flatly. "Does he hold your dick when you piss too?"

"No," I snarled. "I love my boyfriend, okay? And I feel so bad about all the stuff I've been doing."

"Oh shit, you're going to tell me things, aren't you? Don't do that."

"Oh, shut up, Ethan. I'm serious. I've been a very bad boyfriend."

"Good for you, I didn't know you had it in you. Now get some sleep. We're meeting a numerologist at nine a.m., and attendance is mandatory."

"A numerologist? How many times do you have to pay someone to tell you you have a good life?" I scoffed. "By the way, do you even like this place?"

"Ojai? What's not to like?" Ethan went to sit down on the edge of the bed but stopped himself mid-sit. "Ew, no, what am I doing, I'm not staying."

"No, I mean, our fancy hotel. It's very Republican. You're better than this. You're gay. I mean, you used to masturbate in secret to, like, the *A&F Quarterly*."

"How young do you think I am?"

"Or to, like, Rock Hudson. Whatever. The point is, you didn't suffer through years of oppression and, oh my god, the AIDS epidemic. You lived through the AIDS epidemic."

"Yes, I did," Ethan said, his tone tight.

"So, wow, you went through all of that just so you could hang out with boring straight guys like Tom? I get that he's hot, but the dude mansplained the brilliance of octopuses for like thirty minutes last week. Straight guys suck. We have our own culture and it's way better. And it doesn't feature questionable art and an omelet bar."

"All right, thanks for telling me how to be gay," Ethan said, heading for the door. "Good night." I mumbled good night back, and he said, "See you at the omelet bar, faggot!"

◆

The next morning I wasn't nearly as hungover as expected, but my hamstring felt on fire. I knew I should've probably left early and gone to see a doctor, but my dramatic exit would've spawned secret conversations about my disability so I took some Advil and sucked it up. At breakfast Ethan surprised me by sitting next to me and having a real conversation—and not about the night before. He was almost normal, which scared the shit out of me. Trapped on this hellish merry-go-round we call our relationship, it seemed like I was back in Ethan's orbit again, which was my whole point of coming here so, yay? Once Ethan left the table, Tom scurried over.

"Hey, you and Ethan were gone for a while last night," Tom said, trying and failing to hide his nerves. "Were you guys, like, hanging out or something? Are you friends now? Because that's cool if you are. Whatever."

Cindy was next in line to undermine me. "I'm glad you and Ethan had some one-on-one time. You know, just between the two of us, he used to tell me that he didn't like you very much, but I'm so glad to see that's changed."

Think kind thoughts. She's only known toxic environments and power plays. It's not her fault.

Amy was third, but she only wanted to know if Ethan had said anything about her over breakfast. Joan had arrived at the buffet late, hair sopping wet from the shower, no makeup, and plopped down next to me and Amy.

"Why the hell is Amy here?" Joan said, taking a giant yellow bite of reconstituted eggs.

"Joan, why are you so rude to me?" Amy said. "We went shopping that one day, remember?"

"You mean the afternoon I ran into you at the Beverly Center, and I caught you hiding behind a mannequin?"

Amy got up and walked away.

"What the hell is going on here? Did you drink away the part of your brain that registers assholes?" Joan asked.

"Ethan sat next to me at breakfast, and now everyone's worried they're out of his inner circle. It's sad, really. They're, like, fifty-one years old but acting like we're in high school."

"Hey, watch your ageist language," Joan said. "What happened last night? Did Ethan get you home in one piece?"

"Yeah," I said. "And we kinda talked? Oh God, you don't think we're friends now, do you?" I thought for a second what being Ethan's friend would actually entail. He'd invite me to events, terrible events, like parties in Brentwood or the launch of a men's intimate grooming product (electric asshole shaver, which actually sounds useful), and I'd have to endure excruciating conversations with salt-and-pepper-haired men in tailored suits. Together they'd look like an assembly of budget Anderson Coopers, and they'd say things to me like "Fire Island," "Barry Diller's yacht," and "Nineteen isn't too young if you're just fucking them." I suddenly felt sick. My hangover had emerged.

"I don't want to be forced into being his friend, Joan," I said, for real frightened. "He's a bad person. Make it stop!"

Joan laughed and told me not to worry. Ethan would be barely tolerating my presence by lunch.

Joan was wrong. At lunch, he and I sat off to the side at our own table exchanging favorite queer movies—me *Parting Glances*, Ethan *Rocketman* (?!)—and discussing why Sam Smith, when the chips were down, hadn't been an amazing friend to Ethan. Imagine having a nauseating conversation like this against a backdrop of physical pain. I was in hell. Cindy approached our table, and I saw my opportunity to gracefully exit and lie down in my hotel room to ice my leg, but Ethan gave her an unfriendly grunt, so she made a quick 180 and disappeared.

Ethan and I were officially attached at the swishy hip. I admit that the attention was flattering. This was what I'd wanted—to get on Ethan's good side and have him take me more seriously at work. But Ethan didn't want to discuss writing or anything job-related. He just wanted someone to be gay bitches with.

"Remember when Cindy said her daughter was an old soul because her dream day was browsing a Samuel French bookstore followed by a matinee of *Sleep No More*?" Ethan said. "That is a top-ten nightmare. An eighteen-year-old who enjoys discussing immersive theater? Jesus. Pray you never get stuck with her at a party."

I nodded, but before I could add something, he cut me off and started in on a diatribe about the medium of plays: "It's a lot of frantic running around and someone asking a character very loudly if they're really going to take that job in Cincinnati. Who the fuck cares?" Keeping up with him was exhausting. I had to be on when all I wanted to do was fade into the background and discern how badly I had injured myself. One good thing did come out of our new nonconsensual friendship: I didn't drink. I wanted to, trust— the pain alone made me want to grab a bottle—but I couldn't risk embarrassing myself again.

When I got home, Gus immediately noticed something was wrong with my leg. He got hysterical asking what happened, did I hurt myself, why didn't anyone help me, I should go to the ER. His concern should've felt comforting—finally I didn't have to hide my injury—but instead it just made me feel smothered and saddled with the helicopter mom I never had or wanted. I snapped and told him I would go to the doctor tomorrow. But that wasn't good enough. Gus wanted to come with, he wanted to ask the doctor questions, figure out a plan of recovery. I said I could take care of myself, and then, thinking of Ethan, I hissed, "Jesus, what's next? You wanna hold my dick when I pee?"

Gus scoffed and said, "Sounds like you need a drink, honey. . . ." He then made two martinis that looked absolutely delicious—like cloudy nothingness in a perfectly chilled glass—but when he gave one to me, I said, "Actually, I don't feel like drinking tonight," because I didn't, because I'd liked being out of alcohol's iron grip, and then Gus looked hurt and sad and a little angry—more angry than when I had just snapped at him—and he said semi-jokingly, "What exactly happened to you in Ojai?" And the answer seemed complicated, so I just sighed and said I was sorry for snapping at him, because I was. I took the martini and drank it, thinking for a brief moment that maybe Gus was an enabler. An enabler of my disability by indulging my laziness and desire to be taken care of and also an enabler of my drinking because as long as we drank together it was less serious or depressing.

Then I had a second martini to forget all those thoughts because, woof.

CHAPTER 27

"Lie on your back, Elliott and just breathe. . . ," my physical therapist, Ralph, instructed me. My body hit the mat and I looked up at the blinding fluorescent lights. I was in hell. A very bright hell.

The popping sound in Ojai turned out to be a tear in my hamstring. Not a big one. Two to three weeks of icing it and doing physical therapy. Anyone else would've seen it as not an issue, but any minor physical setback leaves me rattled because it's a reminder that no matter how much I run in the gym or look for ways to get stronger, I always run the risk of injury and getting sent back to square one.

"You don't stretch before you work out, do you?" Ralph asked, situating my foot on his shoulder as he began to stretch me. He looked at my tight expression and course corrected by adding, "Not a judgment, my man. You're just very tight."

"I do stretch. All the time," I lied.

"Oh, okay. Super."

Ralph was a real goof. Long hippie hair, Zen yoga voice 24/7 that somehow made me more stressed out because all I could think was *What the fuck is his real voice like?* He worked out of a character-less office in Westwood with one other therapist, Nikki, who was currently bored eating a yogurt.

"I'm going to bring your knee to your chest," Ralph said. "Tell me when."

Ralph slowly lowered my gam to my chest, the stretch getting more and more intense. My body felt like a rubber band about to explode.

"We still okay?" Ralph checked in, registering the look of pain on my face.

"Doing great, Ralph," I said, defiantly.

I wasn't going to let Ralph win. At a certain point, Ralph picked up on that and stopped the stretch on his own.

I looked around the room, trying to distract myself, but everything was so drab and depressing. Then someone walked in, a real beanpole of a man about my age, and walked toward the mat next to mine. Actually, "walked" wouldn't be the correct term for this guy's gait. Hobbled. Limped. He walked like me. His outfit slash whole vibe was unfortunate. Ill-fitting sweat shorts that were two sizes too big. Extra pale skin. A boyish face with a few stray zits. Messy hair that bordered on greasy. He plopped down on the floor as Ralph instructed me to turn over on my stomach.

"Hey guys," the new arrival said to Nikki and Ralph. His voice was deep and gravelly sounding. Perfect for NPR.

"Jonas!" Ralph lit up, his voice finally slipping out of Zen Yoga and into Real Human. They gave each other high fives. Nikki finished up her yogurt and sat down on the mat with Jonas, ready to begin their PT.

While I was on my stomach, Ralph started pulling my leg

toward my butt—a move that made me feel like Stretch Armstrong in a deeply unpleasant way. Jonas looked over and noticed me for the first time.

"Hey," Jonas said, pointing at me. "I know you."

"I don't think so," I said, trying my hardest not to sound like I was in the depths of pain.

"Easterseals, right? In Ventura? I'm Jonas. And you're . . . Elliott? We both worked with Jendy."

Jendy. An example of a normal name getting wasted and doing whatever it wanted. She was my physical therapist at the PT clinic Easterseals from ages four to twelve. And Jonas . . .

My brain turned on. There was a flicker of recognition. "Oh, yeah. Your appointment was right after mine, huh?" I remembered now, with a clarity that almost made me nauseated, seeing Jonas and disliking him because sometimes Jendy would compare the two of us. "Jonas has cerebral palsy too, but his muscles are not as tight as yours because he actually does his stretches," she would tell me. "Jonas pays attention when I tell him what to do."

"Yes!" Jonas exclaimed. "I'm so glad you remember, so I don't seem like I'm doing the 'I'm disabled, you're disabled' thing."

Ralph laughed. He thought that was funny. Nikki performed the same stretch on Jonas that was being done to me, but Jonas was able to take the stretch further. It made my blood boil to see Jonas, yet again, be better at being disabled than me.

"You know, not to blow up your spot," Jonas said, smiling. "But Jendy told me you never stretched."

"Jendy's a fucking liar," I blurted out, stunned by my vitriolic response. I scaled back and tried to adopt Ralph's chill cadence. "I mean, I stretched all the time. Still do."

"I don't think that's true," Ralph said, sweat pooling on his forehead from the exertion caused by trying to move my brittle body.

"No offense, man. You're doing great but, like, wow. You have one of the tightest bodies I've ever worked on."

"Hmm," Jonas said. That's it. *Hmmm.* I couldn't believe how judgmental Jonas was being! It's my body. He should know more than anyone to not comment on it.

"Why are you still here?" I asked, trying to conceal my contempt. "Don't people usually stop going to PT after they're a teenager?"

"Um, yeah," Jonas said, his knee almost touching his face, taunting me with his flexibility. "I just, um, have a lot of anxiety about my body failing me. There's no guide on how to be an adult with CP. You're just kinda set out to pasture. So, I come in to just, you know, do maintenance."

"And you do such a good job, Jonas," Nikki said, crunching on something else in her mouth. Maybe a Kind bar. "You are a star patient!"

"K, I'm ready to go," I said, fed up. I got up from the mat, which took me a humiliating amount of time.

"You have twenty minutes left," Ralph said. "It's your time. Do what you need to do, brother. I'm just saying you should probably stick around because—"

"My body is a hot mess and you can't believe I'm even able to walk right now," I said, snarling. "Yeah, I'm good. See ya."

"Hey, we should hang out sometime and catch up," Jonas called out.

"Sure," I said, speed-walking out before Jonas had the chance to ask for my number.

CHAPTER 28

When I was young, maybe nine or ten, I jumped into a lake while on vacation and almost drowned. My parents told me to stay right on the dock while they brought the boat around, and I said okay, but the second they left I looked out across this large body of water and wondered for a split second how I would feel inside such a big thing. So I jumped in and, obviously, immediately started drowning, and my dad—not my mom, just saying!—saved me. I wasn't relieved or grateful. Instead I was mad at them for interrupting my reverie. They'd placed yet another rule on me. *Stay right there. Don't move.*

My life has been nothing but a series of things I've been told I can't do. The countless doctor's appointments where men named Peter or Robert with medical degrees explained what life would be like for me with cerebral palsy.

"If you don't stretch every day, your body will twist like a pretzel by the time you're thirty."

"You won't grow past five-foot-five, five-foot-six at the most." (Joke's on you, bitch. I'm almost six-foot.)

"He's going to need extra time on tests. His handwriting is illegible. I suggest investing in a good computer."

I did everything they told me. Physical therapy with fucking Jendy four times a week. Surgeries every summer. In school, I was the only disabled kid, and I couldn't shake the feeling that I was engaging in some kind of able-bodied cosplay. Constantly surrounded by people whose lives looked nothing like mine, who didn't have to ponder dilemmas like "What happens if my Achilles tendon keeps getting shorter?" I tried denial, pretending that my biggest hardship was the possibility that my parents wouldn't be buying me Lincoln Logs.

My rage, a small fire at first, began to build. I fantasized hitting my physical therapist, not showing up for surgeries, not stretching for months, destroying my body before it had a chance to destroy itself. The world was a rigged board game, and I was tired of playing. Sleepovers with friends filled me with fear. What if we snuck out at night and they wanted to climb fence and walk down into a neighbor's barranca? I had to learn how to anticipate people's moods, their desires. I had to constrict my life, squeeze it into a routine so that there were no surprises. My adolescence became small and claustrophobic.

When I tell people about almost drowning, they inevitably ask why I jumped. Did I have a death wish?

No, the opposite, I say. I had a life wish. I made a real decision for myself for the first time ever. It was liberating. If I had drowned that day, at least I would've died on my own terms. Nothing else I'd done until that moment had been.

When I think about these last few months, when I think of River and the endless drinking and getting jerked off in a steam room and getting throat-fucked in an older dude's fixer-upper in Van Nuys, I imagine them as versions of that little boy jumping in the lake, all in the hopes of a life. A complicated and risky life but a life that's mine to ruin as I see fit.

By the way: despite the physical therapy, my Achilles tendon did end up shrinking and I had to have surgery to lengthen it. A painful procedure with a long recovery time. A success, thankfully, but, for reasons unclear to me, the surgery also caused my right foot to jut out at an angle whenever I walked. This particular complication, I was told, would require surgery down the line. Another painful procedure. With another long recovery time.

See? Even when you play by the rules, you can still lose.

CHAPTER 29

Things, on paper at least, got better for a while. My
healed and I stopped going to see the Goof Troop at
apy. I was drinking less too, only on weekends. And
me to a new office, right next to his. Worried a
as Ethan's favorite, Tom took to stress-eating
Cindy fucked up her knee again running on
may have hated my job, but at least I wasn't

Now that Ethan acknowledged and
tence at work, it felt safe enough for n
stories. In fact, I got eight jokes int
counted. *I'm a loser, baby, so why don*
me my own episode to write, whic
when he told me the news, I g
eyes welled up with tears. "D
literally writing an episode
at an annual robot conven
I couldn't. I hadn't real'

down at work. I depended on the validation of my coworkers, and when I didn't get that, it threw me off my axis and took away my superpower, which is disarming people and winning their approval. If I wasn't the laser-focused perfectionist perpetually triumphing over something, who was I?

Things at home, meanwhile, stayed more or less the same. Gus kept at his watercolors, which were god-awful, but a step forward from colored pencils, and watching him be proactive turned me on and our sex life heated up. Rimming remained verboten, but I bought a jockstrap and we practiced dirty talk instead of being our usual *widdle babies*.

The one thing I couldn't, or wouldn't, change was seeking out sex workers. I hooked up with Rob, who had a ginormous cock and a love of Astrology, like me. He was a Taurus. I had no choice but to stan. There was Dalton, visiting from Las Vegas, who had ended a long run in the esteemed stage show *Puppetry of the Penis*. He showed me all the ways his dick could stretch and twist, and took my breath (and a little bit of my boner) away. There was nthony, who had the most beautiful hands I'd ever seen and gave a prostate massage and my first no-touch orgasm. We showered ther afterward, and he washed my hair while we laughed about vorite trashy reality TV (he agreed that Kyle Richards wasn't st compelling Housewife but that she's an excellent producer vides access to her sisters, Kathy Hilton and Kim Richards, national treasures).

me a sex-work connoisseur, scouring the message boards, encing customer reviews. I created an account on one par- age board, "M4M Escort," with the screen name "Unhap- and put out a call for recommendations. I never saw the more than twice. I refused to repeat my mistake with as I maintained the proper professional boundaries, I was fine, what I was doing was totally and completely and utterly fine.

I could disappear with these men and experience the double thrill of anonymity and acceptance. They saw me on my terms and did the emotional labor of creating a satisfying sexual experience for me. It's not easy work and I was so grateful to all of them.

Gus never noticed anything, or if he did, he didn't mention it. Besides, we were still baseline happy together. There were moments when I would snap out of my sex worker fog and catch Gus singing to himself while cleaning up the kitchen. He sounded so beautiful and unself-conscious, so himself. I was myself too. As much as I felt like Gus wasn't able to see all of me, there was a deep-seated feeling of relaxation whenever I was with him. I wasn't at work having to perform for anyone. I wasn't trying to dispel expectations or prove someone wrong. There was no adversity to fight against.

So many discussions around relationships feel binary. You're either struggling or you're not. You're either content or you're miserable. These narratives are easier to follow and allow us to think, *Well, if X isn't happening, then we're okay.* The truth is much more complicated and terrifying. You could love someone and want to lose them at the same time.

CHAPTER 30

"Don't you think it's fucked up how gay guys treat Britney?" Augie said, taking a sip of his whiskey ginger. It was Saturday and Gus and I were at the Eagle with our friends. After nobly abstaining from alcohol during the week, I rewarded my sacrifice by getting absolutely obliterated on the weekends.

Augie is the hottest guy in our friend group. He has 11,242 Instagram followers, solely due to his looks and bodyodyody. He's small—like a compact parking space—but he has sinewy arms and a sculpted butt that hangs like a shelf, and his hair is long but kind of tousled and sexy, like he's been places and experienced things. In Provincetown, Augie would walk down Commercial Street solo and return with stories of the scads of men he met. "Yeah, it was wild," he'd say. "I was in this cute little tea shop reading my book and this nice cute guy walked up to me and we got to talking and he randomly invited me to stay at his place in Europe? Like, he offered me his frequent-flier miles. So sweet of him." Augie never brags, if anything he's incredulous. I don't think he understands that this kind of thing doesn't happen to the rest of us. Not everybody can walk into, say, a bookstore and have, at minimum, three handsome men chat them up. I like that naïveté about Augie. Sometimes I wonder why he doesn't leave us in the troll trenches to enjoy the sunlight with the upper-echelon gays, but he is overly sensitive, almost fragile, proving that sometimes nerds are born in a hot person's body.

"What do you mean?" Justin said. "We love her. We want her to be happy."

"Now you do. But at one point, gays were commenting 'my iconic queen' on a video of her in raccoon makeup rolling around on the floor of the gym she accidentally burnt down," Augie said. "It's hypocritical. We're all complicit in what happened to her."

If I'd had the energy I would have said, that's how gay men show love and affection. Camp 101. We mock and celebrate at the same time. But Augie was right. Blood is on all of our hands when it comes to Britney and I was pretty sure I'd said the same thing three weeks ago when we argued about our questionable treatment of Britney the first time. So instead I finished my tequila soda and went to the bar for another. I didn't ask Gus if he needed one because he was a drink ahead of me. We keep score of each other's alcohol consumption in social situations to avoid judgment. SO NORMAL.

At the bar, a finger tapped on my shoulder. I turned around. River, smiling, was standing behind me. He had a sharp new haircut and smelled like palo santo.

"Oh, hey, River, hi," I said, totally taken off-guard even though we were in a popular gay bar and odds are you will run into at least one guy whose penis you've seen and/or touched.

"Hey," River said. "How are ya? It's been a while." I wanted River to act awkward, like spotting me had thrown him, but he was unfazed, or really good at hiding it. Why am I always the one who has the harder time? Why am I always the one who cares more?

"I know, sorry, things have been just so crazy busy with work and stuff," I said, barely committing to the lie.

"Well, that's good, right?" River nodded.

"Yeah. Do you want a drink?" I said.

"I'm sober."

"Oh, right. I knew that, sorry."

I wondered how hard it was for someone sober not to drink in a bar. Was it like going to Magic Mountain and not being able to ride the roller coasters?

"So . . . ," I said.

"You're making this kind of awkward," River said, chuckling. "It doesn't have to be."

"Well, I just . . . yeah . . . I mean, there's no rulebook for when you run into a guy you've paid for sex, you know?"

"I sense a hole in the marketplace," River said. "You should write it."

River's eyes shone like sparklers in the dusky light of the bar. He was infuriatingly adorable. To see him was to want all of him.

I had to leave or I was going to be enveloped by his charm. I excused myself and rejoined Gus.

"Who were you talking to?" Gus said, sucking down the last of his drink.

"No one." It was almost true. How could I explain to him what River was to me? I couldn't explain it to myself.

"Ooh, he's cute," Justin said. "If I wasn't with someone . . ."

"Justin, your boyfriend sucks," Augie said, slightly slurring. "Not only did he vote for Trump, but he tried to fuck me in your pantry after last week's poker game."

"What?" Justin said, mouth agape.

"Wait, you two, back to that guy . . . ," Gus said.

"He looks familiar . . . ," Augie said, squinting.

"Wait, Brian came on to you?" Justin said, on the verge of hysteria. "*My* Brian?"

"People aren't your property, Justin," Augie said. "But, yes. Also, you have rice on your shelf that expired like five years ago."

"I don't believe it . . . ," Justin said. "I mean, we leave for Burning Man Friday."

"Oh shit," Augie squealed, clapping his hands like a drunken gay seal. "I know how I know that guy. He advertises on Rent Men."

Oh, Jesus. My heart began pounding.

"Really?" Gus lit up at the news.

"Yeah, River something?" Augie said. "River Banks. I like to browse."

"Wait," Gus said. "The guy's a hooker?"

"Sex worker," I said, defending River a little too strongly.

"Okay, sorry, PC Police," Gus said. "From over here it looked like he was totally flirting with you. Do you know him or something?"

I had to think fast, which is hard to do on your third tequila and soda.

"Um, not really," I said. "He did a couple days of extra work on *Sammy Says*."

"Wait," Justin said. "Does no one care that Brian tried to cheat on me with Augie?"

"You dodged a bullet," Gus said. "He's an anti-vaxxer."

"Says who?" Justin said, ready to defend his betrayer.

"I remember it being all over his Facebook, which, God, does anybody know why we're still on Facebook?" I said.

"He, he's questioning the facts. I like that about him. He showed me that one book by Jenny McCarthy and—"

"Hey, babe," Gus said, putting his arm on me. "What do you think? Should we have a three-way with River tonight?"

"Excuse me?" I said, as the room began to spin.

"I mean, it could be fun, you know?" Gus said. "Ever since you had your little steam room jerk-off—"

"Whoa," Augie said. "Did you go to the place downtown?"

"Yep," Gus said. "And now he owes me."

"Owe you?" I said. "Where is this coming from? You've been so anti opening things up—"

"I haven't been anti," Gus said. "We just haven't ever talked about it seriously."

"Yes, we did," I said. "When I told you about my steam room moment and you were like, 'Let's not turn this into some massive slut free-for-all.' You said that, Gus. You did," I said, trying to seem more playful than panicked, but not sure I was succeeding.

"Okay, calm down," Gus said. "I did say that, but maybe I've been a little too old-fashioned." Gus was very drunk. His eyes glazed over as he continued. "I mean, you're right, babe. We're gay. Which means we can do shit like this. Plus, the experience might be good for my art."

Everyone in the friend group exchanged side-eyes. *Good for my art?*

"We can't just go up to him and ask. He's off-duty," I said, grasping at coke straws.

"I disagree," Augie said. "Even if he's a civilian for the night, he can schedule you for later."

"Please?" Gus said, now tugging on my arm like a child. "Let's go be gay and free together."

CHAPTER 31

I found River alone on the dance floor moving his statuesque body to "How Soon Is Now?" Every minute or two a guy would try to join him, but he would gently turn away. When he saw me approaching, he waved and said, "C'mere."

"I can't dance," I said.

"Anybody can dance to the Smiths," River said. "All you have to do is sway." River laughed and put his arms around my waist, guiding me back and forth.

"Are you here with anyone?" I asked.

"Nope," River said. "You?"

The confidence to dance alone at a gay bar. To know, at any moment, you could just talk to a stranger who would welcome you and no longer be alone.

"Yeah, I'm with friends," I said. "And, um, my boyfriend."

"Ohhhhh," River said, giving me a knowing nod. "Is that why you stopped texting me? You got a boyfriend? Congrats. I love that for you."

"No, I didn't just get him," I said, removing my hands from his waist. "We've been together for years. I'm sorry I told you I was single. I didn't—"

"Oh my god, I love this song!" River said, suddenly bouncing up and down. I didn't recognize the opening, but it sounded like Rihanna remixed by meth.

"River, are you mad at me? I'm sorry I lied."

"Not mad," he said, grabbing my hands. "Our time is your time. If you want to be someone who doesn't have a boyfriend when we're together, that's your right."

"God, you're so, like, annoyingly chill," I said.

"You kinda have to be to do what I do. You interact with so many different types of people, taking all that energy in. It's not about me, it's about them," River said, as he twirled me around. I prayed my balance would handle the sudden movement.

"That makes sense," I said. "Good, I'm glad you don't care."

I lied. I wanted him to be furious with me. I looked over River's shoulder to see a sloshed Gus by the bar, giving me a hopeful thumbs-up. I cringed.

"So listen," I said. "About that boyfriend, his name is Gus and he thinks you're really cute, and he wants to know if you'd be down for a threesome? Paid, of course, but also he doesn't know about, um, our history. I told him you were an extra on the TV show I write for, random I know, but you do look like you have a head-shot lying around somewhere. Anyway, if you don't mind not telling him that you've been inside me, that would be great. Oh, by the way, please don't think that I think you're just like this sex toy, available anytime and—"

River put a finger to my flapping lips and slipped into business mode. "Threesomes are double. Are you down for tonight? It's cheaper if I host, but I can go to yours too."

I smiled weakly, turned back to Gus, and flashed him a thumbs-up.

CHAPTER **32**

We ended up going to our place. Not my choice. Gus was freaked out about being naked in a stranger's apartment, and I couldn't exactly say, "Don't worry, babe. I've been there, like, eight times. I mean, it smells like vanilla and the water pressure sucks, but out of all the places I've been fucked lately it has the best feng shui."

Gus was gradually sobering up from the bar, and I could sense his bravery evaporating, and for a moment I contemplated convincing him to pull the plug, but it was too late. He offered River some wine and River said he didn't drink and Gus got embarrassed and apologized profusely and I kind of smiled to myself at the familiar scene. Gus and I drank our wine, and River watched us, politely sipping a seltzer. Gus proceeded to ask him a bunch of questions about his job to fill the air and delay what we had come here to do. Gus was nervous and flailing and I refused to help him out. I wanted to see him squirm.

After about forty-five minutes of excruciating "getting to know you"s, River gently reminded us that his fee was hourly and Gus blurted out, of course, yeah, let's move this thing along. We all walked into the bedroom and Gus fretted over our three-way playlist. He put on Portishead but worried aloud that it was too expected, so he put on Billie Holiday but decided it would kill the mood.

Anxious to get this *Looking* storyline started, I suggested to Gus that we skip the music. We stood there for a moment, silent, all looking at each other like unwrapped presents.

"Okay." River clapped his hands together. "I'm going to tell you boys what to do first. You cool with that?"

"Yes," Gus said, his voice wavering. "Tell us."

"Sure, whatever makes the most sense . . . ," I said.

"Great. You two are going to kiss in front of me," River said.

"Us?" Gus said, his disappointment palpable.

"Yes."

Gus nodded. Neither of us made a move.

"Now, boys," River said, sternly.

Gus and I kissed, like we had a million times before. From the corner of my eye, I spied River stroking his dick through his jeans.

"Mmmm," he said. "That's nice. Now undress each other."

I tried undressing Gus, but there were too many buttons involved and I gave up. Gus took the reins, taking my clothes off, then his. A mixture of rage and embarrassment bubbled in my chest. What was so sweet on our hike in Provincetown was humiliating here. Worse, I began to grow insecure comparing my average dick to Gus's nine-incher. River was going to like it more than mine. Why wouldn't he?

"Damn, you have an amazing cock," River said.

Sonofabitch.

"Um, thank you. I know you probably see a lot of dicks, so I'll take your comment as high praise!" Gus said.

"Shit, and you," River said to me. "Your ass. Damn."

Oh, thank God. I forgot that I had my ass.

"Both of you. Get over here."

Gus practically sprinted over like a *Price Is Right* contestant. River pulled off his shirt and placed Gus's hand on his stomach, which, okay, we get it bitch, you have abs. He guided my hand to his bulge which wasn't fully hard.

At that moment Gus lunged at River, kissing his neck, sucking on his earlobe, and landing on his mouth. Unsure of what my role was, I unzipped River's jeans, dropped to my knees, and started sucking his cock (he was freeballing, glam). River and Gus continued to make out, and River would stop occasionally to say something dirty in that fake accent of his. Gus loved it. He didn't know River's real voice was better.

Not wanting to have third billing in this threesome, I stood up and made us triple-kiss like we were in Cancún on spring break. We collapsed on the bed together. River took off his jeans and we were all naked, a bunch of spaghetti limbs splayed out over the comforter. Gus went down on River for a while, and then Gus and I made out while River watched us and jacked off, but our couple's scene seemed perfunctory, like two people being forced to eat their vegetables before allowed our dessert.

"I want you to watch River fuck me," Gus said.

I felt stupid for not understanding until this moment that tonight with River was not about spicing up our relationship and experimenting with a degree of openness or, Jesus, getting inspiration for Gus's shitty watercolors. It was about Gus finally seizing the opportunity to get fucked the way he wanted to. The way he needed to.

"You really want to?" I said, already knowing the answer.

"Oh yeah you do, baby. You want this cock . . . ," River said, hard dick in hand, playing for his audience. I shot him a look that was like, "Babe, stay out of it."

"Is that okay?" Gus asked tentatively.

"Yeah," I said. "Knock yourself out."

Once River eased his way in and the two found their groove, Gus let out these guttural, almost inhuman, moans of pure pleasure I'd never heard before. Watching them move together with such cohesion and fuck in positions I could never force my body into was gut-wrenching. This was the way sex was supposed to be. This was sex without me.

After Gus came, River offered to suck me off, but I declined. He went home shortly thereafter, and I felt a sense of relief when he left. No more hanging out on these dangerous open-relationship streets. I was officially ready to go back to the safe, comfortable cul-de-sac of my long-term relationship.

Look, the outside world is scary for a boy like me. It takes time and energy for a person to figure out how to navigate my booby trap–filled body and understand my disability. I didn't want to lose Gus, but tonight had shown me that I could. I could lose him to someone who was truly versatile, who could fuck for hours without his thighs seizing. The "You're just lucky to be with someone at all!" voice had taken up residence in my brain again. I wanted things to go back to the way they were before River.

The next morning Gus rolled over, looked me in the eyes, and said, "Thanks, babe. That was really fun last night."

"Yeah," I said. "I guess it was fun."

"You guess? That River guy is sexy."

"Yeah." I bristled. "I mean, in a generic way."

"I know but still," Gus said, getting out of bed. "I think I might want to do that again?"

"Do what again?"

"Play around with River," Gus said, a mischievous smirk spreading across his face. "It didn't feel weird or—I don't know, I feel kinda silly that it took us so long to do something like this."

"Really?" I said, trying to appear casual. "I found it more exciting as a one-and-done."

Gus said yeah, okay, that's fine, he was only wondering, but I sensed the conversation wasn't over.

CHAPTER 33

In the Uber to brunch Gus and I sat with our tension, and in an effort to distract ourselves, I struck up a conversation with our driver, Bob, who was a writer and an actor and self-proclaimed healer. He made eye contact with me through the rearview mirror when he revealed that last bit and asked if I was getting enough iron in my diet. I told him to turn up the radio. It was a Pink song. Every song in an Uber is a Pink song. I looked out the window, watching Los Angeles drift past me, and I suddenly felt very tired. When you look at the city for too long, you get exhausted because it's impossible to latch on to anything, when it's all strip malls and hot concrete and cars. LA is the ugliest thing you've ever seen but also the most striking, and it doesn't make sense and never will and you need a nap to forget about all of it. Bob turned down "Raise Your Glass" to ask me another intrusive question about my body, a question you wouldn't ask if you'd stop to think for a single second, and I wanted Gus to be the one to call out his bullshit, but he was too busy looking at house listings on Redfin, and even if he had been paying attention he might not have known that Bob's questions were overstepping, because able-bodied people—even the best ones—don't always register the micro-aggressions. I asked Bob to please turn up the radio again, and the way I said "please" sounded like a hot poker digging into skin. He got the memo. I started to wonder about Pink, if she's ever brought a sex worker into bed with Carey Hart. Are they still married? They were very on-again, off-again, quite the seesaw, but also why the hell did I know this? I'm not remotely a Pink fan. What precious memory in my brain had to die so Carey Hart's name could live?

We pulled up to the brunch spot in Echo Park. "Oh no," I said, before opening my door. A line of people was wrapped around the corner and we had no reservation. Truly an already tense white gay couple's worst nightmare. I predicted in an instant how this scene was going to go down. A woman with bangs and a clipboard would inform us of an hour-and-a-half wait and for a brief moment we would wish this woman were dead. I'd imagine snatching her clipboard, throwing it to the ground, and stomping away while Gus pulled out some scissors and hacked away at her bangs. But instead we'd say to her, "Um, wow, well, it's only brunch, whatever. Give us a second . . ." After a good minute of loaded conversation, Gus and I would admit that the restaurant had us by the balls, and every other place would be just as packed so we were trapped in the ninth circle of brunch hell. And we'd wait outside in the sun, our hungover bodies losing moisture and replacing it with anger, and every time someone else's name was called, we'd wish a pox upon them and their entire family. By the time our table was ready, two hours would have passed.

That is close to what happened, except the woman with the clipboard had a bob instead of bangs. Luckily, there was a bar across the street where we could serve our brunch sentence in relative comfort.

Inside the bar the calendar had been stuck on "sad Tuesday afternoon." A smattering of rough-looking regulars were drinking in silence at the bar while two people played pool. I ordered a margarita—big mistake, I know, ordering a cocktail at a dive bar—and Gus ordered the drink of choice for disordered-eating alcoholics everywhere: a vodka soda. We sipped our beverages and ate the stale bar nuts, making inane conversation until I couldn't stand the tension any longer.

"All right, let's address the sex worker elephant in the room, shall we?" I said. "I didn't give you the answer you were looking for earlier, did I?"

"Regarding River? No, don't worry, I'm fine."

"So you're okay with it?"

"Yes! God . . ."

He wasn't. Wait a beat.

"It's just . . ."

Here we go.

"Like, you've pretty much done whatever you want."

"What do you mean?" I asked, knowing exactly what he meant.

"Like, you've always been this way. You wanted to get jerked off at the spa, you got jerked off at the spa. And you did it without checking in with me first."

"I'm sorry, Gus, I really am, but I thought we moved on from that."

"Look," Gus said, putting his hand on mine. "You know how they say in every relationship there's like a plant and a gardener? Well I've been gardening your ass for five years."

"I've never heard that saying . . . ," I lied.

"Whatever. It's not important. I'm just saying," Gus continued.

"Hooking up with River was fun. I wanted something, I vocalized it, and we did it. Together. I got gardened."

"You got plowed."

"I did, didn't I?" Gus said, wistful.

"But okay, look, Gus, I get everything you're saying. Truly, madly, deeply. I do. But if you wanna get gardened or plowed or fertilized—"

"Too far," Gus said.

"Then why not open up our relationship? No sex workers."

"Because, I don't know, that scares me," Gus said. "I mean, what does an open relationship look like? Us fucking our friends? Too incestuous."

"We could fuck non-friends. . . ."

I was doing everything I could to steer Gus to anyone who wasn't River. Anyone at all.

"And what, spend hours on Grindr trolling for dick? Look, I love you. . . ."

"Same. Obsessed with you. I just don't know how we got here," I said. "I mean, the vibe I always got from you was 'full monogamous bitch.'"

"Yeah," Gus said, carefully choosing his words. "That's fair. I guess I was scared of bringing in any outside elements. I didn't want to mess anything up. But that's the great thing about River. It's no muss, no fuss. He comes, we come, he goes. He won't bleed over into our real lives."

That was exactly my logic in the beginning and look where it got me.

"But, also," Gus continued. "We've been together for such a long time and, you know, we're solid. I need to ease up."

We are not solid. HE NEEDS TO CLAMP DOWN.

"Okay," I sighed, resigned to my fate. "Fine. Let's see River again."

"Yay!!!" Gus came alive.

"Okay, you are way too happy about this right now. I'm honestly triggered."

"Sorry." Gus lowered his voice and said, "Can River fuck you next time? I appreciated the starring role last night—"

"Starring hole, you mean."

"God, once you start, you can't stop, huh?" Gus said. "Anyway, it would be so hot to see River fuck you." Gus let out a big grin before adding, "Oooh, this is so fun. Us fucking people! Getting fucked."

I could do this, I assured myself. We'd get together a couple more times at most, I'd let River fuck me, and we'd move on. Better to indulge Gus now than tell him the truth about, well, everything.

I proceeded to get shitfaced on margaritas so I could believe the lies I was telling to comfort myself. Gus and I lost track of the clock, and by the time we paid proper attention, two hours had passed. We rushed over to the restaurant, where the girl with the bob said, with smug satisfaction, that she had given away our table. Drunk and defeated, we ordered tacos from a food truck on the corner. Fuck brunch forever.

CHAPTER 34

When I was twenty-four, my life didn't consist of many real things. In fact, I couldn't even envision a life that could be good. I don't mean that in a pity-party way. More in a practical sense. Where were my disabled gay role models? Geri Jewell could only shoulder so much responsibility. I assumed, at best, life could be about experiences. Like having an excruciating conversation with a girl you met at a party who's convinced you're instant best friends and wants to tell you about her trauma, eating a peach in Midtown because Joan Didion wrote about it in an essay, befriending boring people who fill out clothes nicely in the hopes that they tag you in a picture and a stranger will see it and think you're cooler than you actually are, going to a foreign country and finally having a reason for people not to understand you, or getting wasted at a bar an Olsen Twin used the bathroom in once. Good or bad, as long as things kept happening to you, you would be all right.

I believed in my theory until I met Devon my last summer living in New York. He was my best friend Maura's roommate—medium-cute, except for his eyes, which looked like the bottom of the pool in that famous David Hockney painting. He was a writer like me but a serious one. He wrote short stories about gentrification and AIDS—nobody had bothered to tell him about *Rent*, I guess—and besides, when we first met, I didn't think about him—or anyone—in a romantic way because I was convinced I was gay Gollum.

"I think Devon wants to fuck you," Maura said to me at Three Lives bookstore in the West Village. It was July in New York, hot and sticky. Everyone wanted to fuck in July.

"No, he doesn't," I said, pretending to thumb through the latest Philip Roth.

"No, he definitely does."

"Isn't he with Ian?" Devon was always with some boy.

"I think they're gonna break up, like, Friday," Maura said, smacking her gum.

"Oh, is there an official breakup date on the calendar?"

"Ian's going to Cambodia Friday."

"Cambodia? Why?"

"How would I know?"

Imagine hearing that someone was going to Cambodia and not asking why. Maura and I stopped being friends six months later.

"Okay," I said, pretending to be distracted by a Franzen novel. God, how I wish a kind soul had led twenty-something me to Lorrie Moore. "Did he say something?"

"Yeah. He said you were hot and he wanted to fuck you."

I hadn't had anal sex in three years. I basically identified as a virgin, so I was thrilled to hear that someone wanted to do sexual things to my body.

"Okay," I said, a little embarrassed. "So what should I do with this information?"

"Don't you want to fuck him too?"

"I'd fuck my radiator at this point, Maura."

"Tight," Maura said. "I'm having people over Saturday. We'll get drunk, set the scene. You can seal the deal then."

Remember throwing parties for the sole reason of inviting your crush? Obsessed with being young.

"HAPPY JULY OR WHATEVER PARTY" the Facebook invite read. I arrived dressed in Opening Ceremony short-shorts and a Buffalo Exchange button-down with a bow tie, looking like a gay temp from the movie *Clockwatchers*. We guzzled vodka and danced to Scissor Sisters. Devon and I hung out for hours, talking about nothing and pretending it was everything. At one point he asked, with those A+ David Hockney pool eyes, if I wanted to read one of his stories.

"Like right now?" I screamed over the music. He nodded and led me over to his room. His bed was a mattress on the floor (classic twenties behavior), and a Morrissey and Marr poster was slapped to the wall (telegraphing your personality via posters in your bedroom . . . also classic twenties).

He handed me some pages, hopeful that I could see him as more than just A Body at a party.

"So, you want me . . . you want me to read this right now? In front of you? While you watch?"

I don't know why I even asked. I read the story. It was about AIDS but not gentrification—he was branching out—and the story was actually kind of funny and moving. I was also twenty-four and drunk and had considered *Eat Pray Love* as a piece of literature that rly made u think, so take that into consideration. Still, I liked his writing and I liked him even more. We made out on his bed and then we blew each other. He came in my mouth as people scream-sang "Party in the U.S.A." in the living room. We started dating immediately, something I had no real adult experience in.

Our relationship was largely unremarkable. We went to see his friends' shitty plays in Williamsburg and moseyed on over to Metropolitan for drinks afterward. We slept over at each other's apartments and walked to our favorite coffee shop (Variety, off the Graham stop) in the morning. Once he locked himself out of his apartment in his underwear, and I brought him clothes that he wore all day, and I swear to God, seeing him in my tank top and black Cheap Monday jeans was such an intimate experience we might as well have been married. These all seem like normal events in a relationship, but to me they were huge. I was a real boy with a real life and a real boyfriend! I knew we were official when we were at the Union Square farmers' market and Devon asked me if we should get ramps for dinner. He was showing me that boring, everyday life could be good, fulfilling even, and that I could expect more from New York than a Didion peach.

The one thing we didn't do was anal. Did we blow each other into oblivion? Yes. Did he once rim me for an hour straight one humid night after four tiki drinks? Absolutely. But not one dick went inside an asshole. He tried. A week into our relationship, he asked if he could fuck me. It was a Sunday afternoon, we were sober. The moment felt right on schedule, a natural progression of our closeness. As we were getting into it though, I became paralyzed with nerves and my asshole boarded up and went night-night. He asked if I'd be more comfortable fucking him. I said no, definitely not. A part of me hoped that he would want to revisit, that he would push me out of my comfort zone and I'd feel brave enough to give it a try with him, but he never asked again.

Devon gave me a peek into a life I never thought I could have, but the more time we spent together the more I began to feel like I was impersonating a person capable of real intimacy. Eventually Devon caught on to my secret turmoil and hit a wall—a wall which

I had built, brick by brick—and he broke up with me. That lazy Sunday afternoon I said no to the nice boy who wanted to be inside me and, who knows, maybe even potentially fall in love remains my *Sliding Doors* moment. It would be a long time till I met Gus and embarked on my first serious relationship. How much damage was done during those in-between years? The ones I spent lost in my bedroom on pills while my friends got into relationships and moved in with their partners and their lives got bigger and bigger while mine got smaller and smaller? If I had just gone through with it, if I had just let Devon fuck me and let myself experience something good, would I be here years later, a bottomless pit of need and validation, fresh from a three-way with my boyfriend and a sex worker? Maybe I was too fucked up when I met Gus for us to ever stand a chance.

Devon never became a successful writer, but he does ad copy in Portland and lives with his husband, Jarrett. We follow each other on Instagram. Last week I "liked" a picture of him kayaking and he wrote "congrats!" on an Instagram post about my career. What can I say? Modern life is hell.

CHAPTER 35

After Gus got me to agree that we could see River again, he didn't bring it up again. I assumed having the conversation might've been enough for him, like traveling with Xanax: knowing it's available can replace the need to take it. The next few weeks Gus and I were homebodies and we splurged on delivery (tortellini en brodo, an ill-advised seafood tower) and watched gay art films with real cumshots and farted freely and fucked after the farting because why not and who cares, and we didn't go to a single gay bar.

Gus continued practicing his watercolors—he was actually getting better . . . kind of—and I'd lie in bed watching him with newfound appreciation, determined to not take him for granted. My heart would experience what I call "surge pricing." You know how with Uber there are times when it's rush hour or raining and the rates go up and it costs $30 to go five blocks? Early in our relationship, Gus and I had gone out for dinner. As I was heading back from the bathroom to our table, I saw Gus talking to a few friends who had run into him and he was laughing his carefree warm laugh, the one that announces "THERE'S AN ANGEL INSIDE OF ME," and his eyes were sparkling with joy and I looked at him, really looked at him, and felt, for the first time, a twist in my heart. *God*, I thought. *I love this man.*

I'd never been in love. My teenage boyfriend Dylan doesn't count. We were embryos and he literally thought monogamy was a type of wood. I didn't know what love was supposed to feel like, but I thought it lived in a big romantic gesture like a surprise candlelit dinner or an impromptu slow dance at an Office Depot. Instead, love lived in the little moments, like seeing the inner light of your boyfriend moments after taking a shit. (JK, I can't shit in restaurants.)

When I sat down, Gus asked me if I wanted to split an order of oysters, and I said, "Gross, no, oysters are living globs of mucus, do you even know me? Also, I love you."

Gus's eyes widened. "You love me. Since when?"

"Since like a second ago. I'm surge pricing."

Okay, the surge pricing thing makes no sense, but it's *our* nonsense thing, and occasionally one of us will look adoringly at the other and smile and say, "Hey, guess what? I'm surge pricing."

This is going to sound snobby—I apologize in advance—but a lot of people don't bring anything to the table. When you talk to them, you know within the first two minutes whether or not they get it and can keep up with you. When my friend Augie broke up with him, I asked Gus out to drinks at this horrible straight bar as, like, a joke. I'd hung out with Gus before in the context of going out with Augie, but never one-on-one. Still, I picked up on things. Like how he was genuinely nice without being boring or a pushover. "No, I don't want to do that," he'd say to Augie firmly at dinner when asked if he wanted to split something. *Hot.*

He could banter with the best of them, always armed with a witty retort or—sorry, I'm unwell—a hilarious pun. How rare it was to be in the company of someone who was quick. It shocked me how many people genuinely had nothing to say. You'd go on a date with them and they'd just sit there in silence until you came up with the next question. I got back problems from carrying so many conversations.

Gus was different. He could carry his weight. He was spiky and yet somehow soft, naturally inquisitive without letting himself fade into the background. We kissed in the terrible straight bar that night after he made a pun about Glenn Close, which I won't repeat in order to preserve his dignity. On the Uber ride to the second bar—a gay one, this time—we started talking in character as two farm boys who had moved to Los Angeles to become influencers, asking the Uber driver if he could take us to the Great Pink Wall for pics. I found his willingness to look stupid all for the sake of a joke to be so sexy. And not very common. Playfulness is an undervalued attribute and one that's necessary, at least for me.

We started our date presenting each other the version we thought we needed to be. I was wearing my aforementioned "I'm rich and able to retire!" outfit. Gus was serving hot slut. But by the end of the evening, those projections had dissipated and we were able to—wait for it—let out the fart that was our true personalities.

A month later, we went to my friend's birthday party—a friend Gus didn't know, a branch of my social life he had no connection to. I was prepared to be his keeper for the night, to hold his hand and introduce him to various people. Instead, he sauntered off in his own direction and started chatting someone up. We barely spoke all night—only reconvening at the end.

"That was fun," he said, wrapping his arms around me. "Your friends are nice."

"Well, thanks for handling things on your own tonight," I said, giving him a kiss.

"Of course," Gus laughed. "You don't have to do social work with me."

Seeing Gus so independent and sure of himself, I knew that if I conquered my toxic brain and actually let myself be loved by him, it would be the greatest gift.

And it was the greatest gift, until time and being with River made me believe otherwise. But now Gus and I appeared to be getting back to basics, showing gratitude for each other, surge pricing when appropriate. In a way, I had River to thank for revitalizing "us." Money well spent.

One night after finishing our third viewing of *Stranger by the Lake* (very French, uncut dicks everywhere, gives new meaning to the term daddy issues), Gus turned to me, eyes clouded with lust, and went in for a kiss. We were making out on the couch, when he pulled away and said, "Hey, wanna call River?"

The question felt like a knife being dragged across my stomach.

"River?" I said. "*The River Wild*? 'Cry Me a River'? The ghost of River Phoenix?"

"Okay, you're short-circuiting. Why the aggressive punning?"

"I'm not. I had kind of forgotten about him, to be honest."

"I didn't."

"Great, good for you," I said, barely concealing my growing resentment.

"Are you all right? I mean, we talked about this, at length. You said you were chill."

"I am, but . . ." I scrambled for an excuse, any excuse. "Fine,

I'll tell you, but it's gross. If you wanted this to happen tonight, we shouldn't have ordered burritos."

"Fuck. I'm not used to thinking about that," Gus said, his anal dreams dashed.

"Well, that's your top privilege!" I shook my fist in fake anger, trying to keep things light. "Look, if River is going to fuck me, which I'm way into and totally one hundred percent up for, I'm gonna need some advance warning, because this bod isn't ready."

"Gotcha. Well, how about tomorrow? We'll make sure to have a light dinner."

"Um, okay . . . ," I said. What I really wanted to tell him was that I had stopped seeing sex workers, that I was back in this, so how could he be going in the opposite direction?

"Great, I'll text him," Gus said.

My surge pricing period had ended. Prices were slashed, like my hopes of never seeing River again.

CHAPTER 36

"Dad, help," I said, massaging his feet. He didn't answer. Instead he let out a bellowing moan. When I was a kid, Dad used to pay me $5 to massage his feet. Even then I knew I was being underpaid, but the tradition somehow followed me into adulthood as a form of charity.

"Between the toes," he commanded. "Ahh, that feels nice."

"Dad, pay attention! Or else I'll stop."

"Okay, okay. Geez. What's the problem?"

"Remember when I told you that I cheated on Gus."

"Ah, yes. With the fella whose real name you don't know?"

"Wow. Good memory for once."

"Your mistakes are seared into my brain, son."

I squeezed his foot.

"Ow!"

"Don't go all judgmental on me, you little bitch."

"Fine," he said. "You got an STD or something?"

"No, but should I get one? It could bring us closer. How are your genital warts, by the way?"

"Getting one frozen off next week."

"Nice. You seem like you're in a really great place." I patted him on the leg. "No, Gus and I ran into River, and for reasons that are too gay and complicated to go into, we hired him for a threesome, except Gus doesn't know that me and River have a past, I guess you could call it. And now Gus wants to see him again. I totally miscalculated his desire to be monog."

"Wow," Dad said. "And to think my biggest mistake as a parent was fooling you into thinking I was one of those Cool Dads you could tell anything to."

"Oh, Dad, you poor thing," I said. "I never once thought you were cool."

Dad rolled his eyes and huffed. "Why are you doing this to yourself? You have a good life, a solid boyfriend, and you've turned it all into some soap opera."

"I did, but now I want everything back to normal and Gus doesn't."

"Well, sounds like you made your bed and now you have to lie in it with your boyfriend and a hooker. How much is this costing you by the way?"

"Sex worker, Dad. And a lot of money. Tons of money. You would die if you saw my bank statement!" I said.

"And this is why you don't own a house," Dad said, shrugging off my attempt to rile him. "Look, every action has consequences. Did I not teach you that?"

"Dad, I know. All people said to me growing up was how things would hurt me and my body if I didn't follow their rules."

"Well, you're a little too old to rebel now, don't you think?"

"Your feet are absolutely disgusting," I said.

"They did nothing to you. Leave them out of it."

I stopped massaging. What's a little more rebellion at this point?

CHAPTER 37

Tonight was the night when two would begrudgingly become three. Gus and I prepped accordingly, eating sad salads for dinner. Earlier I masturbated in the shower so I wouldn't come when River fucked me. My own private little fuck you, even though the whole situation was my fault. I punished myself by getting off to a man who was mean to me in a job interview four years ago. He was wealthy, gay, and of a certain age—well maintained but shiny, like an expensive dessert left out in the sun. During the interview he asked me straight out if I had cerebral palsy. People rarely clocked my particular disability, so I said yes despite being turned off by his directness, and he acted all impressed, marveling at how I was in pretty good shape for someone with CP. "I mean, as a gay man you're average, but for a disabled gay, you're like, wow." He laughed, providing a runway for me to land my crip plane and make him feel okay about the offensive thing he'd said. Normally I would have given him what he wanted, but that day was different. I don't know if it was because the interview was already a bust or I'd spent two

hours in an Uber to get there or I was tired of giving human garbage cans permission to make me feel like *I* was the garbage can,
but I decided—for the first time in my life—not to laugh. Instead
I sat there, unsmiling, and he stopped laughing and cleared his
throat and asked if I needed parking validation. Because my brain is
basically a spoiled vat of coleslaw, our hurtful interaction was then
metabolized into an erotic prompt, and I decided his shiny face was
going to be the one to get my cum tonight.

River texted to say he was running late so I calmed my nerves
by watching an episode of the cult classic Bravo reality show *Gallery Girls*, about women in their mid-twenties pursuing careers as
art dealers, which mostly meant having drama in front of a Henry
Darger print. They were all awful, but different flavors of awful,
like a buffet really, and I loved rewatching episodes because the
show aired in 2012, a simpler time, when America had less of a
stressed-out vibe and soul-killing news about climate change didn't
come out every day. The world was a delicious croissant for you to
feast on instead of a two-day-old churro dropped on the ground at
Disneyland.

Is my life a stale churro? I wondered. I turned off *Gallery Girls*
for something equally pointless: inspecting my naked body in the
mirror. My midsection had gotten fleshier because of the wine, but
my legs and arms were okay. Great for disabled, okay for gay, haha-
haha!!!! God, kill me. I searched through my closet for something
to wear. Does one dress up for the occasion? Gus had put his contacts in, which he does when he wants to feel hot. He knows I can't
wear contacts because of my hand-eye coordination. I sent him a
mental message of *Wow, must be nice to be able to live that contact lens
life. Maybe you can learn how to drive next?* while I slipped on a pair
of old American Apparel briefs.

I decided on white linen shorts from Entireworld and my

tried-and-true Acne measure tee. All white. I looked like a cult member. Wow. This was pointless. I wanted desperately to fall asleep and wake up when the fucking was over. Gus could recap events and I'd nod, a sleepy smile on my face, and we would watch an episode of *The A-List: New York* and I'd snuggle in the nook of his arm and fall back asleep before the end. To me that would've been more intimate than any threesome.

"River said he'd be here in five!" Gus burst out of the bedroom, like it was his birthday and his rich uncle who gives the good gifts had walked in.

I went to the bathroom and brushed my teeth, put gunk in my hair and spritzed on cologne. The ritual of prettying yourself up only to end the night with jizz on your face.

I looked at myself to see if my reflection would give me a sign or insight into anything. Nothing. Instead, there was a knock on the door. Time to tear down what I had built.

CHAPTER 38

River walked in with his dog, Honey.

"Oh, you brought a dog," Gus said, confused. "Is that, like, a prop?"

River laughed. The dog was throwing a tantrum, he said, and he had to bring her or he'd have arrived even later. Was that okay?

"Gus hates dogs," I said. It was true.

"Don't be silly. No, I don't," Gus said. That wasn't true.

River looked self-conscious and apologized, offering to reschedule our "session."

I lit up at the prospect. "Oh, that sounds—"

"Oh please, don't worry about it!" Gus said. Goddamn that horny bastard.

I kneeled down and hugged the dog. "Hi, Honey," I said.

"What's her name?" Gus asked, reaching out to pet her like she was hot lava and not a dog.

"Honey," River said.

Gus said, "Hey, how did you know her name?"

"I didn't," I said, getting up from the floor. "I call everyone Honey."

A slight smile was forming on River's face.

"No, you don't. Since when?" Gus said.

"Okay, not everybody. But I have been known to address people and animals like that. I mean, I'm gay."

Gus was too overcome by the promise of penis to push the matter, and he returned his attention to River.

"So, gentlemen." River cleared his throat. "Shall we go to your room?"

"Sure," Gus said. "Elly, do you have the—"

"Have the what?"

"The money?" he mouthed, embarrassed.

"You pay after," I said, with an internal eye-roll. Then, catching myself, I said, "I mean, at least they do in the movies, I think."

River told us he was fine with whatever.

"Let's do now." Gus set the money down. Two twenties fell to the floor and he stooped to pick them up. *Amateur.*

"All right, boys!" River took off his shirt and bent down to pat Honey on the head. "Daddy will be back!" We headed for the bedroom.

"So . . . ," River said, taking off the rest of his clothes. "Anything you're in the mood for?"

"Not really," I said.

"Wait, babe, we talked about this, remember?" Gus said.

"Ohhhh, so you guys have been talking about me?" River said, playfully. How could we not? I thought. A chiseled sex worker had disrupted the lives of two gay geeks and turned their world upside-down.

"Well, kinda," Gus said, standing up, his semi-erect dick swinging between his legs. "I thought it would be cool if I watched you two fuck."

River and I had fucked twelve times already. Not that I had counted.

"No worries, you don't have to," I said, giving River an out.

"Sure. We can do that," River said, proceeding to compliment Gus's ass with words he had already said about mine. *Shit. Did he have a script he used on everyone? Because I thought he genuinely loved my butt.* This devastated me to an uncomfortable degree. Our asses don't even look the same!

Perhaps sensing my displeasure with the recycled compliments, River walked over and kissed me. My mouth, my chest, making his way downward to random spots like he was trying to Lewis and Clark a new route to my dick, where he eventually arrived and began sucking. Gus crawled behind River and wrapped his arms around him, cupping his ass and kissing his neck. I was determined not to surrender to this threesome, but my shower jerk-off plan was powerless in the face of River's stellar blowjob skills. I wanted his cock up my ass so badly, I was two seconds away from begging for it.

I grabbed the lube and got on top of River. As I guided River's dick into my ass with expert familiarity I made sure to focus my attention on Gus, holding his hands and locking eyes. He was so into seeing me get fucked. I honestly didn't understand the appeal. I mean, I would never in a million years want to watch myself having sex. But part of being in a relationship is acknowledging that people find you attractive for reasons you will never understand. So there Gus was, beating off and watching me glide up and down on River's cock. When Gus asked me to look at River and tell him how much I loved his cock inside me, I was annoyed, but I made eye contact with River and said, with as much enthusiasm as a Kristen Stewart line reading, that I loved his cock inside me. I wished I'd seen anything resembling hurt or at the very least confusion on River's face—something to demonstrate that he felt any kind of attachment to me—but he just looked distracted and hungry (his stomach growled loud enough for me to hear). When I looked over at Gus, he was so horned up it was almost repulsive to see such unfiltered desire. If he were a stranger, it would've made me feel good to be looked at like that. But because he knew me, because he'd wiped dry toothpaste off my mouth, it was unbearable. It only felt like a win to be wanted by someone who knew nothing about me.

I worried that Gus's dopey sex face would show up to haunt my brain when he'd be in the middle of the most arbitrary thing, like flossing, and I couldn't bear the thought, so I focused on River who by now was basically a hologram of himself, probably mentally ordering the kale and quinoa salad he was going to eat right after this, and then I checked in on Gus, who was still mayor of "I LOVE EVERYTHING SEX-RELATED!" town.

There was nowhere safe to look, so I stared at the ceiling, and within seconds I came and Honey barked, like she always did.

CHAPTER 39

I woke up one day and hated my body. Like, more than usual. This was to be expected. Being around River and his horny oil painting of a physique gave me extra dysmorphia. I know that I should be evolved and "body positive" about it. I know there's nothing wrong with being fat and we have been gaslit by a thin-obsessed society, that all these boogeyman fears stoked by doctors about obesity is LOL and you can actually be skinny and deeply unhealthy. I know all of this, and still, sometimes I wake up and jiggle the fat around my stomach and want to astral project myself out of my body. So I went to this place called Sweat Haus in Beverly Hills that identifies as an "urban sweat lodge." You put on this massive silver sweat suit contraption and then you go lie down on a bed that exudes infared heat while you watch HBO on an individual TV screen for an hour. You allegedly sweat a shitload, which in turn makes you thinner? It's ridiculous. I actually feel myself losing brain cells just describing it but, who knows, maybe brain cells contain a lot of calories.

Getting into the sweat suit was NOT disabled-friendly and required the help of two Sweat Haus workers, Heylan and McKinzley. By the time we got it on, I was already sweating profusely. For free! (Hmm, already poking holes in this new weight-loss craze.) Heylan led me to my steaming hot bed and put on the canonically incredible *Sex and the City* episode "Hot Child in the City." After a few minutes of living, laughing, and sweating, I saw a wisp of a man (his tiny frame was extra-exaggerated given the comically oversized sweat suit) walk over to the pod next to mine and lay down. Actually, I could tell by his quirky gait that this was not any man. This was Jonas, the breakout star from physical therapy.

I needed a second to orient myself. It's rare to see a fellow crip out in the wild like this. I immediately imagined Heylan and McKinzley exchanging a look at the front desk after meeting him and asking themselves, "Do you think they know each other?"

Jonas looked over and lit up. "Well, well, well," he said. "Out of all the urban sweat lodges in this town . . ."

I don't think I like Jonas very much. Is that problematic? I just feel like he's always judgmental about my journey. Like, I'm sorry I can't do double backflips like you, Jonas, and I'm sorry that I don't go to PT still as an adult. Plus, am I supposed to like him just because he's disabled? That's offensive too!

"Oh hey. What are you doing here?" I lowered the volume on a scene where Jenny Brier (Kat Dennings) eviscerates Samantha Jones (Kim Catrall) for not taking her birthday party seriously.

"Oh, um, I'm a teacher at a fancy private school and one of the parents gave me a gift card to this place." Jonas took a look around at his surroundings—a sea of LA psychos lying horizontal wrapped in what looked like burritos and drenched in sweat. "They really don't get me there," Jonas said.

"So you're saying you wouldn't subject yourself to this on your own accord? I can't understand why," I said, sarcastically.

"Exactly," Jonas laughed. "What are you doing here?"

"I'm here because being gay and having a body is exhausting," I said. Drips of sweat were falling down my face and I suddenly felt very claustrophobic.

"Having a brain is worse, no matter the sexuality," Jonas said, scanning HBO and stopping on a show. "Now would be a really weird time to start *Game of Thrones*, right?"

"Or maybe the best time? There's a lot of, like, dragons and hellfire, right? You could feel like you're right there with them."

Wait, why was I bantering with him? He didn't get to have my banter.

"What do you do for work?" Jonas asked.

"I write for TV," I said, with a tinge of smugness.

"Cool," Jonas said. "I don't really watch TV—hence, why I haven't seen *Game of Thrones*. But have you worked on anything I might've heard of?"

"Um, right now, I'm working on a show called *Sammy Says*."

"Huh," Jonas said. "Never heard of it."

"It's one of the biggest shows . . ."

"Does that offend you that I haven't seen it? I'm sorry. I told you, I don't watch TV."

"It's fine," I said. "It's actually bad. Don't watch it."

"I bet there's something decent if so many people like it," Jonas said, awkwardly turning on his side to face me. "Hey, would you maybe be down to come talk to my class about writing for TV? I know a lot of my students would be interested."

"Um sure," I said, noncommittal. I had no desire to see Jonas again or do free labor. I found his presence to be unnerving, like I was being given a test and failing. I started to get up from my sweat pod. "Well, it was good seeing you."

"You too," Jonas said before grabbing my arm. "Are you going to give me your number so we can coordinate you coming to my class? Or are you going to run away from me like you did at PT?"

I laughed, impressed by his directness. "You're weird," I said. "You're not supposed to call me out like that. It violates the social code."

"You're the one who spends money to sweat. And yet, I'm the weird one? Interesting."

I laughed again, despite my desire to be a cold bitch. "Fine," I said. "I'll give you my number."

I was still perturbed by Jonas, but now I was perturbed and 2 percent intrigued. He seemed so self-possessed and sure of himself, even though he shouldn't be. Like he was Rob Schneider or David Spade in the nineties or something.

When I left the sweat area, Heylan and McKinzley asked if I needed help getting out of my suit and I said no to prove a point to . . . Jonas? The able-bodied gods? Who knows, but I ended up falling over mid-undress in the changing area and couldn't get up. Heylan rescued me and asked, with a flicker of annoyance, "Where's your friend? Could he maybe help you?"

CHAPTER 40

Something had happened at work. Something bad. I was still somehow in Ethan's good graces. One day, he told me to come sit next to him in the writers' room, which, in the seating hierarchy, meant I was officially being anointed as Ethan's favorite. Tom looked like he was going to throw up as the two of us switched places. I actually felt bad for him—and for myself. I was going to miss being in shit-talking proximity to Joan. However, I knew I had to play the game and accept my new seat assignment with feigned excitement. Oh, and Ethan also started letting me get B_{12} shots from his hunky private doctor who did weekly office visits. No one in the room had *ever* been given B_{12} shot privileges before. I was making history!

But then Ethan, overnight, became withdrawn. He came into work, and instead of holding court and regaling us with anecdotes about his thieving housekeeper (Okay, racist and not funny. Read a book, bitch!) or playing bocce ball with Zachary Quinto, we all got straight to work. Everyone was scared shitless by how reserved he was acting. Later that week the news broke on *Towleroad* that

Joe, Ethan's husband, had left him for a guy named Jordan, who billed himself as a "reiki healer/actor/dancer/dreamer" and posted shirtless selfies in front of tragic historical sites like Chernobyl and Anne Frank's house. (Jordan's Instagram stats: 56,412 followers, following 702.)

Everyone was too scared to give their condolences, so we didn't say anything at all and sometimes Ethan would disappear for hours and come back with a red nose and flushed face. He'd been crying; we knew it, and we hated it. It was inconvenient to all of us that Ethan was becoming layered. It was much easier to see him as a cartoon villain, and in a lot of ways, he still was. After coming back to the writers' room, he'd often start a fight with someone, but this time we saw his behavior for what it was: displaced anger. Cindy's ugly purple eyeshadow wasn't the source of his ire, it was really Joe.

"He's still a piece of shit," Joan said during lunch. "Don't forget."

"I know," I said. "But it's still sad. No one deserves to be cheated on."

Says the person who cheated on his boyfriend and is now trapped in a psychosexual game of his own making.

"He cheated on Joe all the time," Joan said, almost choking on her sandwich. "He fucked the janitor!"

"Wait, the hot one?"

"Yes! He fucked him on-set in Sammy's bedroom. I don't even want to unpack that."

"How do you know this?"

"I have a face that says 'tell me things.' If I could get plastic surgery to change it, I would. Believe me."

"So, you don't feel bad for him? Like, at all?"

"No," Joan said. "Ethan hates himself, but he doesn't quite know it. He needs to go to therapy, do the work, realize his self-loathing, and then turn that hate inward like the rest of us. That's what a real marginalized person does."

"Ethan hasn't been a member of a marginalized community in a long time. He has five bidets in a four-bathroom house," I said.

"Whatever. Ethan's never bothered to see me as a real person, so why should I extend him the courtesy?"

I looked over at Ethan in his office. He was at the computer with his Gucci loafers, fancy-man pants, his cardigan and Tom Ford glasses, looking weathered. There was something devastating about a man who had spent thousands and thousands of dollars on therapy only to end up here, scrolling through *Queerty* looking for mentions of his name.

"Maybe I should ask if he wants to get a drink or something," I said.

"You've gone full Stockholm, honey."

"No, I just, I feel like gay men have to take care of their elders in crisis."

"Ethan isn't community service. He's your boss."

I don't know why I felt drawn to him. Joan was right about everything, but seeing Ethan vulnerable for the first time was intriguing. I also knew he had no real friends. Everyone that was there for him was on his payroll. Maybe it'd be nice for him to talk to somebody. A different kind of person on his payroll. I got out of my seat and walked over to his office.

"Hey, Ethan." I knocked on his door. He was playing a Demi Lovato song through his speakers. I remembered him telling me once, in a misguided attempt to score cool points with me, that he'd had dinner with them. As if I would ever care about . . . Demi . . . Lovato.

"Hi," Ethan grumbled. "Are we starting the room?"

"Nope," I said. "I just wanted to say, you know, what's up."

Ethan regarded me quizzically.

"I mean, more than what's up. I was actually wondering if you . . . have you been to Akbar before?"

"Akbar. The place poor gay people go to? Not since my twenties."

"It's not poor people, Ethan. I mean, maybe some of them are, but who cares and that's not the point. You wanna get a drink there?"

"Why would I do that?"

"Because it's what people do?"

Ethan had fraternized with sociopaths for too long. He expected an agenda.

"Okay, fine," Ethan said. "Tonight. Let's do tonight."

"Oh." I had plans with Gus but knew this was a big step for Ethan, and any obstacle would cause him to turtle back in. "Okay, tonight it is."

I walked back to Joan, who was trying to conceal her laughter.

"Oh, man," Joan said. "You've lost your mind."

"No, I haven't. I'm being a human."

"You can't be human toward someone like Ethan. He's a fucking alien. He can't speak your language."

"Whatever," I said. "It might be sort of fun."

"It won't. But good luck."

CHAPTER 41

Ethan drove us to Akbar in his new Tesla. Zooming through Laurel Canyon, I thought we were going to die because Ethan was doing four million things, like calling his assistant or looking for his vape pen.

"Tell Courteney Cox she can go fuck herself if she doesn't want to do a cameo on *Sammy*. I've been friends with her since she had her first face! And don't tell me I can't make jokes like that anymore. I'm simply stating a fact!" he screamed at his assistant, Gail, a woman in her mid-fifties who had to have endured some childhood trauma to be able to put up with Ethan's bullshit.

"Oh, and tell my shaman I have three words for him: fuck off!" he yelled. It was like this till we arrived in Silver Lake, Ethan rolling calls and screaming at various people, but then Joe's number popped up as an incoming call and Ethan sent it directly to voicemail. He looked at me, knowing I'd seen it, and then averted his eyes.

"This neighborhood is sad," Ethan said.

"Houses here start at over a million dollars, Ethan."

"Are you looking to buy?"

"I'm not really in a position yet. I wouldn't mind starting with an apartment."

"Buying an apartment building is a great investment. I did it when I was your age."

"I didn't mean an entire building. A single apartment. Hopefully a two-bedroom, if I'm lucky."

"Oh," Ethan said, scrunching up his nose like he smelled a fart. "Don't do that." He pulled into an open parking space.

As we got out of the car, a man who looked like John Travolta in *Battlefield Earth* approached.

"Hello," he said.

Ethan took one look at the guy and said, "No."

"I'm going to pray for you," the man said, pointing at me.

"Oh fuck off. You're wearing Crocs. We'll pray for *you*," Ethan said. "Come on, sweetie." Ethan guided me by the arm in an almost paternal way. Being with Ethan in the outside world was like wearing a bulletproof vest. I liked it.

When we entered Akbar, Ethan went from confident to uncomfortable. It was my turn to provide protection, so I found us an empty table and went to the bar to order drinks. (A seltzer for me. I was still traumatized by my behavior in Ojai.)

"Tell me: Do people say stupid shit like that to you all the time?" Ethan asked, drowning his hands in Purell before diving into his vodka soda.

"Not all the time, but it happens often enough."

"Jesus, people are fucking idiots. I had a lisp growing up, and I remember there was this one chubby guy, Don Chamberlin, who made fun of me for it. Years later, I ran into him at a party. He was still chubby and my lisp was gone. So, I won. But then I spilled some wine on his suit, and he made a huge deal out of it, ripping me a new one in front of everyone at the party. So you know what I did? The next day I sent him a brand-new suit, the same designer as the one I 'ruined' except I ordered one a size smaller so the fucker wouldn't be able to fit into it." Ethan started howling with laughter, rubbing his hands together like a gay(er) Mr. Burns. I nodded and smiled, not exactly sure what his tale of revenge had to do with my struggles and that it seems unwise to look at life through the binary lens of winning and losing.

"Okay, so, what's going on?" Ethan asked, taking a giant gulp of his drink. "Why'd you want to get a drink? Are you trying to blackmail me or something? I didn't get fresh with you in Ojai, for the record."

"No. I just wanted to see, like, how you are doing."

Ethan blinked. This did not compute.

"Okay, cut to the chase. Do you want a raise? Because you don't really do anything."

"Well, that's because—oh forget it, never mind."

"No, tell me. What?"

"You run a fear-based room," I said. "I don't feel particularly funny when I'm scared. And I'm doing things now, bitch! I wrote, like, four good scenes yesterday."

"They were all right. But, honey, you need to toughen up. Everyone puts up with shit."

"But they don't have to. That's a choice. And, you know what, while we're here on the subject, why did you turn on me to begin with?"

"Wow. Did you bring me here to confront me? Because we could've just done it in the writers' room in front of everyone," Ethan said, taking a sip and slightly grimacing. "Could've been fun."

"No, I didn't. But we're here now. So just tell me. You were so nice to me at the start . . . well, nice for you, anyway, and then you became *The Devil Wears Prada* overnight."

"Well, I was annoyed with you. You were so, I don't know, performative. You were trying way too hard."

"I was just doing my job."

"No," Ethan said, firmly. "You were giving me a version of 'doing your job' you thought I wanted."

I realized right then that I didn't actually want to hear Ethan's explanation. I wanted it to remain a mystery so I could project all sorts of terrible things onto him.

"Okay," I said, after taking a pause.

"Okay, are we done?" Ethan let out the bitchiest of sighs.

"Look, I really didn't come here to talk about work. I truly did ask you to get a drink to see how you were. You know, with Joe and everything?"

"That's none of your business," Ethan said. "That's not what this is, buddy. You and me, we don't do this."

"Okay, fine. If this is inappropriate, I'm sorry. Let's just talk about your shaman. Do you know 'fuck off' is two words, not three?"

"Not when I say it." Ethan stabbed the ice in his drink with his straw. He sighed. "Joe, he's gone. He left me. What else do you want?"

A tiny breakthrough. I would need to proceed gently.

"Are you guys talking?"

"No. Fuck him." He took another swig. "Look, things change. That's life. When I first met Joe, I knew who I needed to be in order to make it work and I assumed, wrongly, that it wasn't far off from who I actually was."

"What exactly went down between you two?"

"It wasn't like there was one incident. I mean, we'd been together for ten years, and when you're with someone that long, you're going to both change, and you just have to hope and pray that the changes complement each other and happen around the same time. But sometimes they don't. I'd talk to people who'd been in long relationships, and they'd say there's bad years, and it's like, 'Bad years? Are you fucking kidding me? I can't handle a day.' But it was true."

Ethan was being so real. It was like seeing Vanessa Hudgens try to act: alarming and sort of cringeworthy, but you can't take your eyes off it.

"Anyway, we were just evolving past each other. And it made me so fucking angry at him, like stop changing without my permission, motherfucker. And then, of course, we invited all these other men into our bedroom, hoping it would help bridge the gap between us, but it didn't work."

I didn't know what to say, so I didn't say anything.

"That was a mistake how I just told you all of that. I really hated that."

"Don't. I'm glad you did."

"What about you and your guy, Cliff?"

"Gus. For the millionth time, it's Gus. And, um, we've been together for almost six years and, yeah, it can get kind of dull, like going through the motions. And, um, I didn't have a lot of sex in my twenties so I thought I might want to, you know, sow some wild oats."

"That's a good instinct. Fuck everything you can. Because, you know, I'm in my fifties, and it's not the same. I mean, I'll always be able to sleep with hot guys because I'm rich and can give them something, like a laptop or a car or whatever, but now when I walk around West Hollywood, I feel like a chalk outline of a person. No one sees me because I'm old."

"Um, you'll never be invisible, Ethan. Even when you're ninety."

His body tensed up and he said, "I didn't share that with you just so you could say something nice back to prop me up."

I actually meant what I said, but now was not the time to double down so I just said, "Okay."

"Anyway, it's a good thing you're doing. Sowing the wild oats."

"Well, it was. Now I'm not so sure. It's never enough anyway. No matter how much sex . . ." I trailed off, suddenly too tired to finish the sentence.

"Well, if I had strangers coming up to me and pointing out all the things that were wrong with my body, I'd have a hole to fill too."

Without realizing it, Ethan had just summed up all my issues in a single sentence. It went quiet for a moment.

"I don't like silences in conversations," Ethan declared. "You should go."

"All right. I'm sorry if I—"

"Stop. You didn't do anything. I'm gonna stay here and have another drink."

"Ooooh, so you like it here?"

"No, it smells like piss threw up on some lube, but I've been making eyes with a guy at the bar and want to take him home."

I got up and gathered my stuff. "See you at work tomorrow?"

Outside Akbar, the *Battlefield Earth* dude from earlier was there. He started to walk toward me, but before he could say anything, I did my best Ethan impression and told him to back the fuck off. It worked.

CHAPTER 42

When I got home, Gus was wasted and hanging out with Augie and Justin.

"Hey boys," I said. "What's up?"

"We're discussing how my nudes aren't great. Like, I really think you need to see my body in person to fully get it," Augie said.

"Augie, shut up, you have a perfect body," I said.

"I know, but I'm gay so I don't *really* know. You know?"

"My nudes are spectacular," Justin said. His body wasn't as nice as Augie's but he was a top, and tops sometimes have better self-esteem than bottoms because, I don't know, toxic masculinity?

"I haven't taken one in like years," Gus said, refiling his wineglass with an orange wine ($42).

"We get it," Justin said in a snotty voice that made him seem more pitiful than anything. "You're in love, in a long-term relationship, blah blah blah."

I plopped down on the couch next to Justin and patted his shoulder. "Breakup with Brian went bad?"

"He accused me of canceling him," Justin said.

"Oh my god, he's right. Getting dumped is like the original 'you're canceled,'" Gus said, eyes wide.

"What do you mean?" I asked, grabbing the bottle of wine before setting it back down.

"Are you not drinking tonight?" Gus asked, lowering his voice. I shook my head no, and the disappointment practically radiated from his flushed wine-drunk face.

"He called me a left-wing hysteric and that dumping him was part of a larger liberal agenda."

"Spooky! Please tell me had a big dick at least," I said.

"He sounds like he has serious mental health issues," Augie said. "I feel sorry for him."

"Whatever. I don't care. I blocked him," Justin said. "Hey, Gus told me you two fucked that River guy again." Justin moved on from heartbreak rather quickly.

I shot Gus a withering glance and poured myself a glass of wine. So much for being sober.

"You told them?" I said to Gus.

"I'm sorry, my angel!" Gus said. "I didn't know we were keeping a secret."

"We're not, I guess, whatever. Yeah. Rumors are true."

"Is this going to be, like, a regular thing?" Augie asked.

"I don't know. Is it, Gus?"

"Maybe?" Gus teased. He was trying to act Cool Evolved Gay right now to impress our friends. It was so not chic.

"Gus said your sessions or whatever were incredible. Which makes sense. Having sex is his job," Justin said. His excitement over our situation was starting to piss me off. Our relationship was becoming fodder, stories you'd laugh about over brunch, when the situation was so much more nuanced.

"Okay, I'm going to bed." I stood up, taking my wine.

"Are you okay, babe?" Gus asked.

"Yeah, of course, just tired."

I lay in bed with my wine and drank fast, watching an episode from an early season of *Real Housewives of New York* when Bethenny was broke. I wanted more wine but didn't want to have to go back out to the living room, so I stayed semi-sober and fell asleep with my laptop on my dick, probably giving me cancer. I dozed off to Ramona Singer screaming about getting the best room on a vacation.

CHAPTER **43**

The next day I woke to Gus trying to cuddle with me, but I turned away from him, still angry from last night. Gus got the hint and apologized for spilling about our continued experimentation with River. When I told him I didn't want our sex lives to become gossip, he agreed and asked me if we were okay and I said yes, even though no, not really, and Gus said good because he wanted to see if we could call River again this weekend.

"I didn't realize our sex life was in such dire straits that we always needed a guest star," I said.

"It's not," Gus said, defensive. "I just think it's fun. And I thought we were on the same page. Are you not into this?"

"What if I wasn't? What if I wanted us to go back to being monogamous? Is that even an option anymore or has it become the gay slut free-for-all?"

"Honestly, I regret making that comment," Gus said, suddenly very serious. "It just, like, reeks of internalized homophobia."

Wow. Gus: the empowered slut! I was livid. Yes, I recognize the absurdity. All I had wanted was for Gus to snap out of his hetero-normative hang-ups and embrace the perks of being gay, but now I realized I liked him better as a loyal lesbian. That's one of the reasons we worked. I had felt safe, and my insecurities had lain dormant, because I operated under the impression that Gus loved me a little bit more than I loved him. But to know that he also wanted to fuck other guys put our whole dynamic into question and made me feel vulnerable.

"Look, we can do whatever you want," Gus said, not meaning a single word.

It was a choose-your-own-adventure, but every ending was unappealing. I could tell him the truth about River, but things had gotten to Lynchian levels of fucked up, and if Gus knew the whore-igin story he'd file a restraining order against me. I could say that River needs to go, but I'd know it wasn't Gus's choice, that I was denying him something he wanted. Or there was option C: we could continue fucking River and see how weird it got. We eventually decided on nothing and I chose to run away to Ventura and visit my oldest best friend, Amanda.

I took the Amtrak Pacific Surfliner, which is a gorgeous route that begins in San Diego and chugs up the coast to San Luis Obispo. When I was on pills, I'd pop a few Percocet and look out the window until everything dissolved into a smudgy ocean blue. It was euphoric. Now I listen to Jesus and Mary Chain on my headphones and read a book.

I arrived in the afternoon and walked from the train station toward the pier like a moody teen bitch in an episode of *The O.C.*, until I called Amanda.

"Why are you here?" she asked, suspicion in her voice. "You only come back when you're distressed."

"You know I love emotional cutting, baby!" I said. "When can we go to dinner?"

"Well, in case you forgot, I have a child that is still conscious," Amanda said.

"When does it go to sleep?"

"I love when you call my kid 'it.' Gives me all the feels."

"Sorry," I said, watching a seagull circle a pile of trash like it was twenty-four-year-old me looking for dick at the Cock at last call.

"It's okay," Amanda said, now only a pinch aggravated. She was my only close friend who had a kid and a husband, and I wasn't always the most mindful of navigating her new life. I did, in a deeply unfair way, resent her child for taking her away from me. Amanda knew how I felt without me saying it and appreciated me keeping my mouth shut.

"Why don't you come over at seven-thirty? The drugs will have knocked her out by then," Amanda said. She needed to show me that she still had a bit of an edge, that she could still hang. As adults, we were presenting ourselves as versions we thought the other one needed. Like me and Gus. Like me and everyone.

"Great. I'll bring a chew toy. Newborns are like dogs, right?"

"Totally. You really should write a parenting book."

I killed the next few hours by window-shopping downtown. I didn't know how any of these places afforded the rent. They all sold junky antiques or used books no one wanted or art, but the bad art you'd find in a dentist's office. Nobody shopped at any of them, and it seemed like they were just there for charm, like a movie set for a quaint beach town. For me it was like browsing a museum of my teenage years.

I stumbled upon a place that used to be called the Retarded Children's Thrift Store until people started protesting and they changed it.

I passed the Ben & Jerry's where my friends Beth and Alex used to work and give me free scoops of oatmeal cookie chunk, which made me feel like a fucking millionaire.

I passed the parking lot where my friends and I once sat in a rusted-out Jetta and smoked resin out of a pipe. I hated pot but never turned it down because it didn't occur to me until the age of twenty-six that you didn't have to do things you didn't like.

I passed the indie movie theater where I saw films like *Mulholland Drive* and *Lost in Translation*. After I left, I always felt like Belle parading down Main Street in the opening sequence of *Beauty and the Beast*. "THERE MUST BE MORE THAN THIS PROVINCIAL LIFE!!!" Meanwhile, the weather is gorgeous and you can hear waves crashing and everyone votes Democrat. What a prison!

I passed the Habit Burger, where I spent the first day of summer after sophomore year with these brand-new friends who I thought were going to crack my myopic life wide open, but mostly they became different people to be bored with, which still means a lot when you're a teenager.

I put on some old Rilo Kiley to really get into the mood, but it didn't work. As I've gotten older, I've found it harder to connect with music as easily as I once did. When I was a teenager, I was experiencing emotions for which I had no reference point, and Rilo Kiley was there to give me all the answers. But by the time you're an adult, you don't need music to fill in the dots anymore, because you've gone through it yourself. The other day this song called "New Romantics" by Taylor Swift came on my shuffle.

The song is all about being young and bored and vaguely sociopathic. If it had come out when I was in high school, it would've been my AIM away message in two seconds. *DRAMA! JADED YOUTH! YOU FUCKING GET IT, TAYLOR!* That joy of being seen and heard in a song: it's a drug. And here I was in my thirties so fucking jealous of people who could still relate to a Taylor Swift song. Because, let's be real, life gets simultaneously more mundane and thornier as you get older. Like, where's her song about the sex worker she fell for because her loving, stable relationship had lost its sparkle? Where's the single about not-so-secretly resenting your best friend's baby because it means you can't get day drunk with her for at least eighteen years (barring an "adults only" vacation which would require a ninety-five-page email thread to plan). Where's her song about growing closer to your emotionally abusive boss even though you're not sure you'll ever respect him as a person?

> *You make me feel bad at work*
> *Oh yeah*
> *10 percent of me wants to fuck you*
> *But I'm not far enough along in therapy*
> *To understand why*
> *(Pop, Boom, Understand why!)*
> *And you're so rich*
> *That even your shaman is an enabler*
> *(Shaman! Enabling!)*

It's not exactly "Shake It Off," is it? I was lost in hypothetical lyrics when a man about my age approached, smoking a cigarette. An actual lit cigarette, not a vape pen. How retro. His hair gave off big mullet energy and he was lean and tall. The Trip Fontaine of Ventura, California.

"Oh my god, hey!" he said, giving me a surprise hug. I did not know this person, but the smell of tobacco lingering on his clothes was so novel that I did not mind the physical contact.

"Hey . . ." My eyes searched for any recognizable features.

"You don't know who I am, do you?" He smiled, revealing his own set of yellowing teeth.

"Yeah, I do," I said, unconvincingly.

"Wow. That hurts."

"Okay, you got me. Can I at least have a hint?"

"We went to Foothill Tech. We had chemistry together."

It was coming back to me. He was the boy on muscle relaxers who fell asleep with the Bunsen burner on and almost blew up the lab. His name was . . .

"Robert. Robert Colangelo."

Me and my friends called him Joe Dirt.

"Right! Of course. How are ya, Robert?"

"Good! I'm gay now! I mean, I always was, but now I'm, like, actually gay."

"Oh. That's nice. Congrats!"

"You're gay too, right? I remember you dating Dylan and stuff. But you're like still gay?"

"Yup, still gay," I said. "That is, until they kick me out of the club."

"Who's they?" Robert asked.

That exhausting feeling when you have to explain a joke. A beat passed before he understood and then he started laughing. Like a psychotic hyena.

"Man, you're funny," he said, slapping me on the shoulder. "You've always been so funny."

"Thanks. . . ."

Robert stared at me like I was an exotic species and said, "Well,

I'm working at Paddy's tonight. I get off around nine if you want to stop by. We can have a drink and catch up."

I had not been friends with Robert. Hanging out with him would make zero sense. But I also was curious to see what would happen. Plus, he looked really good in his jeans.

CHAPTER 44

"Why are you doing that?" Amanda said, putting her hair up in a bun. We were eating dinner at an Italian place that served baked rigoletti smothered in cheese, and I was pouring a mound of marinara sauce on it.

"I don't like dipping each individual bite of rigoletti into the sauce," I said, shrugging.

"No, I mean hanging out with Robert Colangelo. Didn't he stab someone?"

"That was Kevin Samson. Robert almost blew up chemistry class while on muscle relaxers."

"We weren't friends with Robert. Who cares about any of these people?"

"Well, he's gay now."

"Does that make him more interesting?"

"No, but it does make him gay."

"Whatever."

Amanda had been in a mood all night. Her baby was still awake when I came over, and watching her do bedtime was like the first twenty minutes of *Saving Private Ryan*. In about ten minutes, we would segue into shared memories of our youth and not have to deal with the uncomfortable present. The first half of our hangouts were always a little strained, trying to pretend like we still made complete sense in each other's life, but we've also earned the right to not make sense. After so many years of friendship, you become family and everything else is beside the point.

"How's Gus?"

"He's good," I said. "Still a little miserable at his job, but he's doing these paintings now and seems pretty happy. Oh, and we started having sex with this sex worker."

I loved trying to shock my straight female friends. Whenever I'd share an anecdote about a gay couple with an open relationship, their minds immediately went to their husbands. Did they want to fuck somebody else? *IS THIS HOW ALL MEN ARE?!*

Tonight, Amanda didn't take the gay bait. She replied warily, "Oh, that sounds like a nice arrangement. I hope he can cook, since neither of you can."

"I actually want us to stop seeing him. I think Gus likes him too much. It makes me feel weird."

"I don't know how you guys can do that kind of stuff," she said, crinkling up her forehead. Amanda's husband, Jeff, worked in insurance and was far cooler than any straight guy working in insurance had a right to be. He was also extremely hot—a fact I had no problem telling Amanda every time I saw her.

"Well, actually, I was sleeping with the sex worker before Gus, but he doesn't know that," I said, trying to seem blasé. "It's all a little messy."

"You mean you were cheating?" Amanda clarified.

"I mean, I guess? I was paying for it. It makes it feel a little different."

"I don't understand. Are you two having problems?"

"It's not about specific problems, per se."

"Then why? Gus adores you."

"I know."

"You can't just do that to him. It's fucked up."

"Okay, stop," I snapped. "Gay men do relationships differently."

"This isn't about being gay. You were sleeping with someone, and Gus didn't know about it. Did you guys use protection?"

"Of course. I'm not, like, some terrible person, Amanda."

"I'm not saying you are—"

"And it's not like you and Jeff are perfect. You told me you guys didn't have sex for nine months. And he's so hot, I don't understand it."

"It was after the baby. It's normal. And sometimes there are lulls in a long-term relationship. It doesn't always need to be exciting."

"But I want it to be."

"Just because you want something, Elliott, doesn't mean you get to have it. What are you, Veruca Salt?" Amanda stopped, surprised by the level of her frustration. She sighed and rubbed her eyes. "Sorry. Can we just back up? I didn't mean to be all judge-y. I guess I'm confused. Like, I'm missing a step or something as to how all this happened."

"I know I shouldn't feel entitled to anything. It's just hard to have sex with the same person for so long, especially when you haven't had much sex to begin with."

"Yeah, I remember. You didn't even kiss anyone when we lived together," Amanda said, taking a giant bite of pasta. Tomato sauce splattered on her shirt but she didn't notice, and I didn't have the heart to tell her. I could tell this was an outfit that had taken time to put together.

"I remember riding the subway and feeling alive when a cute stranger brushed my shoulder. It was pathetic. And I honestly think I have this gross thing inside of me where I just . . . I want to be objectified by strangers."

"Are there other guys you've been hooking up with?"

"Yes," I said, after some hesitation. "For a few months now. I've fallen down this rabbit hole, and at first I thought I was empowering myself. Like, I was having this sexual reawakening or whatever but . . ." I trailed off. I could feel myself getting emotional.

Amanda rubbed my hand. "Don't see Robert tonight, okay? Come home with me. We'll watch *Hey Paula* or something."

I nodded and we ate the rest of our dinner, feeling more comfortable with each other than we had in years. We didn't have to take a trip down memory lane, because finally we were making new ones.

CHAPTER 45

I did meet up with Robert, after Amanda fell asleep, like a surly teen sneaking out his window once his parents were knocked out. When I entered Paddy's, there were only a smattering of gays playing pool and "Firework" by Katy Perry was blaring through the jukebox, and it was like the movies, where someone goes into a bar and everyone there immediately looks up and sizes them up. In Ventura, it's rare to see a gay man you don't know. A part of me wished they would see me as exotic and clamor for my attention. "Who are you? The new girl in town!" But after taking me in briefly, they went back to playing pool and drinking their drinks. Wow. A flop in LA *and* Ventura. At least I'm consistent.

Robert was on the patio chain-smoking cigarettes, and he was wearing black tight jeans with a very visible bulge and a button-up T-shirt with the top and bottom button left undone, and he looked sexy, like a lost Strokes member circa 2002, and he knew he looked sexy, and instead of it being a turn-off, it actually made him more appealing because to have that confidence while having once accidentally almost blown up a chemistry class in high school is impressive. He said hello. I said hi. Our conversation was dull and stilted. Possibly a level up from a conversation you would have with your dental hygienist. What's important is that, unlike my dental hygienist, Robert kept touching my leg or arm for emphasis, and he'd smile at me one second longer than you would with people you don't want to fuck, and what kept me there, shivering on that patio, was the possibility I could see Robert naked. I know it's beyond pathetic. I felt like a total junkie. It reminded me of the time I was addicted to painkillers and took what was essentially an extra-strength Tylenol, thinking, *This will do*. Robert was the Tylenol, and I couldn't wait till I could swallow him dry and keep the sickness at bay. But it didn't happen. Arm-touching. Leg-touching. It was all looking promising until there was a shift in the conversation and Robert confided in me about a recent breakup and how he'd been having a really hard time and there were not many people he could talk to about it—no one seemed to care, their version of a remedy for heartbreak was a shot of alcohol and a pat on the back—but Robert knew I had experience, you know, being gay, and when he saw me walking downtown earlier it was like a sign from God. *He'll know what to do*, Robert thought. *He'll get me out of this rut.*

He looked at me with pleading, sad eyes and my heart sank. Here I was, yearning to be validated and seen by this person, but was I bothering to see *him*? I hadn't even remembered Robert when we ran into each other, but Robert remembered me. Maybe I meant something to him in high school for being out. A shame, because he meant nothing to me. Just a hard cock. And I was the one who had the audacity to feel rejected tonight? What a joke. I felt so guilty and gross about my behavior that I became Robert's Emotional Support Gay for the night and helped him through, even letting him literally cry on my shoulder at one point. I tried to focus on him and how he was feeling rather than how he was making me feel. It's so embarrassing that this is something I had to think about, that it took concentrated effort. But the ultimate irony of being insecure is that you're consumed with your least favorite subject: yourself.

CHAPTER 46

To be disabled is to understand, at a base level, that your existence, your experiences, do not matter. Your life isn't reflected in TV or movies. If it is, your options are an able-bodied savior (*The Upside*) or a tragic suicide (*Me Before You*) or an actor donning cripface so they can win an award (Leonardo DiCaprio, *What's Eating Gilbert Grape* . . . it almost worked!). We're given these slots to exist and then able-bodied people get to feel proud of themselves, even though they've given us no meaningful advancement. In fact, all they did was make money off of our trauma. But sure. . . . *Clap clap clap. Pat pat pat.*

I don't see myself on screens, and I also don't see other disabled people around me in real life. I used to think that was fine but not anymore. You can't measure the psychic toll exacted on someone when they've never interacted with a single person who looks and acts like them. Why don't people care about disabled people? How am I supposed to care about myself when no one else does?

Here's a theory: people choose not to deal with disability because deep down they know it will happen to them. It's like aging. When our loved ones get older, we hide them away in nursing homes. We can't bear to see what's eventually coming for us. We'll do anything to delay the inevitable. Lotions, potions, bring it on baby. When people see someone disabled, the illusion is punctured. They imagine themselves slipping and falling and breaking a hip and being bedridden. They see themselves with a cane or walker, unable to go on the hike that helps them stave off death. And there's the issue of work. So much of our value as Americans is tied into our productivity, which is super-unfortunate since disabled people are not seen as particularly valuable in a capitalist society. Could someone please hire disability a better publicist? We are the most creative and hardworking individuals out there because we have to constantly navigate a world that isn't made with us in mind. Literally. Nothing is handicap-accessible! It's not subtle. The message is clear. No one wants us here. Which is a shame because being disabled gave me such amazing qualities, not least of which is my work ethic. I once had an internship that required a lot of transcription work. It was stressful, considering I could only really type with two fingers, but I managed my workload. I compensated by staying up until the early morning to finish, never once telling my boss that I was working over sixty hours a week. Every day I had to prove my worth. Like how I was at the start of *Sammy Says*.

The conversations around race and gender identity and sexism have deepened over the years. We are nowhere near where we need to be, but measurable progress has been made in certain areas. Donations pledged. Petitions signed. Protest signs made. Jobs given. Message received. We must continue to do better, but I'm sitting here waiting for that conversation to happen around disability. I'm waiting for able-bodied people to be like "Oops, babe, we fucked this one up, didn't we?" and feature us on magazine covers and give us ramps and meaningful employment and pass real legislation. It's wild to be ignored in a culture that currently has such a hard-on against injustice. When the fuck will it be our turn? Which Kardashian do I need to throw down the stairs and paralyze to get a disabled person on the cover of *Vanity Fair*?

These societal prejudices seep into our bones, telling us we should hate ourselves. I am in the best position imaginable. I am the most privileged form of disabled. My case is mild, not wild. I'm a white guy who owns many Diptyque candles. And I still feel myself getting deleted every single day and spend so much of my energy begging for people to notice me.

It's hard not to feel resentful. It's hard not to feel angry that because of our convoluted ideas about disability I'm paying guys to positively rail me so I can feel good about myself for the next twenty-two minutes. *When will I stop needing them to touch me? When will I stop filling my hole to feel whole?*

Never. I'm learning the more you want things, the more likely you end up with nothing.

CHAPTER 47

"How was Ventura?" Gus asked. He had a sunburn and was folding his laundry on the bed.

"It was okay," I said, setting my luggage down.

"Did you see Amanda?" Gus said, folding the Modern Amusement shirt he wore to our first date at the straight bar.

"Uh-huh."

"How's she?"

"Fine. She's good."

"Gee, you're really selling this trip to me," Gus said.

"No, it was fun," I lied. "But I'm glad to be home."

That part was true.

"Why do you have a sunburn?" I said, pointing to Gus's salmon-colored arms.

"I got drunk at the beach with Augie," Gus said, embarrassed. "Do I look insane?"

"Not more than usual."

He sighed. I hated when he sighed. The way he did it was so

over-the-top and reminded me that he had once been a musical theatre major.

"My widdle angel," Gus said. "I did something weawy bad."

"You fucked River, didn't you?" The question came so quickly to my tongue because it was already there.

Gus seemed shook. "How did you know?"

I was nauseated, unsteady. To center myself, I focused on Gus's shirt, a reminder of a time when we had yet to disappoint each other.

"I was super-trashed . . . ," Gus said.

"We drink too much," I snapped. "We're both functional alcoholics who get off on keeping score of how much the other is drinking. It's fucking scary. We should stop."

"Okay. Where did that come from? I think it's a little dramatic to say we're alcoholics. We like our wine, sure. But—"

"Why'd you do it?" I asked, sparing Gus the introspection on his drinking. The shirt had a torn collar and there was a stain, even though Gus had just washed it. Why didn't he just throw it away?

"It wasn't that deep, Elly," Gus laughed. An exasperated laugh. "I was horny and just texted him."

"Where did you fuck? Here? On our bed?" My eyes wandered to our duvet cover. The one Gus always put on for us because it perplexed me and I refused to figure out how to do it on my own. Or maybe Gus did it even without asking. I can't remember.

"No, I went to his apartment." Gus was cycling from guilty to defensive. "Is it really that big of a deal? You got jerked off by some guy and told me after the fact."

"That's different."

"How?"

"Did he top you?"

"Why does that matter?"

I looked at the wall. It needed a coat of paint.

"Can you please look at me? Elliott. What are you doing?"

I told him I had to go. I ran out of the apartment as far and as fast as my faulty legs could carry me. I ran down streets with old 1950s apartments, the ones with parking garages underneath the units, which in The Big One would most assuredly collapse. I ran past dying Russians and people posing in front of murals (90 percent of Los Angeles is people taking pictures in front of colorful walls). I ran past a Whole Foods and a store called Food for Dogs that had recently started selling non-dog food. I kept on running and I liked the feeling of my deeply flawed body supporting me. I didn't know where I was going, which meant I was headed to River's apartment.

CHAPTER 48

"Wow," a shirtless River said. "No one just, like, shows up at people's places anymore. Hi."

Too fatigued for small talk, I dove right in and asked, "Did you see Gus this weekend?"

"Gus? Yeah. We met up last night." River's half smile disappeared once he saw that I wasn't giving one back. "Did you not know . . . ?"

"I didn't. I mean, he told me twenty minutes ago."

"Okay," River said, staring blankly. "Is there, like, a problem?"

"Not really. But, you know, if it's okay with you, I want you to stop seeing him. Like, if he texts you, just say you're busy or on vacation or whatever. We need to be alone right now. Together. Just working on our relationship."

"Huh," River said, clicking his tongue against the roof of his mouth. "Well, I'm just doing my job, you know? Like, you're cool dudes and everything, but—"

"*Cool dudes?*" I said.

"Yeah. We have fun together."

"Did you like fucking him more?" I asked, ashamed of myself for asking but not enough not to.

"What?" River laughed.

"You can tell me," I said. "I can take it."

"Look, I'm there to do whatever a client wants to do. It's not about what gets me off."

"But you do get off. You've come on my face multiple times."

River paused. "I don't understand why you're here. What is it that you're looking for from me?"

"I don't know. Did you like having sex with me?"

"Yeah. I like giving pleasure to people. Making them happy."

"No, did I give you pleasure?"

"Sure." River shrugged.

"Sure? Sounds convincing."

"Why do you care so much what I think about you?"

"Because," I said. "I have feelings for you. Sorry, had. Past tense."

"Tell me how exactly did you have—sorry, had—feelings for me?"

"What do you mean 'how'?"

"What parts of me did you like?"

"Um, all of you? Is this a trick question?" I asked.

"No, I just don't see how it's actually possible you had feelings. You never asked me a single question about myself."

"Yes, I did."

"Really?" River said, incredulous. "Name one thing about me."

"What?"

"Come on," River said. "One thing." He seemed agitated, which was a change for a man I'd only seen erect, mildly bored, or hungry.

"You're going to optician school," I said, triumphantly, as if I had correctly answered a question on a game show that would award me millions of dollars.

River snorted. I mentally added snorting to his repertoire. "Uh, yeah. But I told you that unprompted. You never asked."

"I don't know. I guess I just saw you as a sex worker and didn't think about it too much. Is that wrong?"

"It's not wrong. None of it is wrong because you are paying me to fuck you by the hour and I don't blame you if you don't want to spend, like, a big chunk of that time talking about my hopes and dreams. But I also find it lame that you're trying to make me feel bad for fucking your boyfriend which is literally my job."

I looked down, replaying in my brain every interaction River and I had ever had.

"Look, I get it. I'm your manic pixie sex worker," River continued. "Which is cool. That's the vibe with a lot of my clients. But this isn't a normal relationship, and if you really think you have—sorry again, HAD—feelings for me, just take, like, a second to think about it. They weren't real feelings. Trust me."

"Don't tell me how I feel," I said, with zero fight. River moved closer and took off my glasses and said softly, "Your lenses are filthy. Be right back."

He disappeared and returned with a cloth and some lens cleaner. After wiping, he placed my glasses on my face. His anger had evaporated and been replaced by pity. I loathed seeing him look at me that way. To me there's nothing worse than pity. Hate my guts, call me a terrible person, but please, please, please, don't ever feel sorry for me.

River took my hand in his, looked into my eyes, and placed the lens cleaner in my palm. "Here, keep it. I get a ton of free samples at work."

"Thanks." I put my arm on his shoulder because I knew it would be the last time I touched him. "When you topped Gus, was it—he really liked it, huh?" I asked, resigned.

River didn't respond. He just looked at me gravely concerned, realizing for the first time probably just how far gone I was.

"I'm sorry I only saw you as a way to make me feel good about myself," I said. "If it's any consolation, I do it with other people too."

River fidgeted, ready to leave the conversation and my issues behind. He gave me a signature hair tousle and said, "Well, I hope you and your boy work things out. You guys seem like you really love each other."

River said it almost like a question, like he wasn't sure if he believed it. It hurt my feelings until I realized I wasn't sure either.

CHAPTER 49

After leaving River's, I remembered Gus was probably waiting for me at home, ready to unpack the litany of failures in our relationship, so I decided to delay the inevitable and stopped at Musso and Frank for a martini at the bar. I stared at my phone and read the website www.Twitter.com, having the courtesy to not force the bartender into a conversation. After forty-five minutes of scrolling, I realized we're not supposed to know this many people's thoughts and feelings, so I finished my martini(s) and stumbled back to my apartment, drunk enough to handle anything.

Everything around me looked blurry, and I was glad I'd brought my headphones, because I put on "Maggie Says I Love You" by No Joy and pretended my life was a movie, and the song helped, it made me walk with purpose, and all I could think about was how do I fix myself? My dealer, River, had cut me off, so where was all this pain going to live now? It needed a home. It couldn't live in my brain anymore.

Somebody needs to tell me they love how my body looks naked, somebody needs to tell me they would invite me to an exclusive orgy, somebody needs to tell me that if they saw me walking down the street, they would invite me to a romantic weekend in Palm Springs, and I would tell them "I hate Palm Springs" (I do—no good food, unforgivable), but they would convince me and I would go and I would tell all the Sailboat Gays and they would nod in unison, having each had that same experience. I'd be a part of a club, I would speak the language, people would never ask for my opinions on anything, they would follow me on Instagram but not on Twitter: a true sign of body over brain.

I hate that I'm like this. I hope that's clear.

LA was so pretty. I was so drunk. I played "You Can Have It All" by Yo La Tengo and was briefly enveloped by such lovely warmth. I passed the donut shop from *Tangerine* that had been replaced by another donut shop. I remembered seeing the movie high on pills and falling asleep and lying to everyone afterward. "Wow, it was phenomenal. Game-changing, holy shit." How shameful. But everyone's secretly in a lot of pain, right? They are. They have to be. Existence is painful. I'd like nothing more than to quit drinking and hiring sex workers and be content and that would be my story. But I'm not stupid enough to believe life is that easy or clean. I could quit those things and still not be okay. Sometimes I think I surround myself with conflict so I have reasons to justify the sadness. That it's circumstantial. That it doesn't live deep in my bones.

"You say I choose sadness. That it never once has chosen me"— "The Good That Won't Come Out" by Rilo Kiley. There. I still relate to a Rilo Kiley song in my thirties.

I arrived at my door. The lights were off. Gus was in bed asleep, thankfully. I wanted to keep on drinking. We had a bottle of Malbec left ($29) and I choked it down while watching *Below Deck*.

I don't remember how the vomiting started, but I do remember not making it to the bathroom in time. That was okay, I told myself, the rug would absorb it. I rested my face on the floor a couple feet from the vomit. Burying my face in the rug gave me temporary relief, the shag tickling my face. I made a mental note to rewatch my episode of *Below Deck* the next morning. I bet it was a good one.

CHAPTER 50

I woke up on the rug to Gus shaking me. The fear on his face made me instantly self-conscious and when he asked about the vomit I apologized for getting sick, and then he sighed one of his theatre major sighs because he would be the one cleaning it up, and I felt too ashamed to watch, and I didn't want to allow any opportunity for us to have a serious conversation, so I went in the bedroom, and when I looked in the mirror I was stunned by how hungover I was, almost impressed I could look and feel this terrible, and there was no way I could go into work, so I emailed Ethan that I was sick and I crawled into bed and fell back asleep.

When I woke up that afternoon, Gus was at work and I felt physically better, which was good and also not, because I now had the space to process my emotions. Out of muscle memory, I started to type in a sex worker website where I could delay the pain and compartmentalize, but my brain was beginning to resemble the

Container Store and I knew I couldn't divide it into any more sections. Instead, I had to expand it. Sit in my feelings. The thought of doing that filled me with panic, though, so I stared at the wall instead and thought about whether or not buying Farrow & Ball wallpaper would solve all my problems.

CHAPTER 51

That night, during my bath, Gus came in and started brushing his teeth. We still hadn't talked.

"Hi," I said, meekly.

Gus turned around, relieved I had broken the silent treatment. He spit out his toothpaste and immediately apologized for River. I did too.

"But you didn't do anything," Gus said. His eyes were like two beads of kindness.

I told him that I did, that I did lots of things, which is why I thought we should break up.

I couldn't believe I'd actually said the words. It felt like casting a spell. Good or bad, something would now have to change. Gus looked winded, even though he hadn't moved. He asked why.

"I've been sleeping with other people. Sex workers. I'm fucked up. Every day it feels like I discover a new flavor of fucked up inside me." I noticed he had no remnants of toothpaste around his mouth. What would it feel like to do a simple task, like brushing your teeth, and not worry you did it wrong?

"For how long?"

"A couple months. I fucked River before we met him at Akbar too. I'm sorry I didn't tell you."

Gus held on to the sink and processed the information. "You . . . How did you know River?"

"He fucked Ethan. Ethan told us about it at work. I looked him up. Then we fucked." I said it calmly. I wanted to practice being cold and detached. I remembered a fight I'd gotten in with my best friend from college. She called me one day furious—about what, who could remember? I decided that instead of matching her tone, I would choose my words carefully and be very matter-of-fact. I figured anger could only survive by feeding off of more anger. If I didn't give in or indulge it, she would have nowhere to go. It ended up working. She quickly deflated like a balloon and ended up apologizing to *me*, even though it should've been the other way around. I was so impressed with myself. And, you know, also mildly concerned I was a manipulative sociopath.

Gus bit his knuckles and said, "We can work on this."

"What?"

Gus seemed fearful. "Whatever you're going through, we'll get past it. I mean, I fucked River without telling you, didn't I? I haven't been perfect either."

Suddenly I was furious. How could Gus be so okay with what I did? *Be pissed off! Call me names! Don't just take it.*

I said, "No, you don't get it, Gus. I can't be with someone right now. I'm not dateable."

"Jesus," Gus said, spitting everywhere. "We can't just end a six-year relationship over a rough patch."

"Five and three quarters," I corrected him. "Gus, I'm getting fucked by random men multiple times a week. This is not a rough patch. This is who I am right now. You have to let me go and figure my shit out."

"That's selfish," Gus said, tearing up. "That you just—you do this and then you also end things because it's easier that way. That way you don't have to deal with what you did to us."

"What are you fighting for? I'm giving you a chance to find someone who makes sense with you. Someone who can do all the things you can do."

"Like what?" Gus yelled.

"Like go on hikes—"

"Are you fucking high? I hate exercise."

"Well, you shouldn't," I said, feeling another wave of anger rise up. "You're lucky and you don't even know it. You're able to do anything you want with your body and you choose to do nothing. Go fucking ride a mountain bike! Like, every day!"

"What are you talking about? I don't know how to ride a bike! Fuck bikes!"

"That's my point," I said. "Go learn! And while you're at it, learn how to drive. How can you not have a license?"

"The freeway is terrifying!" Gus said. "It's not like when you're sixteen and think you're immortal, okay?"

It was like a piñata. One good swing and it all came spilling out. My resentment over his able-bodied-ness. My resentment over his complacency regarding exercise and his career. His lack of desire to do whatever he wanted when he had every option right in front of him. So much of my existence was spent conquering anything that resembled weakness. This made it intolerable whenever I saw someone like Gus not trying to constantly optimize his life. *I'm trying so hard to be perfect. Bigger. Faster. Stronger. Why can't you do the same?*

"Okay, look, what exactly is happening here?"

"I'm just saying you should be with someone who is on your

level. Wouldn't that be nice? You could find someone to, you know, fuck you the way you want to get fucked," I said, shrugging my shoulders.

Gus softened and said, "This is about your topping anxiety, isn't it? Come here, honey." Gus got on his knees and hugged me in the bath. I could feel his relief. *Oh my god, if this was our only problem, we'd be fine.* I didn't embrace him back. I just hung there like a bag of wet bones as he continued. "I don't know how many times I have to tell you: I don't care, all right? I don't give a shit about your disability."

I pushed him off of me. "Well, maybe you should. Maybe *I* should. It's a part of me, you know."

"Well, you never talk about it," Gus said.

"I do now," I said. *Do I?*

"Okay, let's talk it out," Gus said.

The thought of having an honest conversation regarding my cerebral palsy made my heart jump out of my butthole. "Never mind," I told him. "I need to get out of the bath," I said, holding on to the sides to my lift body up. Gus held out his hand, like he always did to help me out. I looked at his hand and became angry at it.

"No," I said. "I got it."

"What?" Gus said, a little stunned. "Look, I know you're upset right now, but you don't need to go and fucking hurt yourself to prove a point, okay?"

"Don't tell me what to do," I said. "I'm not going to hurt myself. Stop doing everything for me."

"Okay, so I either don't acknowledge your disability or I acknowledge it too much." Gus sighed. "Please. Just tell me how you want me to be."

I ignored him, turned off by how easy it was for him to surrender parts of himself so that we could still work. I lifted my right leg out of the tub. That was easy. It's the stronger one. The left one, however, was the troll. I steadied myself on the toilet to anchor myself—my hand now touching pubes and dried piss—and started lifting my left leg out. I became overwhelmed immediately and put my leg back in the water.

"See?" Gus said. "Let me help."

I waved Gus away and he backed off. I concentrated, really gripping the toilet to help me push my leg out and over the tub. Finally, it worked. I got out of the tub on my own for the first time in years. I looked at Gus, equal parts satisfied and annoyed at him.

Gus scoffed. "For the record, you were the one who first asked me for help getting out of the tub. Not me."

"That doesn't mean you had to keep doing it," I said, grabbing a towel and starting to dry myself off.

"So what? Now I'm becoming the representation of everything that's holding you back? Too simplistic, Elliott. You're really letting yourself off the hook here."

"Fine, I'm the asshole," I said.

"You are the asshole! I can't believe you're just done," Gus said, his voice breaking. "Whatever solution I offer up won't even matter, will it?"

"Why are you being so pathetic?" I yelled, suddenly self-conscious the neighbors could hear us. I lowered my voice and said, "I'm terrible. Tell me I'm terrible."

"I already called you an asshole."

"Tell me more," I said, noticing that my leg had started shaking and my lip was quivering. "Tell me I'm despicable. That I'm a piece of shit." My eyes were welling up with tears. "Do it, you fucking coward."

Gus looked at me like River did. Almost frightened, like he'd had no idea so much ickiness lived inside of me. I could feel the tables turning in the argument now. I was unraveling, which allowed Gus to gain strength.

"No," Gus said. "I won't. Because then a part of you will just be relieved. I'm not going to alleviate you of your guilt, Elliott. You made this decision. You fucking stand behind it."

"Fine," I mumbled. "I will."

Gus said okay then, we're over. The finality stunned me for some reason and filled me with panic instead of relief. Was this really what I wanted? There was a chance no one would want to be with me ever again. Meanwhile, Gus would assuredly float on to his Great Love. I'd be a footnote in Gus's relationship history. He could be my whole goddamn book. Who's the pathetic one now?

I wanted to say, "Sorry, I changed my mind, please take me back." He'd buckle and say yes because us apart is scarier than us together. But I didn't. I needed to do the decent and honest thing. For him. And for myself.

CHAPTER 52

It's uncomfortable when the breakup sticks. You'd think with a long relationship like the one Gus and I had, there would at least be a process of getting back together and then ending things for real. At the very least, there would be breakup sex, right?

There was none of that. After I broke up with Gus, he moved out and crashed at Augie's. Texts were sent but only to deal with logistics like moving out his things, who could keep what, and coordinating the move-out date. (Gus asked that I not be home.) It was heartbreaking, even though it's what I wanted. My drinking intensified. And now without the comfort and rationalization of drinking with Gus every night—it's our routine, it's us getting loose with each other, he enables me—there was nothing to hide behind and no one to blame but myself. *Am I the problem and was Gus merely the scapegoat? Did I let myself off the hook, as he suggested?* I drank a bottle and a half of wine, sometimes two, every night alone and trudged through every day, almost disappointed in how high-functioning I continued to be. Part of me wanted to fuck up at work, lose my job, hit some kind of rock bottom, but I continued to exist in a frustrating gray area, dedicating most of my emotional real estate to hollow attempts to manage my drinking—when to drink, how much to drink—which would inevitably lead to me tearing down my newly constructed parameters little by little, but not enough to create the kind of damage that would necessitate quitting. Every day had a flat, blank quality. With the edges dulled by alcohol, my life resembled some sad, tedious blob.

I tried to heal myself in embarrassing rich Goop-y ways. I went to a reiki healer in Santa Monica who kept calling me Paul. I saw a gay therapist who was too good-looking for me to be vulnerable around, so I spent our sessions making him laugh, fishing for validation. I exercised more, which produced zero results because my alcohol consumption was canceling out the gains. Ethan recommended me to his shaman, with whom he had recently reconciled, but our "session" was a true lol. First of all, shamans should not look like soap opera stars. I feel like they should have enough of a spiritual foundation to forgo veneers and Botox. I lay down on a mat on his floor, and he began by pressing on my stomach, asking if I sensed any black energy escaping, but all I could focus on was how much his pressing made me want to fart. There was a hypnotist with an office on the Paramount lot (?!) who charged me $2,000 for an eight-hour session where I mostly napped.

Sometimes I'd start to text Gus some anecdote from my humiliating journey to enlightenment, only to realize halfway through that he was no longer the person I told things to. Is that why people stay in relationships? Just so they can have someone to tell their stories to, someone who cares if they got home dead or alive, someone who's thinking of them first thing in the morning and last at night?

I'm not asking as a judgment. It makes complete sense.

CHAPTER 53

"You know, Elliott, when you get to my age, you can come blood," Ethan said, eating a forkful of chopped salad in his office.

I spit out my falafel. "How did we go from talking about the gay guy who ran Katherine McPhee's social media presence to blood in your cum?"

"Because I've been watching you be a sad girl for the past thirty minutes and I'm losing my appetite. You have it so good. You have two decades of bloodless cum ahead of you," Ethan said. He had lettuce in his teeth.

"I'm going through a breakup," I said. "I'm sorry I'm not grieving in the way you'd like me to."

"I've been going through a breakup too, dummy."

"You've already moved on with Luke Evans's stunt double," I said. "He's moving into your mansion next week!"

"Nico's between places, he's not moving in, and our situation is irrelevant. I'm fucking someone new but I'm still in mourning. I'm letting myself feel all the feelings."

"Yes, and you have a lot of them," I said. "You said Cindy looked healthy today, and she's been on edge ever since."

"She does."

"You knew that comment would trigger her food issues, but you said it anyway. You like to dominate people."

"Wow," Ethan said. "What searing insight into my psyche. You're getting pretty comfortable with me, aren't you? Don't forget that I'm your boss."

"God, Ethan, could you not lord your power over me for one fucking second?"

The mood in his office shifted. I was afraid that I'd overstepped.

"I'm just trying to help you," Ethan said, in a measured tone with a hint of bubbling rage. "But you don't want that right now. You want to get trashed every night and come to work hungover while you collect your inflated paycheck and go home, convinced that I'm the bad person." Ethan laughed. "Well, guess what? I know I'm a moody bitch. I know I can be cruel, but so can you. I mean, look what you did to your poor boyfriend."

Ethan got up from his desk. On his way out of his office, he caught his reflection in the glass and said, "Jesus fucking Christ, would it have killed you to tell me there was fucking lettuce in my teeth? You really are an asshole."

I left work early—said it was a migraine, Ethan didn't push, he was glad to be rid of me—and decided to walk home. Burbank to West Hollywood. It's not easy, you have to dodge a freeway and the walk can take over two hours, but I liked putting my body in motion and tricking itself into feeling anything other than stagnant.

I was afraid of everything. Afraid to keep drinking. Afraid to stop drinking and have to experience everything without the brain condom alcohol provides. I was afraid of losing my job and not being able to spend $200 whenever I felt a bad mood coming on. I was afraid of keeping my job and my heart becoming a Bank of America. I was afraid of never seeing Gus again. In my grief, I'd almost forgotten the reason why we broke up. Key word being "almost."

I was afraid of getting older and injuring myself, something worse than a torn hamstring, and getting cut off from exercise: the one thing that allowed me to have a healthy relationship to my body. I was afraid of fucking sex workers again until everything got pulled down by gravity, and I became another creepy old man they'd have to grin and bear it for.

I was walking for an hour, deep in my k-hole of pity, when I got a text message from Jonas of all people: "U on your way?" After a moment of confusion, I remembered that today was the day I'd promised I would visit his classroom and give a career talk. I looked at my phone's clock. I was already ten minutes late. Motherfucker. I'm a Virgo. I'm never late. Luckily, I opened up my maps app and saw that the school was only a mile away, so I decided to run, Forrest, run.

I arrived to Jonas's classroom red-faced and wheezing for air. A bunch of baby-faced teens with expensive haircuts looked up at me, borderline disgusted. I bet they all had rich people names like "Hale" and "Juniper."

Jonas was dressed in beige pleated pants and a deep blue button-down. Very Kurt Russell in *Unlawful Entry*, except less chic. Jonas had a way of making normcore look just "normal" instead of purposefully ironic and elevated.

"Hi?" Jonas said, communicating a very clear "What the fuck?" to me.

"Hello!" I said, with an exaggerated enthusiasm. "Rule number one of television writing: when you're in the writers' room and in the thick of breaking a story, it's really hard to tear yourself away and, in fact, your coworkers will judge you for it. One time I was writing for a show about housewives that turn out to be aliens with hearts of gold, and we were going to have to rebreak an episode and pull an all-nighter, and the staff writer, who is like the lowest rung on the totem pole, said he had to go because he was taking a ceramics class. He was fired the next day, obviously."

Okay, wow. "Ramble On" by Led Zeppelin much? The teenagers just stared at me, unwilling to process anything I had just said. They were too busy focusing on my sweat stains.

Jonas went into salvage mode and said, "Wow. Sounds pretty cutthroat. Maybe you should start by telling the kids who you are, where you come from, and how you got your start."

I nodded, acutely aware I needed to get things back on track. I told them about my humble beginnings in Ventura, my obsession with television shows, and how I would watch them with closed captioning on so they would resemble dialogue in a script, and how I wrote a pilot that was very gay and noisy and full of sex, which got me representation and then staffed on a TV show that was also considered noisy and full of sex, but none of it gay, of course, because Hollywood is quietly homophobic.

"But don't gay guys, like, run Hollywood?" a teenager, clearly gay, who looked like a barista at your second favorite hipster coffee shop, asked.

"Well, sort of, but it's mostly run by old straight white guys named Tim," I said. "And so much of your career will be spent worrying if Tim likes your work and will give you the money you need to make your show, even though your work isn't for fucking Tim—" I stopped myself and turned to Jonas. "Oh, sorry. Can I curse?"

"These are rich prep school kids," Jonas sighed. "I'm pretty sure some of them have smoked crack as, like, a joke."

The class erupted in laughter. I couldn't tell if Jonas was being serious or not. I smiled and continued on. "Anyway, things are a little bit easier now because of streaming platforms. Corporations no longer have to create their content with, like, Kraft macaroni and cheese in mind. They have subscribers and that's who they are beholden to. But it's still really bleak. Everything that gets ordered to series has the same logline: 'Overprotective mother moves in next door to her children who just started college.' Or 'Free-spirit sister moves in with her uptight sister and together they learn to become just sisters.' It's depressing. And the people that make those shows, they're not artists. They're essentially company robots. But they're absurdly rich, which is great, I guess. But nothing they've done has improved the culture or been remotely meaningful."

"Well, what have you made?" a Juniper-looking motherfucker asked.

"Um, nothing." I cleared my throat. "I've made nothing."

I looked around the room. Here were some of the most privileged kids in America. They were going to do amazing things because the system was rigged in their favor. And here I was, from a middle-class background occupying a space in one of the most competitive industries. I'd had to fight to get there. To do what, though? To just say I accomplished the unthinkable? To be able to say to someone at a bar "I'm a TV writer . . ." and watch their face be overcome with jealousy and have my ego fed? What did I actually want? What did I have to say?

I was apparently lost in thought when a Hale-looking motherfucker raised his hand and said, "Um, Mr. Jonas? Is Elliott going to say more stuff or is he done?"

CHAPTER 54

"Are you sure you can just take a break?" I asked Jonas. We were sitting down on a bench in a playground that had been donated by Ron Howard.

"Yeah," Jonas shrugged, "there's, like, four teachers per kid."

"Glam," I said.

"Not really. I miss working in public schools and actually feeling like I was making a difference, but the lack of support from the higher-ups made me feel like I was constantly drowning, and I almost had a nervous breakdown. Speaking of those! You were really 'on one' back there. What's up?"

"No, I wasn't," I said, folding my arms.

"Okay, I don't understand why you're even denying it. I don't care. I just told you I almost had a nervous breakdown. And by 'almost' I mean, I kind of did."

"Yeah, okay," I said. "I'm full *Boy, Interrupted* right now."

I looked at Jonas, wanting to tell him everything, because if anyone would understand, it would be him, wouldn't it? I mean, I don't know a lick about his life but both having mild cases of cerebral palsy, there's a shared experience there. A Cliff's Notes to your misery. There has to be.

I took a deep breath and said, "Jonas, I'm burning down my life. I want to stop but I don't know how so I just keep burning it down and soon there will be nothing left and I just, I need help. Somebody needs to tell me how to be a better person."

Jonas didn't say anything back. He just pulled me into a hug. I barely knew him, and I still wasn't even entirely sure I liked him, but when he hugged me, it felt correct.

CHAPTER 55

Four days later, Jonas sent me a voice text. I listened to it in my office during a break from discussing what headshot Ethan should use for his next *Deadline* announcement. He had just sold a show to CBS about an uptight brother who moves in with his slacker brother and together they learn to become . . . brothers.

"Helllooooo," Jonas said, a choir of kids screaming in the background. "So, one of the teachers here invited me to a Halloween party at his house and, well, first of all it's September, so, um, calm down, but I feel like I should go because all my coworkers think I'm weird because I don't talk to anyone but . . . I don't talk to anyone because I don't want to. Anyway, I realize I should make more of an effort and I was wondering if you'd like to come with me? I need backup and you seem like you could use some fun right now, let's be honest. Okay. Bye."

I was confused. Was Jonas trying to become my friend? Can you even make friends in your thirties? I mean, the clay has dried. Furthermore, did I *want* to be friends with him? We had a nice moment at his school, and he made me feel better, but he's completely random. How would I even marry our friend groups? The anxiety! Plus, he's straight. I don't hang out with straight men unless I'm being paid for it. Then I thought a gross thought. Would I be feeling *any* of this hesitancy if Jonas wasn't disabled? Like, how much of this resistance was fueled by my own self-loathing and calculating all the stares from strangers we would get when out in public together?

I knew the answer. Which meant I had to go to this Halloween party.

CHAPTER 56

"Who the fuck lives in Altadena?" I said, approaching an admittedly stunning Craftsman bungalow. I was dressed up as nothing because there are much more interesting ways to feel stupid than donning a fake mustache. Jonas was dressed normally—i.e., terribly—save for a potato chip that was taped to his shoulder.

"I have a chip on my shoulder. Get it?" he said with tepid enthusiasm.

"You're really starting things on the right foot," I said.

"Both my feet are fucked, actually." It's true. They jutted out to the side like mine.

Jonas said he was more interested in how a teacher could afford to own property like this. Definitely family money.

When we entered the foyer, it smelled like a pumpkin spice candle had fused with mediocrity. The host—a thirty-something nerd/dude/bro dressed as a pie—approached.

"Yo, yo, yo," he said, high-fiving Jonas. "I'm so glad you made it, Jonas. We didn't think you would. We were all, like, taking bets and shit."

"Oh," Jonas said through gritted teeth. "Well, apologies if my presence made you lose money."

"Only five bucks. Aka what we make in a week, right?" Rob shoved Jonas, playfully. Jonas almost fell over, but I caught him.

"Now, Rob, you must make more than that," Jonas said, stabilizing himself. "This house is 1.2 mil. I checked the Zillow, bro!"

The host tensed up with uncomfortable laughter and then, looking for an exit, turned to me. "Hi, I'm Rob! What are you dressed as?" Before I could respond, he said, "Wait. Don't tell me. Hipster?"

I stood there, offended, taking stock of my outfit. Skinny jeans, a striped shirt, and my giant Gloria Steinem glasses. I'm sorry, but this is just how people dress. To identify it as "hipster" ages you ten years and makes you instantly uncool. I didn't say that, though. I just nodded and said yes. Rob then excused himself and Jonas and I exchanged a look. "I'm sorry," Jonas said.

"It's okay. Not my first bozo convention."

"Can I get you a drink?"

I reflexively nodded but then stopped myself. Eighty percent of my thoughts today had revolved around whether or not I should drink tonight. (The other 20 percent was wondering what outfit would make my face look less puffy. The answer was none, obviously. It's your fucking face.) I was still drinking a fountain's worth of booze every night, blaming it on the breakup while also realizing it was probably just good old-fashioned alcoholism. I wanted to get wasted tonight. I was in a new environment with people I'd never met before. Jonas and I were getting to know each other. But I also didn't want to get too fucked up and I knew better than to lie to myself and say I would only have two drinks. If I was able to say no tonight, it would be such a boon to my self-esteem. I'd get to delude myself for at least a day that I had control over alcohol.

I must've looked like I was lost in my inner monologue because Jonas gently said, "If you don't want an alcoholic beverage, there's probably LaCroix." I nodded and said, with every ounce of strength, I would actually love a LaCroix.

Jonas went to go retrieve our drinks, and I found myself accidentally checking out his ass as he walked away. It was big like mine. Are big butts a cerebral palsy thing? You know, from all the limping we have to do? Someone get Nancy Drew on the case.

I wandered around the party by myself for a moment. Since everyone was in costume, I couldn't judge them properly for who they actually were, which was annoying. There were three people dressed up as the guy from *Tiger King* though. Sad. It's like, "Babe, that was forever ago. Try harder." But then I remembered that straight people have no culture and rely on viral Netflix docs to fill the gaps in their personality.

When Jonas returned with our drinks, he had brought a girl in a wheelchair with him.

"Oh my god, it's Elliott!" she exclaimed, gliding up to me with her hand extended for a shake. "I'm Kings. Jonas has told me so much about you. Well, not so much. He literally just told me about you today when he talked to me about this party. Wow. Do you ever find yourself just saying things out of a script and asking yourself why?"

"Yes," I said, already into her. "Hi. Nice to meet you." I was too nervous to lean over and give her a hug. Was that the appropriate thing to do or was it insulting? Also, what if I lost my balance and fell on top of her? It's hard for me to lean. Honestly, our disabilities were not well matched so I decided to just stand there and wave, like a total freak on a leash.

Jonas leaned down and gave her a hug and said, "I didn't think you were going to come!" *Of course, Jonas is able to lean and hug. The bastard.*

"Why? Because house parties are the least accessible thing on the planet? I know. But when you told me there was a way in from the backyard. . . . I mean, I'm really just trying to get laid tonight, all right?"

"If you're successful, you'll be the first person in history to get laid in Altadena," I said. Kings laughed. She had long brown hair. Like, down to her ass. And these giant expressive Shelley Duvall eyes. Like me, she hadn't dressed up. Just then, Rob, the host, waltzed up to us, clearly buzzed, and looked at Kings.

"Let me guess," he said. "You're an accident victim? Genius. Where's the fake blood, yo?"

My, Jonas's, and Kings's souls died in unison. This fucker. Without missing a beat, Kings said, "Yup. That's me. An accident victim! What are you? An incel?"

Not getting it, Rob clarified. "Oh, you mean Excel. Like the spreadsheet? No, I'm a pie. Which has a double meaning because I'm a math teacher and, you know, the mathematical constant? Pi?"

Kings closed her eyes and said, "I hate it here."

CHAPTER 57

Here's how the rest of the party went. I stayed sober, which was hard for two minutes and then easy. Honestly, I stopped thinking about whether or not to drink when Jonas and Kings got absolutely blotto and Kings ended up making out with the vice principal of Jonas's school who had recently gone through a divorce, and Jonas started tripping and falling down, like, every three minutes. It was sort of a cringe-y scene and served as my own personal anti-drinking ad. Jonas apologized to me for getting so drunk, said it was nerves and that he never gets like this, he can count on one hand how many times he's been wasted, and I said, trust me, I understand getting too drunk.

Being sober in a room full of drunk strangers emboldened me to act insane. I approached partygoers and introduced myself as someone from the Make-A-Wish Foundation. I had only five weeks to live and my one final wish was to go to a house party full of teachers in the suburbs of Pasadena. It meant a lot to be there tonight so thank you. Their faces dropped—two women burst into tears—but

I was lol-ing on the inside. A lot of people use alcohol to lose their inhibitions, but for me it was the opposite. I drank to calm down and basically become catatonic. To be sober at a party reminded me that this is who I truly was: a Dennis the Menace weirdo who liked trolling people and acting kooky. I drank alcohol to suppress that, to quiet the nonstop energy and constant turning of the wheels in my brain. But why? This was way better. I mean, not to sound straightedge and boring, but is being sober low-key more fun than drinking?

Looking at Jonas answered the question. He was falling asleep on the shoulder of a lesbian gym teacher who was dressed as Michael Cera. I asked him if he would like to get an Uber home. I could ride with him, make sure he got back okay, and he smiled at me all dopey and said yeah. It was strange to be on the opposite end of a situation like this—to be the Gus or the Ethan. I liked it. It was a sign I was getting better, which is huge because it seems like I'm almost always getting worse.

The Uber driver rolled down the windows in case Jonas vomited. Jonas lived in Atwater, which isn't far from Altadena, but it took seven freeways. When we arrived at Jonas's apartment—a 1960s stucco nightmare—I said good night to Jonas, but then he got annoyed and said I was coming in to make sure he didn't trip and kill his spastic ass by accident.

I unlocked the door for Jonas and we walked into his apartment, which had hardwood floors and was sparsely decorated. I filled up a glass of water and made him drink it and then led him to his bedroom. There was a mattress on the floor—yikes but at least the bed was made—and a desk and a *Star Wars* poster, which I tried to un-see. Jonas took off his shirt and his pants, and I tried to avert my eyes, but Jonas laughed and said, "It moves like yours. It's like you've already seen it without seeing it so don't worry!"

I stared directly at him but not in a perv-y way. He was kind of scrawny with big nipples and thin arms. Nineties heroin-chic vibes.

"I eat a lot," Jonas said, picking up on me assessing his body. "I think I have, like, a tapeworm or something. Two disabilities, mothafucka!"

Jonas got into bed and I went to go fetch him some more water and an Advil. I came back and placed it on his nightstand. Jonas looked at me, bleary-eyed, and said thank you.

"Elliott, I never get like this. I swear . . . ," Jonas said, yawning, rubbing his nipples like they were two body pillows.

"I know," I said. "You told me."

"I hope this doesn't scare you off because I'd like for you to be my friend," Jonas said, eyes half-open.

Aha! It was confirmed. Jonas did want to be fronds ("friends" but more fun to say). The sincerity of his statement kind of embarrassed me, and then I felt embarrassed for being embarrassed, because being too cool is actually the worst. "It hasn't scared me off," I said.

"Good," Jonas said. "Because I have a feeling you don't know, like, any disabled people."

"We're hard to find," I said, defensively.

"We're not that hard," Jonas said. "But who am I to judge? Besides Kings, I have, like, no friends. Disabled or otherwise."

"Yes, you do."

"No, I don't," he said, plainly. "I'm an introvert. And not in that fake-ass way extroverts say they're introverted so they can sound deep or whatever. Jonas keeps to his goddamn self and Jonas likes it that way. That's why, when I met you, I was a little surprised that I wanted to be your friend, but, um, you're funny and more social than I am, and being around you makes me, um, like, more energetic, but honestly, you're also kind of fucked up so you really should work on that. Why don't you make a list?"

"A list of what?"

"Every disabled person you've ever met," Jonas said, eyes now fully closed. "It'll be good for you. A nice exercise, mmmmkay? Great, goodbye."

"Why?"

Jonas was snoring, fast asleep, before he could answer me. I tiptoed out of the bedroom and let myself out, registering his sad IKEA futon in the living room and what appeared to be a lava lamp. Straight men are so broken.

CHAPTER 58

Bad news hit. Lisa, the lead actress of *Sammy Says*, was told from her homeopathic doctor who once was a prominent hairstylist that she had a rare bone disease that could only be cured via three weeks of bedrest. No one believed her, the studio was furious, but she ultimately got what she wanted and production shut down, along with the writers' room.

I was terrified. The workplace at *Sammy Says* wasn't exactly a beacon of joy, especially after my breakdown/breakthrough at Jonas's school. I was wondering now more than ever what the fuck I was doing there. Surely, I was capable of doing something more meaningful than writing robot jokes? But it was a way to distract me from the *American Horror Story* that was my life. Left to my own devices, was I going to go on a soul-deadening sex worker + natural wine–apalooza? I'd been sober since not drinking at the Halloween party (six whole days, bitch!), and I hadn't seen a sex worker since River. It wasn't easy. It was very hard. I felt like a toddler in need of a thousand distractions.

The first day of forced hiatus I reached out to Augie to hang, but he was in Joshua Tree watching a hot person he met on Instagram do mushrooms, and I thought about texting Justin, but I finally admitted to myself that I just didn't like him as a person, and then I texted Jonas, who had sent me a million apology texts for his drunken behavior the day after the party, but he didn't respond.

I then did what every bored person in LA does: I went to the outdoor dystopian mall, the Grove. I almost got run over by the trolley, which, to my knowledge, only goes around the perimeter of the shopping center on a constant loop, its route resembling some kind of capitalist purgatory. I bought expensive bars of soap from Le Labo and shorts from J.Crew that only made me feel medium-bad about my body. Daytime was safe. I could busy myself during the day. But then the sun went down and brought literal and metaphorical darkness with it. After leaving my shopping spree, I contemplated going to a bougie wine shop and picking out a new and exciting natural wine. Drinking problem or not, I am a genuine wine enthusiast. I, um, love the craft of winemaking. It's, uh, a really exciting time for wine. The old guard has been replaced and, well . . .

Ew, shut up, you Bon Appétit *bitch. You've been here before with this rationalization. Next piece of pretzel logic please.*

What if I went out to eat and sat at the bar having one martini? Just one.

Lol, babe. Are you getting lazy? One martini? No one has ever had one martini. Even people who aren't alcoholics! Try again.

How about I'm just an alcoholic ruled by emotional and physical cravings, and it's exhausting to go through life white-knuckling it, so why don't I just make it easier by letting myself become a full-blown drunk?

OMG, wait, no. That's too dark. You should really go back to coming up with some far-fetched justification. It works better that way.

Exhausted, I settled on the second best of my addictions: seeing a sex worker. That way I could fulfill a less harmful itch without jeopardizing my paper-thin sobriety. Great decision. Go team! (Team = my anxiety and depression.)

This particular sex worker lived in a neighborhood I'd never heard of, sandwiched between two freeways, and he was standing outside when I arrived. He looked nothing like his photos, which made me feel uneasy, but I stayed because my Uber didn't. He invited me into his dark, creepy studio, which sat behind a dilapidated house. His voice had an unsettling nasal quality, like he had been sucking on some helium. He pointed to a massage table and offered to do some "bodywork" and I was relieved. Maybe he wouldn't want to have sex, even though it's what I had asked for by coming here. I undressed and climbed onto the table. He touched me. His hands were clammy. My body tensed up.

"Oh, you're a shy one."

I tried to laugh but nothing came out. He resumed massaging me, and within five seconds his fingers landed on my asshole. I jumped and told him I actually had to leave. I'd gotten the time wrong and had to go to a friend's thing. People were expecting me.

He asked me where. I told him a place an hour away. He said he would drive me. I said that's okay. He called me a tease. This time a laugh did come out.

I surveyed my options. Best-case scenario: I let him jerk me off. Maybe he'd blow me. I hopped off the table. I stared at him and forced a look that could convey happiness. He looked odd. Everything about him was odd. I hate when people throw out terms like "bad energy," but he was the embodiment of a cool draft of wind you did not expect. If we did have sex, I was going to have to fold myself into smaller parts origami style to get through it.

He tried to kiss me on the lips. I gave him a little. He said, "Don't you want to fuck?" I said not today. I blamed my stomach. Big lunch. Ha ha.

He hesitated but not enough. I would have to work a different strategy. Music was playing. Mellow music. Music that reminded me of Mazzy Star, so I steered the conversation to shoegaze and he got excited, so I kept that discussion going in an effort to direct us into a friend zone. *What kind of music do you like, oh wow, you have a playlist full of music like this, yeah, definitely send it to me.* When that reached its natural conclusion, we were left with our naked bodies, nothing else, and he started jerking me off. I got hard in a second. I couldn't believe I could still get an erection. My body betrayed me.

I came, but it was a sprinkle of an orgasm, not even a lot of cum came out. He walked me out. He looked old and decrepit under the moonlight, more like himself. The pictures weren't from ten years ago. They were from never. His teeth were brown and his skin had dark spots all over the place, like moles, or at least I hoped they were moles, and, whatever, the point is he lied. He lied hoping a boy would take the bait and then be stuck with him and be too polite to say no and then eventually have to pay him for an experience the boy never wanted.

I did pay him. He kissed me goodbye. Salamander tongue. I thought about Mazzy Star and promised myself he would be the last one.

CHAPTER 59

The day after my sex worker relapse, I got an email from my agent about an all-expenses-paid speaking gig at Emerson College the following week. I would just have to show up and talk about how I broke into television writing, like I did with Jonas's class, but this time I wouldn't use it as an opportunity to have revelations and free therapy. I agreed. This was the life raft I needed to get through these next few weeks. I decided to bring my dad along, partially because I wanted to live, laugh, and bond, but I also wanted to have a safeguard against drinking. Afterward, we would go to Provincetown. It was the middle of September. The weather would be perfect. The streets not so crowded. We'd make a whole trip out of it.

"We'll take a plane from Boston to Provincetown," I told my dad on the phone.

"Fuck no," my dad said, audibly slurping down what was most likely his seventh Coca-Cola of the day. "I want to drive. Route 6 is supposed to be gorgeous. We'll rent something cheap. Fifty bucks a day. I can probably get a very good deal, actually."

"Whatever." I rolled my eyes. "Just don't bring your Gregorian chant music. It literally ruins my hearing."

My dad let out a loud, disgusting burp on the phone.

"Dad!" I sighed.

"Sorry," he said. "It's a medical condition."

Because my father thrives on chaos, we barely made our flight. But I got the final troll when he realized we were flying first class.

"Don't worry about it," I said. "Emerson is covering both tickets."

That was a lie. Only mine. Hehehe.

My dad spent the entire flight organizing his three(!) massive pillows so he could get comfortable. By the time he finally settled into sleep, there was only forty-five minutes left on the flight. Which turned out to be a blessing because he ended up snoring so loud, I heard other people in first class whisper to the flight attendants about it. You can't take my dad anywhere, which is unfortunate, because you want to take him everywhere.

After consulting his *Zagat* (he doesn't trust Yelp's "algorithm"), we decided to eat at an Italian place that read very Buca Di Beppo. Everything was covered in butter and finished off in a layer of fat. My dad was in absolute heaven. Growing up, I thought he was a foodie. He'd drive me to far-flung places in LA from Ventura to go eat a bahn mi his trusty *Zagat* guide had raved about. But since he's gotten older, I think his taste buds have died, because unless the dish is six thousand calories and so rich you feel like you're going to keel over and die, he calls the meal "bland." Come to think of it, maybe this is why he requires six different kinds of dressings for his salad.

I drank sparkling water at dinner. My dad is a teetotaler and considers drinking to be "low-life behavior," so his judgment made it easier to not imbibe. Plus, I was getting used to the whole "not walking around with a perma-mid-grade hangover" thing. I had fourteen days, which was my longest stretch of sobriety since I had a really bad flu in 2017.

"I don't miss him," I said to my dad, at dinner, looking at two sad meatballs on my plate.

"Miss who? Our waiter? I do. Where the fuck did he go? This needs more sauce."

"Dad, you can't just ask for more sauce. It's like sixty percent of your meal," I said.

"Watch me."

"I don't miss Gus," I said. "I mean, I do. But I've never regretted my decision to break up, which feels more important than missing him."

"Well," my dad said, chowing down on his food, not realizing that by the time he got the attention of the waiter, there would be no food left to put sauce on. "You don't know what you feel right now. I bet you do miss him. I bet you do sometimes regret it. Your brain's just not letting you access it."

Thinking about all the feelings I had yet to meet or realize made me want to drown in a vat of spicy tequila cocktails. I abstained, though.

My dad and I ate the rest of the dinner in silence, a luxury we've earned. My dad did get an extra side of sauce, and he poured the entire thing on his last little bite of chicken parm. It looked obscene.

I spent the next day wandering Newbury Street while my dad stayed back in the hotel, suffering from indigestion. The man spends 90 percent of his life having stomach problems and the other 10 percent eating food that will give him stomach problems. Then my phone pinged. A voice text from Jonas! Well, well, well. I thought the li'l bitch had disappeared on me. I pressed play.

"Hello, hi," Jonas said. "I'm sorry for going off-the-grid there. Did I tell you that I am a fragile introverted soul? I think I did when I was drunk. Anyway, the rumors are true. I sometimes go AWOL to recharge my batteries. But I'm back, baby! And I went on a date with this girl Ingrid who works at the Laemmle in Pasadena. My first one in a long time. It wasn't great. She's a Scorpio, and I don't know if I can take that on. Also, she asked me if my dick worked. So I suppose I was offended by that. Anyway, what are you up to? Did you make that list of disabled people you've met? I remember telling you to do that. I remember everything from that night, unfortunately. Oh, P.S., sorry for the voice text. It's just, my hand-eye coordination leaves a lot to be desired so this is easier."

I smiled hearing Jonas's voice. I missed him! Which surprised and delighted me. *C'mon heart. Make room for this straight* Star Wars–*loving spastic geek. I know you have the room.* I sent a voice text back that said, "OMG, I'm bad at texting too. I only type with, like, two fingers, so this is very soothing for me. I can't believe she asked you if your dick worked. Why wouldn't it work? Did it seem lazy that night? Sorry, I just feel the need to defend your penis on behalf of disabled penises everywhere. My dick, for example, works perfectly." I sent the voice text and then immediately felt embarrassed. I sent another one. "Sorry, I don't mean to tell you about my . . . I mean . . . I want to stop talking about both of our penises. Okay, bye."

Jonas's next voice text was sent as I was in a fugue state at an Urban Outfitters—the only way to be in an Urban Outfitters. Jonas said, "No, I'm happy for your penis. Ingrid, she immediately apologized, but like, the damage was done. I was bummed because, well . . ." Jonas's voice lowered. "I was really looking forward to, um, hooking up. It's been a while. Anyway, where's the list?"

I got distracted looking at a $200 Polaroid camera, but I responded the second I left. "Don't be that bummed," I said. "Sex hasn't changed since the last time you had it. It's still simultaneously the best and worst thing to happen to anyone. And I'm going to write it, okay? Just give me a minute. I still don't understand why it's so important." I pressed send. No messages after that.

CHAPTER 60

Everyone at Emerson was cute and impressionable and asked a lot of questions I actually didn't know the answers to, but when that happened I just distracted them with jokes. My dad sat in front and guffawed his little head off, to the point of wheezing and scaring the students. He always says to me, "You're really funny, you know that?" And I say, "Yes, I do. It's how I make my living."

That night I was buzzing with adrenaline, but my dad, being old, with a stomach held together by Silly String, passed out shortly after we returned from Emerson. I wanted to not drink, but I was wracked with nerves and just needed to pass out. Ugh, it is SO FUCKING BORING to talk about this shit. Maybe people wouldn't get so addicted to things if they knew how fucking tedious it was. Did D.A.R.E. cover this? A substance problem is the opposite of crazy drama and destruction. It's like being a hamster on a wheel. Here we go again. The same thing. Day in and day out. Dominating your thoughts, taking up all the space, pushing out anything new and exciting.

So, with that in mind, let's just cut to the chase. I raided the minibar and found some shitty wine. My dad was sleeping in the bed next to me, so I quietly downed a bunch of mini bottles of red while watching *Southern Charm* which is, yes, as depressing as it sounds.

I woke up in the morning to my dad puttering around the room, getting ready for our road trip to Provincetown. I panicked for a moment, thinking I'd left some booze next to me in bed, but luckily I'd remembered to throw it in the trash before falling asleep.

My dad managed to rent a car that made a Pinto look high-end, but he was happy because the car was so old it still had a CD player, which meant he could play his handmade mixes of religious music. My dad is a staunch atheist, but for some reason he loves listening to Gregorian chant music from five million centuries ago. These singers are belting their tits out in a foreign language and my dad will start tearing up and I'm just like, "Babe? You know they're singing to God, right?"

I sat in the car in my own little world with my hangover. I resolved to not drink in Provincetown. There would be no stress, no need to take the edge off. I'd be surrounded by beauty. My dad was right. Route 6 was gorgeous. It takes you down the Cape, past all these adorable little towns you convince yourself you could live in one day, and then it leaves you in Provincetown, which is on the outermost tip of the Cape. People have often said Provincetown is located at the end of the world. I like to think of it as being at the beginning of a better one.

After two hours of driving, we arrived at our hotel. The weather was mid-seventies and perfect, almost like it was flirting with you. Most of the tourists had fled after Labor Day, and Commercial Street, which is the main drag that runs through the town, was just the right amount of populated. How do you describe a magical place like Provincetown? It's like if someone painted the perfect picture of a quintessential New England seaside town. And that someone also happened to be really gay and horny. Husbands and wives eat ice cream with their children right next to a group of leather gays. You can see beautiful pieces of art, eat your saltwater taffy, and then mosey on over to a place called the Dick Dock, which is pretty self-explanatory. In P-town (okay, I'm a local!), the wholesome coexists with the hedonistic. You can bring your dad one week and your daddy the next.

Once we settled in, my dad needed to nap, so I walked to a place in the West End that had a stellar happy hour and a deck with a view of the ocean. I ordered a cocktail. I know I said I wouldn't, but "we tell ourselves stories in order to live" by Joan Didion. I thought about the assignment Jonas had given me. Write down every disabled person I've ever met. I sat down with my lemon drop and started composing the list on my iPhone, but then I quickly stopped, pre-triggered and exhausted.

A man came up on the beach riding a horse, and a gaggle of gays who all looked like if the suicidal Lisbon sisters had a secret hot brother, gasped, saying they wanted to play with the horsey. They ran down the stairs and gave the horse a giant hug. The owner, a silver fox, seemed amused by the attention. The hottest Lisbon brother asked if he could ride it. I didn't have to stay to know the silver fox said yes.

CHAPTER 61

The sunsets in Provincetown are so beautiful. The town must be positioned in such a way geographically that it soaks up most of the sun? Soak up the sun. Huh. I wonder how Sheryl Crow is doing.

My brain is at its least compelling when buzzed. My dad and I were eating dinner on a patio. I was already medium-sloshed from my lemon drop, and now I was nursing my second glass of Savvy B.

"You're drunk," my dad said, resigned.

"What?" I said, swallowing rubbery chicken. "This is only my second. . . . I'm only having two drinks."

"I smelled alcohol on you when you came back to the hotel," my dad said. "Don't bullshit me."

"Whatever." I rolled my eyes. "I had a little cocktail moment. I'm on vacation. It's normal to drink on vacation."

"Is it normal to drink the entire minibar when I'm asleep? I found the little bottles in the trash."

"Well." I cleared my throat, distancing myself from my drink to prove a point. "I just needed to wind down after my talk. You don't get any of this because you've, like, never drank."

"Yeah, why would I? Alcohol is ethanol. It's poison."

I pointed to his glass of Coke and said, "They use Coke to clean car engines and clear out rust from drains. It's not exactly from the earth."

"Oh, shut up." He gulped some down, like a surly teen. I did the same with my wine. We were in a petty standoff.

"Look," my dad said, cracking his knuckles because his body is incapable of not making noise for two seconds, "they used to say cigarettes were good for you. People actually smoked when they were pregnant and shit. And now we know that it kills you. Alcohol is the same. And yet, everyone fucking drinks. It's disgusting."

"No," I said. "It's just how normal people who have, like, friends and are a part of this world do things."

"I have friends," my dad said, genuinely hurt. "I talk to Carl in Florida regularly."

"He manages your rental property."

"Son, don't be a dick," my dad said, getting pissed. "I tried alcohol once. You know what it tasted like? Poison. Because it is."

"You already told me that," I said, averting my eyes to look at the sun, which didn't look so beautiful anymore. In fact, the light felt oppressive.

"The only reason why it tastes good to you is because you've had practice. Your taste buds realized you weren't going to stop drinking poison, so they had to adapt and learn how to like it."

"Is that even real?"

"Yes," my dad said. "Carl told me. He read a book about it and got sober."

I didn't say anything. Finally, my dad took a deep breath and said, "You had to fight to be here, you know. When you were born, you were in the ICU for a month. And I would come visit you every day and see you all determined to hang on. And now what? You don't care anymore? You done fighting?"

My dad never talked to me like this. Mom was The Bad One. Our common enemy. We shared an implicit understanding that we were each other's safe harbor, that everyone and everything else could be shitty but we had to make sense.

"Maybe I don't want to be your miracle child anymore," I said, drinking the last dregs of my wine.

The next few days my dad and I barely spoke. He spent his time mostly in the hotel room burping and napping. When he did leave, I had no idea where he went. I read books and wandered around town. When the sun went down, I wanted to drink. I even went to a bar and ordered a gin and tonic, but before drinking it, I imagined it to be my first sip of alcohol ever: a screwdriver a friend had given me on my seventeenth birthday. I spit it out and my friend kept telling me, "Just keep going. It gets easier." *It gets easier.*

I lapped up a little of the gin and tonic and visualized it as that screwdriver, burning my throat and the edges of my mouth, my body trying everything in its power to hold it down. It actually worked. The gin and tonic tasted disgusting. (It also wasn't top-shelf booze, so it wasn't that much of a stretch.)

From then on, I didn't drink. Every night I would come home from a solo dinner and slyly demonstrate to my dad how sober I was. I would skillfully take my pants off without losing my balance. I'd unbutton my shirt with focus and intention. I don't know if he noticed, but it wasn't all for him anyway. A part of this was for me. I'd been living in that purgatory of knowing things needed to change but being unwilling to actually do anything about it. I felt myself, for the first time, being nudged toward doing something.

Finally, after a few days, my dad broke the silence and told me he would like to go to the beach.

"Oh," I said, scrolling on my phone in bed. "The beach is kind of a trek. Plus, gay guys have legit sex in the dunes, and I know you're evolved and everything, but it's a lot even for me."

My dad was resolute. He was tired of eating shitty food and lying in bed all day. He wanted to experience Provincetown and he was going to do it with or without me.

It was about forty-five minutes into our walk to the beach that my dad realized I wasn't joking about this being a schlep, but he was too stubborn to turn back around. We continued walking on a winding road and then down an embankment onto sand that burned the soles of my feet, and then it was about another thirty minutes until we finally reached the BEACH portion of the beach.

A beautiful symphony of gays were sprawled out on their beach towels, some leaving their marked territory to hike up the dunes to have the aforementioned sex I told my dad about. I could tell he had so many questions but was still pissed at me so he had to pretend to be unbothered by everything.

My dad took off his shirt. There were bruises on his skin and random rashes—I swear, this man looks at something cross-eyed and it leaves a mark. His belly hung over his swim trunks; his skin was pale. His body was defiant in the face of the chiseled beach bodies that surrounded us, and for a moment, I felt self-conscious that someone would think we were dating. And then, of course,

I felt bad for thinking that. My brain should be an attraction at Knott's Scary Farm.

I lay in the sand and read Eve Babitz's *Slow Days, Fast Company* (I picked it up after seeing it on River's bookshelf), and my dad switched positions from lying on his stomach to lying on his back, slow-roasting like a rotisserie chicken. He eventually went in the water, and I put down my book and stared at him as he walked through the waves—balding, descended gut, patches of psoriasis—and I felt this sudden urge to protect him. To take him out of the water and bundle him in a blanket and feed him Propecia and psoriasis medication and a salad. "Take these," I would say. "So you can live forever."

My dad got out of the water and looked at me. "You have a bad sunburn."

"Um, okay," I said. The surge of love I'd just felt for him evaporated and was replaced with frustration. "Can you put some sunscreen on me?"

"I forgot to bring it," my dad said, shrugging.

"Great," I said, getting up and quickly putting on my shirt. "Well, let's get out of here then before I get, like, sunstroke."

"The drama, Jesus," my dad said, exasperated.

We started walking back to civilization. With every step, I found myself more and more agitated.

"Why can't you just be a dad for one second?" I said. "Bring some fucking suntan lotion for your child."

"Excuse me, sir," he said, out of breath from walking on the sand. "You're a grown adult." He burped loudly.

"Stop fucking burping, Jesus."

"I told you, it's a medical condition."

"That's not funny. It was never funny. Stop saying it." Now *I* was out of breath. Who knew sand could be so difficult?

"You're just pissed at me for rightfully calling you out on your drinking."

"And I find it rich that you're calling me out for my lifestyle choices when all you eat is garbage and your cholesterol is through the roof. I remember growing up, you'd leave me all alone so you could go on these dates in LA. There'd be no food in the house, except for like old hot dogs and ten condiments so I would just starve."

"What's that have to do with anything? Are you just free-associating your grievances with me now?"

"Maybe I am. It's like, Mom left and I was never able to criticize anything you did because you stayed. So I thought I should just be grateful for that and shut up."

My dad and I were both struggling physically at this point. Hunched over, gasping for air. I really am my father's daughter.

"So now you have the freedom to admit I was a terrible father too? Delightful. I'm really glad—" My dad paused, winded and catching a breath. "I'm really glad we took this trip together."

We didn't say anything until we started walking up the embankment. Our bodies were both tired. I tried to grip a rock to steady myself but I slipped and fell. My knee started to gush blood, and my dad lifted me up and walked ahead of me, with his arm held out behind him for me to grab on to. But then my dad also slipped.

"Dad, oh my god," I said, crouching over him. "Are you okay?"

My dad looked at me fearful and said, "Just . . . go. Leave me here and save yourself, son." He started fluttering his eyes, until closing them entirely. After playing dead for a moment, he opened his eyes again. "Gotcha!"

I rolled my eyes, not giving him the satisfaction of a laugh, even though it was funny. We tried going up the embankment again. This time my dad didn't assist me. He needed all his focus to be on

himself. The two of us started climbing together, sending supportive vibes without actually helping. Eventually we made it up. Feeling triumphant and emotional, I went in for a side-hug, but my dad
brought me in for a full embrace, kissing my forehead and nesting
my head into his shoulder.

"Love you, son," he said to me. "Sorry for everything I didn't
know I did to you."

"Love you too. And it's okay. Between you and Mom, I think
I'm just the right amount of fucked up."

We broke apart. I looked at what we had conquered and realized that this was the same embankment that Gus had helped me
up years earlier.

This was the first time I'd thought about Gus in Provincetown.
Strange, considering we'd gone here so many times together. Every
corner of this small town held a memory and had been marked.
But maybe, like my dad suggested, I wasn't letting myself feel it.
Or maybe all the memories I had revolved around me being drunk
or helpless and I wanted to erase that person and, in order to do
so, I also had to erase Gus. Whatever the reason, one thing was
clear: that beach is not designed for disabled people and I should
definitely stop going.

CHAPTER 62

The first person I saw when I got back to LA was Jonas. We made plans to get dinner together, settling into our friendship rhythm. *You are going to be a person I see regularly,* we would ESP to each other over plates of cacio e pepe. *You're becoming sewn into the social fabric of my life.*

Jonas offered me a ride to the restaurant, since it was on his way. I said yes, assuming we would share an Uber, but, twist, Jonas can actually drive. He pulled up in his car—a Rabbit, the kind Alyssa Milano's character in *Fear* drives—and zigzagged us to the restaurant, effortlessly weaving in and out of traffic, expertly using his turn signal and side and rearview mirrors. He even drove barefoot. A brief thought flickered of me sending Gus a picture of Jonas driving and writing, "See bitch? This man's disabled. What's your excuse?"

To be fair, no one officially told me I couldn't drive. I just figured it was not in the cards. Too many split-second decisions to make, too much reliance on fine motor skills and reflexes. But seeing Jonas drive with such ease made me wonder: Where does my cerebral palsy end and my learned helplessness begin?

During the car ride, Jonas told me more about the origin story of him and his date Ingrid. She took his ticket when he went to go see an art-house movie that wasn't very good but had an amazing soundtrack. He liked the way she said, "Theater two to your left," and so he saw this movie four times just to say hi to her, and anyway he eventually asked her out and he wasn't nervous about Ingrid not being into him because of his limp because nobody cares about these things as much as you think, but it turned out Ingrid did care. At least a little, which is already too much, so fuck her and the horse she rode in . . . Oh God, why is every old-timey saying ableist?

Jonas had a quiet confidence about him, an innate calm, and being around him felt like being back in the womb. I was grateful to have found him.

"Well, there are other girls," I said, my hair blowing in the wind like a movie star's on a perfect California night. "I feel like if you're a straight guy and you are, at baseline, not a sexist monster, you'll have no problem getting dates."

Jonas laughed, pulling up to the valet. He turned to me and said, "Oh, Elliott. I'm not straight."

CHAPTER 63

I've been writing for TV for too long, because when Jonas told me he wasn't straight, I could actually hear the sound effect of a record scratch. I'll admit, I was shook. Since when was Jonas not straight? The man owned a futon as a couch and slept on the floor! Also, was Jonas hot? I did love his giant butt.

Wait. Why was I suddenly thinking about Jonas's oversized gorgeous ass? I didn't have feelings for him, did I? It couldn't be that fucking easy. Someone is strictly platonic and then they give you the tiniest whiff of gay and all of a sudden you want them?

I didn't want Jonas, at least I didn't think I did—but I did feel a little flip-of-the-switch. When I assumed Jonas liked women and only women, I didn't experience any emotion other than *I am intrigued by his brain. It's not smooth, it has wrinkles.* Now things were different. Sorry! They were! It's just, everything felt possible now. I even felt a little high. When I was seventeen and met Dylan, I also felt high, but I didn't quite have the language to describe the constant buzzing, euphoric feeling. Now, years later and having extensively dabbled in substances, I can say with certainty there is no more powerful drug than "gay boy with a crush." I had experienced it with Gus, but that hit me slowly because I'd known him as an off-limits boyfriend-of-a-friend first. With Jonas, I was quickly operating at a different frequency, which I knew was ridiculous. Was this merely a by-product of a devastating breakup? And in the dark recesses of my brain lingered the most troubling question: Could I date another disabled person?

I never had to think about a situation like this before, which, in a way, was a blessing because I didn't know if I would have liked the answer. My relationship to my body had improved, but I easily slid back into thinking I was a wild, unruly, unfuckable thing. If I couldn't feel a sustained tenderness toward my own body, how could I extend that feeling to someone else's, one that looked and operated like mine?

Here are the facts: After Jonas's "not straight" reveal, I was transported back to seventeen, dancing around my bedroom to "Spin the Bottle" by the Juliana Hatfield Three, a giddy, happy, naïve faggot. Gay men are so adept at nurturing crushes, partly because we're used to such things being withheld from us. When Dylan and I were dating, the bedroom was safe, the outside was not. Ventura is liberal(ish), but it was still 2004. We only kissed each other in public twice—once on a trip to LA and once at California Pizza Kitchen. I always wanted more from him. The desire never went away, was never fully satiated even when we were together. This constant longing kept me company. I actually didn't mind it. When you're in the closet, you learn to flatten your insides as a means of survival, so longing, by contrast, wasn't so bad.

Now, here I was again, all these years later, shocked by this rush of new feelings. After dinner (I can barely remember it, too stunned by the news of his sexuality and also bummed I didn't have a view of his butt), Jonas drove me home, and when we reached my apartment, I asked if he wanted to come in for a drink. The night needed to keep going. I had to know more.

"I mean, I don't actually have any alcohol in the house," I said. "I did, but I'm trying not to drink right now. Or, like, ever. Tonight, when they presented the wine list, I imagined the wine to be rotted. Because alcohol is poison. Did you know that?"

Jonas laughed and said no but he's not surprised. He really wasn't kidding when he said he didn't drink. The Halloween party was an anomaly. He said he would have some water, though.

Now that we were together in my apartment, I realized I didn't have a plan. I wasn't going to try to kiss him. I wasn't sure I could trust how I felt right now. Things needed to settle for a minute. I decided on doing a version of foreplay that required no physical contact: I showed Jonas my favorite YouTube videos and gauged his responses to see if he understood the true complexities of my being. I showed him the video of the lady who fell while stomping grapes in a bucket, the supercut of Liza Minnelli cracked out on *Larry King Live*, Elizabeth Taylor howling like a wolf on the red carpet, Janice Dickinson getting wasted on *America's Next Top Model: Finland* and falling down the stairs, and I ended it with an episode of *The Avenue* starring Gigi Gorgeous. Jonas didn't really get the last one—he found the show to be more creepy than funny—but even that response was refreshing, a nice respite from gay causticity.

Jonas went next and was struggling because he really doesn't go on the Internet that much (okay . . . he needs to be preserved in amber), but he eventually showed me a Black Sabbath performance of "Never Say Die" on *Top of the Pops* in 1978 (he loves Black Sabbath, unclear), and then he chose a sweet video of a lioness being reunited with the person who raised her. It was an eclectic pairing that did not bring me any closer to figuring out his queerness, but I enjoyed it nonetheless. I realize I also could've just asked him right then and there to elaborate on his sexuality, but that felt like skipping levels on a video game, and it also would make me seem a little too horny.

I walked Jonas out. He said good night and drove off. I imagined him gripping the steering wheel again and accelerating the . . . whatever it is you accelerate. I don't understand cars. The point is, I could just see him doing a very good job and I felt equal parts jealous and aroused.

CHAPTER 64

This is Jonas, according to the Internet. Three years ago, a local Los Feliz newspaper reported on him winning some teacher of the year award at a public high school called John Marshall—the place where he probably had his mini nervous breakdown. There was a full-body photo printed with Jonas sporting a closed-mouth smile, holding the award, and looking very tired. He was wearing khakis and a polo: very similar to his uniform now, except this time I didn't find his clothes boring. I found them endearing.

He has an Instagram with only one post from 2016. It's a picture of fried clams with the caption "fried clams."

No Facebook, which is great, fuck you Mark Zuckerberg! I'm so glad a girl making you feel bad about yourself in college led to you inventing a site populated by aunts with pyramid schemes.

No Twitter. Wow. Jonas wasn't fibbing when he said he didn't really do the Internet.

I did somehow manage to unearth an old dating profile of his from a website I've never heard of called Plenty of Fish. There was a picture of him smiling on a patch of grass wearing a—and this is hard for me to type—sweater vest, giving that same closed-mouth smile from the Los Feliz newspaper. His interests were listed as "education policy, sci-fi, and general fluidity." I couldn't relate to any of those things but go off, king! Oh, and it said he liked ice cream. Jeni's in particular, but he fucks with Salt & Straw and sometimes the frozen yogurt that tastes like the mall from the nineties.

I love seeing people present what they think is the best version of themselves in order to attract a mate. Jonas looked so earnest on that patch of grass, like he was ready for something to come along that would transform his life. If I were on Plenty of Fish, would I have messaged his profile? Absolutely not, but I think that just speaks to the failure of dating sites in general. They're giving you the tiniest curated piece of someone's personality. Flops can come off as charming or witty. Meanwhile, unicorns like Jonas fail to translate. They become nothing more than A Sweater Vest.

I scoured the World Wide Web, like an old-fashioned hunter and gatherer, looking for information on Jonas, but there was nothing else. His digital footprint was itty-bitty, and it was clear that he had built a life that was more IRL than URL. How fucking sexy.

CHAPTER **65**

Production shut down again after Lisa got pinkeye (but actually)—so the next few days I could do as I pleased. So far that had amounted to masturbating twice a day, looking at photos from when Gwyneth Paltrow and Winona Ryder were friends (before Gwyneth allegedly stole the *Shakespeare in Love* script from Winona's house), running at the gym, and yes, still not drinking. Three whole weeks. Can you believe? Instead, I just looked at Boomerangs on Instagram of people clinking glasses and photos people posted of martinis with some "funny" caption justifying their drinking, and I thought about how our society worships at the altar of booze and how it's more socially acceptable to drink than not to drink. That, along with seeing booze as toxic poison rather than something delicious, was keeping me dry.

I also made plans with Jonas. There was so much more to know about him. His coming out as bi (pan? no label?) and his first sexual experience with a man. I wanted to know it all. He asked me to meet him at his school at 3 p.m. Remembering his interests from Plenty of Fish, I suggested we go to Jeni's for ice cream. He wrote back "love Jeni's sounds cool." I felt kind of sneaky knowing information from stalking him online rather than hearing about it from him organically, but this is how we do things now. The modern world gives everyone a cheat sheet and it's not like we're *not* going to look.

Sitting on a grassy knoll at his place of work, waiting for my crush to come out: I literally and metaphorically felt like I was back in high school. Jonas walked out looking actually dapper in an Oxford shirt and tight black jeans. It was still "Teacher's Uniform" but a little more "Fun Gay Teacher." Or maybe he was dressing exactly the same and my newfound feelings for him were turning me into an unreliable narrator.

Walking down the entrance stairs, Jonas gripped the railing. I took mental notes on how his body moved. His was definitely jerkier than mine, more spastic, but he seemed to have more of an awareness of or a control over how it worked than I had with mine. Or maybe it wasn't about control, maybe it was that he liked his body more than I liked mine, which meant that when he moved, he worked with his limbs rather than against them.

"Are you experiencing PTSD?" Jonas said, approaching with a wide hug. He smelled like fabric softener.

"Excuse me?"

"Being back in school."

"I've been here before, silly. I'm used to it. Besides, elementary school was lame, but I loved high school," I said, smugly. "I was really good at being a teenager. Like, if you could've gotten a grade for it, I would've aced the class, for sure."

"Okay, brag," Jonas said. "I was weird and deeply unpopular. Kind of like now, actually!"

"You're very socially adept for someone who identifies as awkward," I said.

"Well, yeah," he said. "With you. Because I'm comfortable." Jonas smiled at me, a knowing smile that suggested a hint of flirtation. My dick wrestled awake in my jeans, almost to be like, "Babe? Do you need us for anything?"

Jonas and I went to get ice cream, and as we stood in line I stared at him, allowing myself to notice how handsome he was. He had a defined jawline (mine is like a time-share that spends two weeks a year on my body) and green eyes and that heroin-chic body that honestly would have looked a little better if it had had some more weight on it, but I was in a place where everything about him read as attractive.

I asked Jonas for a bite of his ice cream, thinking it might be sexy, but I slobbered all over it and spilled on my shirt. Still, I wasn't embarrassed because I was with him. Jonas then asked about my boy journey, and I was relieved, thinking it could be a natural segue into asking about his sexuality. I told him about my breakup with Gus and how amazing he was but I messed it up in a million ways because I am defective and will probably die alone forever, and as I said that narrative, I knew it wasn't correct. It just felt like an easy way to describe the breakup. Jonas licked some ice cream that had dripped on to his hand and said that, although he didn't know the particulars, it probably wasn't that cut and dried. Both parties are usually complicit in the unraveling of a relationship.

"Sometimes it's easier to just look at yourself as the fucked-up one because it gives you a pass on doing any work on yourself because like, well, at least you're self-aware," Jonas said, biting into his waffle cone. "I don't know. Maybe you guys both couldn't give each other what the other one needed." Jonas paused and laughed. "Full disclosure, I've never had something last longer than six months, so please take all of this with the tiniest grain of salt."

I thought of Jonas's love life, of him going on dates with his hair combed, wearing an outfit that took some thought to put together. Then he meets his date—maybe it's a boy this time. His name is Skyler, they met off Plenty of Fish. Skyler shows up to the restaurant and his face falls when he sees Jonas struggle up the steps. He doesn't know what to do with Jonas or his body. (Jonas didn't say he's disabled in his profile. He doesn't want to be dishonest, but he also feels like his disability is pretty minor and no one should care anyway.) Jonas can sense Skyler's discomfort. He's used to this. Maybe he even ends the date early. Maybe he says something like "This is clearly not a good match. Perhaps we should just call it." Jonas doesn't seem like he fears an awkward moment. Skyler's taken aback by this, maybe even a little insulted. If anyone was going to end it, it should've been him. Jonas shakes Skyler's hand and says "Best of luck out there!" and he means it. Skyler's rejection doesn't represent a general indictment of his worthiness as a person. Jonas knows who he is. He doesn't need Skyler to tell him. The situation has left him unfazed.

Jonas and I may've had similar bodies, but we were very different people inherently. Jonas didn't have the luxury of being disarming to people. His rhythms were too strange. He would oscillate from being shy to being direct in a way that bordered on rude. I don't think he made the same mental calculations as I did while interacting with able-bodied people. For me, that was a primary mode of survival. Successfully diverting attention away from my CP used to be a point of pride, a proof of assimilation, but telling that to Jonas would've had the opposite effect. He would've looked at me with overwhelming empathy and said something like, "I'm sorry you felt like you couldn't discuss this very important part of yourself." And he would have been right.

Looking at Jonas I couldn't tell if I wanted to fuck him or if I wanted to inhabit his body and see what it felt like to be so comfortable and relaxed. Did it matter, though? People have sex with each other for a variety of reasons. Doing it because you looked up to the other person, because you wanted their essence to somehow rub off on you, well, I could have (and have) done a lot worse.

I decided not to ask Jonas about boys after all. I had done enough creepy sleuthing. He would tell me if he wanted to, when I'd earned it.

CHAPTER 66

"You're manic," Dad said, matter-of-factly. We were at a Caribbean restaurant in Los Feliz. Dad wanted to try the jerk chicken, which translated to "I want seven different sauces, and if I happen to pick up some notes of chicken, God bless."

"That might be true," I said.

"You've recently gotten out of a long-term relationship and you're obsessed with this guy who you just met? Yeah, textbook manic."

"We actually met when we were kids at Easterseals and he's not just anybody," I said. "He's—he's like me. You don't know what that's like. Everywhere you go, you're surrounded by straight white guys like you. Imagine never meeting someone who reminds you of yourself."

"I take offense to that," Dad said. "Everyone at this restaurant is at least twenty years younger than me."

I looked around at a gaggle of young people with their mimosas and choppy hair and laughed.

"But you are right. And I'm not trying to downplay that. I imagine it's a very powerful feeling. The issue here is that you barely know this guy. And he likes women too? Greedy little bastard."

"Dad, don't be embarrassing. It's called being bi or sexually fluid or whatever."

"My best friend Bobby and I jerked off together once in middle school."

"Ew, Dad." I grimaced.

"What? Now you're silencing MY sexuality? Who's the old fogy now, huh?"

The waiter came to take our order. As expected, Dad made substitutions for every ingredient and asked for six sides of different sauces. I gave the waiter a sympathetic look, and didn't change a single thing on my order.

"Look," I said after the waiter left. "I don't know how he identifies. All I know is that he likes girls and isn't straight."

"I can't believe they charge a dollar extra for each sauce. Ridiculous."

"Dad, focus. Regardless of what happens, I feel medium-okay for the first time in a while. I mean, this is huge. I finally have a friend who's disabled."

"Is his case of CP more severe? Because you got off pretty light."

"I think so. His limp is a little more pronounced and he slurs a little. But he can drive."

"Yeah, you definitely can't drive."

"I know."

"You'd kill yourself instantly. Maybe others too. Cause a seven-car pileup."

"Thanks for the vote of confidence." I rolled my eyes. "Wait. You know what, maybe I can drive. Maybe I've been underestimated my entire life by everybody, including me."

I picked up my drink for a sip but stabbed myself in the eye with my straw.

Dad started laughing. "Yeah, no. I think I have a pretty accurate read on your abilities."

"You're a jerk," I said, rubbing my eye.

"Okay, fine," Dad said. "I don't want to fight again."

"Me either. That was terrible," I said, sighing. "I haven't drank since Provincetown, you know. I'm really making a go at it. Being sober."

"Kick ass!" Dad exclaimed. "Did you read the book Carl read?"

"No, but I will," I said.

Dad beamed and grabbed my hand across the table, locking our fingers together. Here we were, back to making sense again.

CHAPTER 67

"Are you fucking someone new?" Ethan asked me. We were eating Kardashian salads in his office.

I pantomimed picking up a phone. "Hello? HR? My boss is asking me questions about my sex life. Send help. I feel unsafe."

"Oh, shut up. Did I tell you I'm fucking Adam Levine's stunt double?"

"I thought you were fucking Luke Evans's stunt double."

"No, that's over."

"How are you finding all these stunt doubles? Also, what does Adam Levine do that requires him to use a stunt double?"

"He does a lot," Ethan said, without a hint of humor. "Anyway, the sex is great. God, I love sex."

"A groundbreaking statement, Ethan. How much do you make per week?"

"You don't want to know," Ethan said, adjusting his tie. "I'm grossly overpaid. It'd only make you upset."

"Okay, don't tell me."

"I make fifty thousand a week. Anyway, I had a point with my 'I love sex' thing." Ethan paused, cleaned his Gucci glasses. "I'm being really adventurous with this guy. I mean, I bottomed for him, for fuck's sake."

"Wow, so selfless of you."

Ethan said thank you, oblivious, and went on about how Adam Levine's stunt double was opening up this new carefree side to him.

"Carefree? When do I get to meet this side? This morning you screamed at Gail for confusing a picture of Blythe Danner with one of Patricia Clarkson."

"You might not ever meet it, asshole. All I'm saying is, sex is a great way to learn about yourself. Self-discovery doesn't always have to be painful."

"Says the man who bottomed once."

"I'm saying, go fuck someone. It'll be good for you."

"I've been fucking enough people. All I've discovered about myself is that I'm deeply messed up."

"You're not deeply messed up," Ethan said. "You just started paying attention. Good for you."

"Thank you," I said, accepting Ethan's version of a compliment. Then, taking advantage of our softer moment, I cleared my throat and said, "Ethan, I've been thinking. What if I didn't come back next season to *Sammy*?"

Ethan shrugged and said, "Do what you gotta do."

"You're not going to ask me why? Or scream at me?"

"I thought you wanted to see me chill," Ethan said, smirking. "But fine, if it's important to you, tell me why."

"Well, I think I've forgotten why I'm even here. I've bounced from job to job, afraid to jump off the moving train and be rendered irrelevant or something. I want to take a beat to figure out what kind of stuff I want to make rather than just be a cog in a joke machine. Like, maybe I wanna make gay shit! Or disabled shit!"

"That's a lot of shit."

"Whatever! This business is fucking awful and filled with rejection. I might as well do something of substance to make it worth my while."

"Is this the part where I tell you to follow your dreams and make important TV and be an artist? Is that what you need from me?" Ethan asked.

"I don't know," I said, searching. "You don't have to say anything. I guess I'm just telling you."

"Okay," Ethan said, throwing his salad in the trash can from his desk chair. He missed. "Gail, can you come in here?" Ethan yelled. "Salad just went everywhere. I have no idea what happened."

What was I expecting? For Ethan to beg me to stay? To give his blessing and tell me how much he'd enjoyed our unlikely friendship? None of that occurred. In fact, we never talked about it again. But we didn't really need to. I knew that Ethan cared about me as much as his unresolved trauma allowed. Some people are just limited. You have to meet them where they are. In Ethan's case, that was his office, where I currently helped a beleaguered Gail pick up croutons off the floor.

CHAPTER 68

I finally bought the book Dad's "friend" Carl read that got him sober. I put it off because I knew that once I read it, it would trigger a perspective shift and I wasn't sure I was ready, but after weeks of sobriety on my own using willpower, my brain was like, "Okay, this isn't sustainable. Let's dig a little deeper." The book was called *This Naked Mind*, by Annie Grace, and after finishing it, I realized my brain's been wearing, like, seven layers of clothing. Here are my main takeaways.

The past few years, I've tried to scale back my drinking, to no success, and each time I betray myself, I feel more powerless and alcohol's grip tightens. But the reason why quitting is so hard and there is such a disconnect between what I want to do and what I end up doing is because my subconscious and conscious are at war. (Yes, I'm bringing my subconch into this, but please bear with me.) Your conscious mind makes a decision not to drink and then sends the memo to your subconscious, which is where years of messaging and brainwashing lives, and your subconscious is like, "Wait, what?

But drinking is amazing. I just binged the new season of *Dead to Me* and those women are always drinking a bathtub's worth of wine, and it's fun and flirty. So, no, sorry, I think I will be drinking this glou-glou red tonight!" So, of course, the subconch wins, and that's why I end up getting wasted and DMing Antoni from *Queer Eye* on Instagram, complimenting him on his recipe of "gourmet" Rice Krispie treats, which he definitely didn't eat, and also, how complicated and chef-y can Rice Krispie treats get?

My dad was right. The tobacco industry is an apt comparison to alcohol. Both are selling a lie perpetuated by capitalism. We've been led to believe that alcohol is an elixir, a social lubricant necessary to have fun and relieve anxiety, when we know through experience that drinking actually intensifies shitty feelings, especially when you wake up the next morning hungover. Like cigarettes, alcohol is an addictive substance that's also progressive, which is why I could drink "normally" for years and now I can't. Part of me is always thinking, *Oh, if I could just go back to being a social drinker, everything would be fine.* But there's no going back. And you shouldn't even want to. The thesis of the book is that alcohol is a giant scam that doesn't deliver on any of its basic promises. I remember once doing a dry January and feeling so proud, but every night I'd have a moment where I'd crave alcohol, and I would have to say to myself, "Yes, a glass of funky red would be heaven right now but I must abstain." And I would white-knuckle it until the desire went away. The problem here is the inherent belief that alcohol is EVERYTHING and you'd be making a giant sacrifice in giving it up. You wouldn't be. In fact, you'd be gaining so much and losing nothing.

It was life-changing to fully know the insidious slippery-slope nature of addiction, that after doing something for so long, you're more inclined to get addicted than to not, and I *am* addicted. I'm not afraid to admit that, because it isn't my fault. Every time I don't fulfill my promise of not drinking, I am competing against years of societal conditioning, of seeing Kathie Lee and Hoda drinking wine at 10 a.m. on the *Today* show. Hahaha, Mom Juice!

I read the book and had my first drink in weeks—a farewell, if you will—but the alcohol hit different, felt joyless, almost like keeping a doctor's appointment. I looked at my wine and said, "I don't want to believe in you anymore. I want to believe in something else." And even if I continued to drink, even if the books weren't enough and I had to join a program, I knew I meant it. I knew I was ready to build something new.

CHAPTER 69

I hadn't seen Jonas since our ice cream date, but we continued to send voice texts to each other. We also sent funny memes (Okay, I did. Jonas doesn't know how), news about global warming (that was Jonas), an article about Bethenny Frankel donating horses to a war-ravaged country ("I've never seen the Housewives. Who is this woman? Why horses? Shouldn't water be at the top of the list?" Jonas voice texted me), and the occasional selfie.

I started masturbating to thoughts of us hooking up, to imagine what sex between us could be like. In these fantasies, I was focused on Jonas's ass. I was rimming, I was pressing my dick up against it. Jonas was on his hands and knees writhing in pleasure, and I flipped him over and fucked him and, unlike with Gus, I was doing a great job. In my mind I was the dominant one, the one in charge, and Jonas couldn't get enough.

I masturbated to images of Jonas topping me too. For the most part his disability wasn't prominent in these scenarios, and when it was, it would only manifest to pose a potential problem. These thoughts made me so uncomfortable. Was my brain an ableist troll? Why couldn't I ever get fully lost in my fantasies?

Jonas's disability is what had drawn me to him initially—a desire for a reflection, any reflection, of myself—but what we shared was also the thing that kept me at bay. Any negative thought I had about him was a negative thought I had about myself. When I was getting turned off by Fantasy Jonas struggling to undo my buttons, I was getting turned off by all the times I was unable to do that for Gus. Sex and shame are intertwined, but my baggage was never more obvious than when I pictured Jonas in bed.

Despite my hang-ups, I was turned on by Jonas. I wanted to fuck him. Or him to fuck me. Or for us to take turns fucking each other. Fuck.

CHAPTER 70

Augie and I had lunch at a "cool" restaurant that had made the bold choice to charge $26 for a half rotisserie chicken with a side of garlic sauce. I knew what this lunch was all about: it was a post-breakup check-in, making sure I hadn't gone off the rails, and if I had, *oooooh, how crazy had I become, must relay this information to our mutual friends under the guise of concern.* Maybe this is unkind. I do love my friends and believe we genuinely care about each other. I also believe we genuinely love gossip. Both can be true.

Anyway, Augie asked if I'd talked to Gus. I told him no, and that I missed him but us being broken up was making more and more sense. I wasn't drinking anymore, and being with Gus, alcohol was basically the third in our relationship. Well, when it wasn't River. And I was also trying to tap into a part of my identity that I'd ignored for so long—my disability—and it hurt me that Gus didn't totally understand it, which, how could he? It's not his fault. In fact, the only way disability factored into our relationship was how I used it as an excuse for Gus to take care of me. Which, of course, made my life seem small, and now I wanted to be more independent and discover what I was capable of. I didn't know if I could do that with Gus. Our dynamic felt fixed.

Augie had never heard me talk so frankly about my disability, and I could tell, without making a big production out of it, that it meant a lot to him. Augie said that it'd been three months since our breakup, wasn't there a version where Gus and I become friends, get the occasional lunch together, and catch up?

I'd thought about this possibility a lot, and I wanted to tell Augie no, I didn't think so, that there were some people you can't ever get lunch with. For almost six years, I had all of Gus. I was given a road map to explore every bit of him. I had a front-row seat to his good moods, his bad moods, I could grab his dick whenever I wanted, play with his asshole. So why would I want to have a catch-up lunch? Why would I settle for a watered-down relationship when I once had everything? It'd be like a sad diffusion line. I couldn't be honest with him. I'd have to pretend to be surprised when he told me about his new boyfriend. (His name is John, he's a software developer, lives in Playa Del Rey, and likes to post pictures of what he eats at restaurants. I'd been cyberstalking him for months.) We would need to be drunk in order to achieve any kind of emotional honesty, and the third drink would turn into five and then we would let it all hang out, accusations would be thrown, one of us would cry. We'd feel better briefly, only to sit with the shame you feel when you've exposed too much to someone who no longer makes sense, has an old set of keys to your body and brain that they hope still fit.

I didn't say any of this to Augie, I just said "maybe one day," and then the check came.

"Oh, look," Augie said, examining the check. "The waiter left me his number. Isn't that sweet? Maybe he just moved here and needs friends."

"Augie," I sighed, grabbing the check. "For the millionth time, this means he wants to fuck you."

I knew Augie wouldn't call him and that it would just go into his "numbers written on checks" graveyard, so I left the waiter a big tip.

CHAPTER **71**

Of course, the day after my lunch with Augie, I fucking ran into Gus. It was at the Arclight. I was going to a solo 2 p.m. showing of the new Mission: Impossible movie. I know it's off-brand, but the action sequences are impressive and Tom Cruise can get it in a "Daddy Needs to Go to the Mental Institution" kind of way. Gus and I both loved watching them, which is why I guess I shouldn't have been totally surprised when he walked in. Gus looked neither good nor bad. Just the same. He was also alone. He didn't see me. I was in the back, thankfully. He blazed right past and took a seat in a middle row, on the aisle. Gus always needed to sit on the aisle because if he had to pee, he didn't want to have to step on people's feet and block their view to get out. Too much anxiety and attention. I didn't mind. I liked sitting smack-dab in the middle.

So, there we were, free to live our movie theater seating truth. How liberated we were to be unshackled from each other's choices! He was holding a glass of wine. Even in the depths of my drinking, I would never stoop so low as to drink movie theater wine. I would get drunk at the nearby chic restaurant before coming to the movie. But today I was sober. Gus was not. Noted.

The movie started. I couldn't really focus on it. I was too pre-occupied with Gus. Wondering what he'd been up to, where he'd been, if he thought this new Mission: Impossible movie was a worthy addition to the franchise. I missed being best friends, but even that pain had subsided. I'd stopped reflexively texting him, and it had gotten more normal having him not know the ins and outs of my days. I had stopped feeling so vulnerable going through life without an emergency contact. Honestly, committing to being sober was a huge reason why the transition wasn't so gut-wrenching. It made me feel like a superhero. What else was I capable of doing on my own? What other ways could I rewire my brain and allow for a healthy perspective shift? I won't say I didn't long for some kind of companionship. I just didn't feel like such a terrified raw nerve all the time. My life belonged to me again. Not alcohol. That sense of ownership over the good, the bad, the all of it, was empowering.

Tom Cruise was having a cheesy sincere romance moment on the screen, and I heard Gus cackle. He was such a heckler during movies. I liked it, to a point, but sometimes it would get obnoxious and people would start shushing us. But still, he had a nice cackle. The perfect amount of edginess and warmth.

When the movie ended, I waited for Gus outside the screening to say hello. It would feel like a violation if I didn't, like I'd been spying on him or something. Besides, a part of me wanted him to also endure the emotional hurricane of seeing an ex. When he opened the doors, he was looking at his phone and then he was looking at me. I asked him if he liked the movie.

"Uh," Gus stumbled, trying to collect himself, "I think I liked the last one better."

"Me too," I said. "He and the love interest had no chemistry!"

"Well, it's Tom Cruise." Gus rolled his eyes. "He has chemistry only with himself and Xenu."

Here we were, both trying to wear our old costumes. They felt nice, if a little itchy. No, actually, a lot itchy. They needed to come off.

"How are you?" I asked, trying my best to not make it sound loaded.

"I'm, you know, okay," Gus said before hastily adding, "I don't think I'm ready to do this yet."

"Yeah," I said, relieved. "Me either."

"Okay," Gus said, clutching his empty wineglass. "Well, I'll see you."

I imagined this moment to be like a scene out of a movie so it wouldn't hurt so bad. I took a dramatic pregnant pause and I said, "I'll see you."

Gus walked away. I continued to watch him, wondering what he was feeling, who he was going to call first to say that we had run into each other. Gus and I worked until we didn't. When you get into a relationship, you both implicitly sign this contract that says "I'm going to be this person for you and you're going to be this person for me and that's why we'll work." I knew I could no longer be that person for Gus. I knew I needed to evolve and I didn't want to be held back by him. I didn't want to wonder what parts of myself I'd have to stifle so we could still make sense, so we could still have someone to watch TV with and know there'd always be someone to call the second something interesting happened to either of us.

It was a privilege to be loved by him, though. I really do believe that. I used to believe it was a privilege to be loved by *anybody*. Not anymore.

CHAPTER 72

I wrote my list for Jonas. Every disabled person I'd ever met.

First was Katie, a girl with a more severe case of cerebral palsy, who was two grades above me in junior high. We'd pass each other in the hallways and we would flash smiles—"DISABLED PRIDE, I GOT YOU, GIRL!"—before I'd turn to my friend to ask him if the circus was coming to town. Not once did I consider, *Dude. You're essentially dissing yourself.*

There was Jeff, my grandma's next-door neighbor. He could barely talk. I never asked about his disability, and I avoided him like he was contagious.

Tess Butner. I didn't know her. She was in some PBS special on disability and she used a wheelchair and used a breathing tube. I watched with my mom, who chain-smoked through the whole show and said to me when it was over, "See? It could always be worse. You could be her."

I saw countless disabled people begging for change on street corners, and each time I promised myself that they wouldn't be my future. I would work extra hard to avoid the cycle of poverty that is often associated with disability. And I succeeded, partially due to hard work but mostly because systemic oppression doesn't affect cis white men with minor limps.

There was my Spanish teacher who wore an eye patch. Sydney in my sixth-grade class who had scoliosis. She loved the show *Friends* and invited me over to watch it one day, but I said no because her back brace placed a magnifying glass over the things I didn't like about myself.

Teenage years. Let's see. There weren't many. A strapping blind boy from a rival high school who asked me out on Myspace. I didn't respond. A successful architect with muscular dystrophy who gave a talk on career day. People clapped. We all moved on. In college, I don't remember anyone, but I probably blocked them out. In New York, disabled people were everywhere and nowhere at the same time. They're hyper-visible until you look away and allow them to fade into the crowds as if they never existed. I've experienced it many times and I've done it to others, this form of passing on the pain, not wanting to be burdened. Like a game of disability hot potato.

Looking at the list, I knew why Jonas wanted me to do it. It was important for me to look at all the ugliness that had lived—no, *still lived*—inside of me. Because only when you're honest about the ugly can it start to become beautiful. I made a promise that the next name I put on that list would matter. I would see them, I would honor them, and I would keep my pain where it belonged: with me. And one day I would harness that pain into something I could eventually use, something more powerful for the benefit of all of us.

CHAPTER 73

Now, whenever I walked, I tried to channel Jonas, head held high, a spring in my step even if it dragged. I liked how I felt when I carried myself this way. The more I did it, the more it could feel less like Jonas and more like me.

I hadn't heard from Jonas in five days, which is an eternity in the beginning of a friendship that you maybe want to turn into something more. On the sixth day, my phone buzzed. It was him.

"hi sorry I was MIA. come over?"

CHAPTER 74

Jonas answered the door in sweats and a wrinkled T-shirt. He looked tired and took me to his bedroom, which had gone from plain to unkempt and chaotic. I liked that he hadn't bothered to clean up. That meant he truly was comfortable with me. Jonas pushed a pile of clothes from his mattress and motioned for me to sit down.

"So," Jonas sighed. "Sorry I went off the grid again."

"Oh my god, don't worry," I said. "I didn't even notice."

Jonas raised an eyebrow and said, "Yes, you did. We were in a whole communication groove and then . . ."

I liked that he admitted our momentum had been lost. It was brave of him to acknowledge how important voice texting and sending memes and our hangouts were.

"Look, here's the deal," Jonas said, rubbing his eyes. "Sometimes I get these things, I call them Blue Periods, where I get really sad and take to my bed for a few days. It happened after the Halloween party. It's like coming down with the flu or something, but in my brain rather than my body."

I told him I totally got it, which I didn't completely. I am familiar with sadness, but it manifests mostly as anxiety and it propels me forward rather than stopping me in my tracks.

"I just thought you should know that," Jonas said, his voice scratchy. "I don't want you to think I'm ignoring you, you know."

"Thank you for feeling cozy enough to share with me," I said.

"Of course," Jonas said. "I feel like you and I—I mean who knows, it's so early—but I feel like we're going to . . . we're going to matter to each other, maybe?"

"Really?"

Jonas laughed and said, "Well, you have more experience than I do in the relationship department. And friendship department. And everything department. So, maybe I don't know what I'm talking about."

"No," I said. "You do know. I feel the same."

Jonas lay back on his pillow and stared up at the ceiling. I looked around awkwardly, wondering if he would like for me to join him. As if reading my mind, he patted the space next to him. I reclined and tried to locate the spot on the ceiling that had captured his attention. Jonas then wrapped his arm around the back of my neck, his hand resting on my chest. My body froze as I attempted to identify what his touch was trying to say.

"Sorry, can you move over?" Jonas said, wiggling his arm out from underneath me. "I'm cramping."

"Oh, um, sure."

I moved. Jonas did too, turning his body in the bed to face mine.

"Hi," he said.

"Hi," I said.

Jonas leaned over to kiss me and everything went still. I could hear only the squeak of the bed, the rustling of leaves outside. His tongue started dancing with mine, and I picked up the gentle rhythm. I shifted my body, draping my arm around him, bringing him closer while also using the move to anchor and steady my body.

The sounds of kissing have historically always made me feel self-conscious, but with Jonas I loved hearing how we sounded together. We continued to kiss, finding new homes for each other on the corners of our mouths, our lower lips, underneath, right smack in the middle. We clanked our front teeth together a few times. If this had happened with an able-bodied person, my boner would've ghosted, but with Jonas our mishap felt ordinary, expected. Two spastic people trying to find out how to fit together. Being patient with each other, embracing the mess, creating the necessary space. Sex and sex-adjacent activity had always been an exercise in adapting to the able-bodied person and meeting them where they are. Even with Gus, a person I was with for years, I experienced stress and anxiety coming up with new ways to contort myself so my body could be viewed as erotic rather than a nuisance. Being with Jonas was the opposite. I didn't shy away from my imperfections. I basked in them.

"You're the first boy I've kissed in a year," Jonas said, giving our mouths a break. "I like it. I forgot how much I missed the stubble action."

"You're welcome," I said, delighted to be getting my first sprinkling of information. I guess I'd earned it.

We continued kissing. Our shirts were riding up with our little bellies touching, our folds becoming friends. There was none of the usual buzzing in my brain, only clarity and warmth.

I liked Jonas's scent. It was sweeter than most men's. Less woods, more jasmine. It made sense, like another piece of the puzzle coming together. Of course he would smell like that. Why would he smell like anything else?

It was 2 p.m., the light was peeking through the windows, our bodies were in focus, there was nowhere to hide. Not like I wanted to. If anything, I yearned to compare notes. Trace our scars together, make them into a heart. I caressed his cock through his jeans but I didn't want to meet it yet. I didn't want to cheat us out of any time. We took our shirts off and held each other. Jonas told me about the first boy he ever kissed, a boy in his neighborhood whom he liked, and about the sour surprise of seeing him with a girl at school two days later, putting on a show to say, "I'm not like you."

We resumed kissing. This was our routine. We would kiss, take off a piece of clothing, then stop and share stories. It was like reading a book you didn't want to end so you put it down after every chapter, stretching out the experience.

We took off our pants by ourselves. We didn't attempt to do it for the other person or while we were standing, because it'd be too much work, we'd be sweating from exertion, why put on a show and pretend? We went to our respective corners on the bed and took our sweet time. It was revolutionary to be able to sit while getting undressed and not worry if I was coming off as weak or unsexy.

We stripped down to our underwear and got into bed, the tight muscles of our thighs touching. We swapped stories of how we lost our virginities, getting turned on and pressing our hips together, shapes growing in our underwear. I could've stayed like that forever: two boys in bed, giving themselves permission to be known.

Jonas pulled down the top of my underwear to gently stroke my cock, but after a while I asked him to stop because I was about to come. I wanted my turn to explore. I took Jonas's underwear down. He was uncut.

"It's my other disability," Jonas said. "My pesky foreskin."

"Are you kidding? Uncut is the best."

Truly. Friction for your dick, easier to come. It's natural. Untamed. I went down on Jonas. His penis fit perfectly in my mouth. I hoped to express how much I cared about him through this blow-job. It would tell the story of my feelings, become a heartfelt country ballad.

We stopped occasionally to rest. At one point, we even took a break to eat a sandwich. (Jonas made them, they looked like throw-up, exactly how I make sandwiches, and I loved it.)

The sun was spilling its last rays onto Jonas's window, but neither of us reached for the light switch. We didn't want to break the spell. After hours of kissing, talking, and touching, we came. Me first, Jonas second. I drank up his cum with gratitude. It tasted sweet, like the jasmine he smelled of but slightly rotted.

We were both out of breath. Jonas's leg was cramping, my hamstrings were on fire. We shared how spent we felt, unashamed, like our fatigue was a badge of honor. I could have lain in bed for hours and not worried once about perspiring on the sheets. I had never felt so free, so open about my body and the ways it rebelled against me. Jonas and I, we had the same reference points, the same parameters, an innate understanding.

I studied Jonas's body in the dark for all the ways he could be seen as different or like me. I imagined molding our bodies together into some kind of super-disabled form. We'd be stronger together than apart.

Sex is a way of announcing yourself, of telling another person who you are, and that night I realized I'd been presenting myself as someone I wasn't and using sex as a way to escape my body rather than inhabit it. I rested my head on Jonas's chest, and I peered up at him and told myself that if this stopped here, it would be enough. I had been on a hellish journey to be seen and validated by an army of inconsequential men. *Tell me who I am. Tell me I am worthy.* But it was over now, or it could be over, because by allowing myself to see and accept Jonas, I was also seeing and accepting myself for the first time. He had given me the gift of finally being present in my body. I felt everything. Every stiff fucking muscle, every blemish, every crooked nook, and it was beautiful. It was wrong to see my body as anything else.

I looked at him and saw a future absent of distractions, of pure unfiltered reality. No more alcohol, no more sex to disassociate. This could be my life if I allowed it. All of it mine, every last bit.

ACKNOWLEDGMENTS

I want to thank Kent Wolf for reading this book in literally two days and getting it in great shape in record time. You're a delightful one-of-a-kind queerdo and the publishing industry is better for it.

My editor, Michelle Herrera Mulligan. What a dream collaborator. Thank you for immediately getting what I wanted to do with this book and enhancing my vision with your brilliant thoughts. IT'S SO GOOD WHEN IT'S SO EASY.

Everyone at Atria for getting behind this weird sex- and limp-filled novel and treating it like it's going to be the new Sally Rooney. It probs won't be. Sorry!

Melissa Broder, Isaac Oliver, and Karley Sciortino: thank you for reading early drafts and encouraging me to keep going. All of your work inspires me, which should be illegal to say since we're friends, but it's true.

Clifford Murray. In an industry full of scared little bitches, you've always supported me in making the gayest things. Thank you for believing in me when everyone else was too nervous to.

My lawyer, Kim Jaime. You're a real one. Thank you for being so sweet and amazing to me and a terrifying bulldog to everyone else.

Greg Berlanti. You were one of the first people with power in Hollywood to be like, "He's good." You've been such an invaluable mentor. You're also one of the few people in this business who is not crazy and actually nice and fun and not evil? HOW DO YOU DO IT?

Ashley Fox. Every time I try to make something, it's met with such resistance and I have to convince 40,056,555,544 people to give me two dollars. Thank you for immediately being like, "This is a movie. Let's make it." You are so fucking smart. A true Virgo queen with taste.

Sam Lansky, Carey O'Donnell, Adam Roberts, Craig Johnson, Henry Slavens, and Liz Elevenri: my gay tribe.

My dad. Thank you for only knowing how to be yourself. I love you.

My stepmom, Pamela Eells. I would not be writing if it weren't for you.

My muses: cerebral palsy, shoegaze, good sex, bad sex, unclear sex, Easton Gym, homosexuality, sex workers, toxic bosses who need to read *The Velvet Rage*, Los Angeles, Ventura, and Province-town. Sometimes New York.

Clare Tivnan. You're my puzzle piece, my family, my heroin, my love.

And to Jonathan. You've made my life better than I ever thought possible. It's a privilege to love and be loved by you.